Praise for

Books in the
Captain Lacey Regency Mystery Series
By Ashley Gardner

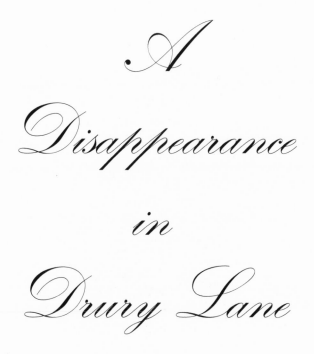

A Disappearance in Drury Lane

Ashley Gardner

Captain Lacey Regency Mysteries
Book 8

Chapter One

Late December 1817

Marianne Simmons came to me on a cold December day when I was packing away my old life in order to begin my new.

Tomorrow, I would journey through sparkling frosts and possible snow to Oxfordshire. I would travel via warm, private coach, but no amount of luxury could keep away the winter winds that were decidedly blowing now.

"I need your help, Lacey," Marianne said without preliminary as she entered my front room.

I did not lift my head from my task. "On the moment? I am rushing off to be married, as you can see."

"I thought you did not leave until the morrow."

"I do not, but Bartholomew and I must clear

everything from these rooms and have my baggage ready for Lady Breckenridge's coach in the morning. Her coachman is not the most patient of beings."

"Good. Then you have this evening to help me."

I straightened up from where I packed the contents of the drawers of my chest-on-frame. When I'd moved into these rooms three and more years ago, I'd had little in the way of possessions. Things tend to accumulate, however, especially in drawers.

I'd thought to discard or sell some of the objects, but each one I lifted out to transfer to an open crate told its own story. Many, like the snuffboxes from Grenville, had been gifts. Others, such as the small stack of letters written to me by Lady Breckenridge, were dearer still. Memories accumulated as thickly as the objects, and I could not remove the one from the other. Hence, they all went into boxes to be moved to my new abode.

"This evening I must pack," I said to Marianne. "You would not wish me to be late to the happiest day of my life, would you?"

Marianne plunked herself onto my wing chair. "Well, if it will be the happiest day of your life, then all the others can only be less happy, can't they? Perhaps you ought to miss it altogether."

Marianne herself had changed over the few years I'd known her. Tonight she was resplendent in a gray frock topped with a black and silver long-sleeved bodice, a silver-gray spencer, gray leather gloves, and a bonnet trimmed with feathers and gray ruched ribbon. A far cry from the tawdrily dressed, rather desperate young woman who'd let the rooms above mine. Rare was the day Marianne had not come down the stairs to filch my candles, my coal, or my snuff, and anything else she could carry off.

She was now the mistress of Lucius Grenville, one of England's wealthiest and most fashionable gentlemen, and he believed in turning his ladies out well. The muff she slapped to her lap attested to the cost of Marianne's ensemble, as did the well-made boots that peeked from under the hem of the gown.

"I fear my good lady would not see it in that light," I said, returning to my task. "Besides, her mother is going to much trouble for this wedding."

"To which I am not invited."

I ended up simply dumping the entire contents of the drawer into the box to sort through later. "No one is invited to the wedding but members of Lady Breckenridge's family. *Her* family, that is. Pembrokes, all. The only Breckenridge attending is Donata's son, Peter, and he with his nanny."

"Grenville will be there."

And now we came to the heart of her sour mood. "Grenville is standing up with me," I said. "I assure you, the rest of the party will be elderly matrons along with gentlemen related to Lady Breckenridge's mother and father. My family will be represented by my daughter."

And my heart sang.

I had not seen Gabriella since the summer, when she'd come for a too-brief visit to the country house of Lady Aline Carrington. We'd spent two weeks together, but Gabriella had been shy with me, preferring the company of her chaperones—her stepfather's brother and wife who'd traveled with her from France. Just as Gabriella had begun to grow more confident with me, her visit had come to an end, and she'd returned home. Her mother, my former wife, had not wanted Gabriella away for long.

This time, however, my friends, abetted by Gabriella's French uncle and aunt, had convinced the former Mrs. Lacey to allow Gabriella to spend the entire Season in England with me. She'd live with us, after my marriage, in Lady Breckenridge's Mayfair home. Gabriella had arrived at Dover a few days ago with her chaperones, and Earl Pembroke had dispatched his personal carriage to take them from there straight to Oxfordshire.

Marrying Donata Breckenridge was one reason I hurried to leave dank and cold London, but the thought of seeing my daughter again put wings on my feet.

"The matter is a simple one," Marianne said, breaking my thoughts. "I am certain you can clear it up in a trice. You generally do."

Not quite. The last problem I'd cleared up had taken two weeks, and I'd ridden miles, had seen gruesome sights, and been battered and beaten for my pains. I'd also done things, and looked the other way at things done by others, that still made me uncomfortable in the night.

But I knew trying to put Marianne off would never work—she could be persistent to the point of madness. "What matter?" I asked.

"A friend has gone missing," Marianne said. She stroked the fur of her muff, the short, jerky movements telling me she was more worried than she cared to reveal. "An actress from the company at Drury Lane. I thought you might look into it for me, since you excel at finding the missing."

I hated that word—*missing*. I'd looked for missing women in London before, to tragic end.

Unfortunately, people went missing all the time. Young men were impressed onto the large merchant ships that gathered on the London docks and Isle of Dogs, young women were lured by procuresses into houses of ruin. The elderly wandered away from home and were never found again.

Compassion stirred beneath my haste. "How long has she been gone?"

"Going on for a six-month now."

I set the drawer down with a thump, some of the anxiety leaving me. "A six-month? And you expect me to find her in the afternoon before I leave for my wedding?"

"Of course not. But I hoped you could make a start. One of her pals told me that Abigail went off in early summer, saying she'd return for the theatre's season, as per usual. But she's not been back, and her pal is getting worried. Abigail's not written, though she was never one for writing letters."

"A moment. Are you speaking of Mrs. Abigail *Collins*?"

"That's the one."

Abigail Collins was one of the most famous tragic actresses of the stage these days, the next Sarah Siddons, everyone called her. I'd watched, enthralled, as Mrs. Collins transformed herself into her characters, from those in great Shakespearean plays to ones from lesser-known modern melodramas. She blossomed as soon as she walked onstage and held the audience in her power until she left it. She and Mr. Kean, a great tragedian in his own right, between them filled every seat in Drury Lane theatre.

"You know Mrs. Collins well?" I asked.

"Abby?" Marianne studied her muff. "Yes, we're acquainted. You know everyone when you're in a theatre company. Better than you wish to, sometimes."

I sensed something more in the reply than Marianne wanted to say. However, I was familiar with Marianne's stubbornness and decided not to try to pull the information from her at the moment.

"Perhaps she decided to do more traveling," I said. "Or is engaged in a series of performances elsewhere."

Marianne shook her head. "Abby would never leave it so late. The new plays open the day after New Year's."

"Perhaps she is with someone then. A lover."

"Abby? Run off to see a man? Not likely. When she has an affair, known or discreet, she never lets it interfere with her performances. She'd never risk missing an opening night for a lover. Abby's life is the stage. She's devoted to it and nothing more." In Marianne's tone I heard resignation and exasperation at the same time.

Marianne herself had once had the habit of disappearing from London and returning when she pleased, refusing to answer questions as to where she'd been. Grenville at first had assumed she'd gone off to a lover—spending all the money Grenville gave her on him—and I admit, I had thought the same. The solution to the mystery of Marianne's disappearances had turned out to be something quite different, however. Perhaps Mrs. Collins kept similar secrets.

"Can you come round and talk to Abby's pal at the theatre?" Marianne asked me.

I opened another drawer. "Let me go to Oxfordshire for my very important appointment. When we return to London, I will begin some inquiries."

"Oh, do not bestir yourself. My friend might be in danger, but it is quite all right for you to hurry off to bask in comfort with your friends. Tell *him* I'll be busy spending his money on clothing and snuff and who knows what else? I will be sure to find comfort on my own."

"Marianne," I said, trying to hold on to my patience. "I am getting *married,* not puttering about at a garden party. Grenville has been kind enough to agree to be my groomsman. This is not a slight on you. Have I ever mentioned that you are a bit selfish?"

She did not look contrite. "If *you'd* had to fend for yourself against the world all your life — not easy for a woman, believe me — you would become a bit selfish too, would you not?"

She had a point. When I'd first met Marianne, she'd had nothing and no one, which was why I'd leave my door unlocked so she could eat my leftover food. She'd never told me where she came from or who her family was. In spite of her working-class idioms, she spoke with a timbre that sounded of the genteel, not one originating in the slums of London.

"Please, Lacey," she said.

I looked past her prickly demeanor and into her eyes, which held true worry. She was trying to make lighter of this than her fears wanted to.

"Very well," I said. "We will go."

Marianne jumped up from the chair. "Excellent. Shall you hire a hackney?"

"It isn't far. We can walk."

"You're rich enough now to never let your boots touch London's cobbles again, you know."

I put my boxes aside and limped across the room for my greatcoat, hat, and walking stick. "I enjoy a good tramp. Nothing like being told you'll never walk well again to give you a passion for it. Besides, the theatre is only steps around the corner."

"You'll change your tune once you are married, I vow. It isn't fashionable to walk anywhere. You never catch *him* doing it."

"I catch Grenville walking all the time. Don't exaggerate."

Marianne made face at me, but at last she stopped her needling, and we went.

We departed down the stairs and out to Grimpen Lane. The bakeshop beneath my rooms, run by Mrs. Beltan, my landlady, was doing a brisk business as usual. The day was bone cold, which rendered the warm, yeasty smell of the shop enticing.

Grimpen Lane, a narrow cul-de-sac off Russel Street near Covent Garden, was lined with houses in which the respectable but meager dwelled. Our cobbles were always swept, indigents encouraged to move along. Few of us had more than two coins to rub together, but the women who lived here made certain the world knew we were *not* of the working classes. So few trudged down this street that it was a hollow victory, but the spinsters, housewives, and widows of Grimpen Lane were adamant.

The two ladies who lived in the house across the lane, leaders of the army for respectability, were just departing the bakeshop. The pair of them, Mrs. Carfax and her companion, Miss Winston, glanced askance at Marianne in her finery. They had never approved of Mrs. Beltan letting an actress live above her shop. As for me, Mrs. Carfax was still shy with me, though painfully courteous. She was terrified of all men — though I knew there had at one time been a *Mr.* Carfax.

"Good evening," I said to them, tipping my hat. They curtseyed politely, tightly arm in arm, gave Marianne a frosty nod, and walked on.

"Cows," Marianne said as we moved on to Russel Street. "As though it's a virtue to be cold and hungry. Let us hold our heads high while we quietly starve to death. Ridiculous way to live."

I did not bother to answer; it was an old argument. We turned left to Russel Street and walked a short distance to Drury Lane. The doors of the Theatre Royal at Drury Lane opened onto Russel Street, but Marianne led me down a narrow passage beside the building, dark now as the walls shut out the weak winter light, and around the theatre to its back.

A notice had been pinned on the dark gray brick next to an unmarked door, announcing that *Next Saturday after the New Year, Mr. Kean will perform the Tragedy of Othello, with a melodrama, The Innkeeper's Daughter.* Coming later this spring would be *The Bride of Abydos,* a tragedy in three acts based on Lord Byron's poem, promising *Choruses of Soldiers, Warriors of an Ancient Tribe, Slaves of the Seraglio, and splendid new scenery prepared for this play,* which would include, apparently, a pirate galley and gardens of the harem.

Drury Lane had the patent to produce what was known as "true" plays, meaning spoken drama, anything from Shakespeare to Sheridan. No opera or musicales, but plenty of dramatics, lavish stage sets, and effects. I'd once watched a play here in which a rainstorm had been created on the stage with real water. The rain had thoroughly drenched the actors as well as members of the audience in the first few rows. In another play, a lighter-than-air balloon had taken an actor aloft.

Marianne knocked on the door beside the notice. I was surprised she thought anyone would be inside the theatre in this week between Boxing Day and New Year's, but she did not seem worried. She knocked again—three short raps—and waited.

After a few moments, the door was opened by a giant of a man. I'd never seen such a huge specimen. My footman turned valet, Bartholomew, and his brother were both large young men, but this man beat them on bulk and me on height. His coat and waistcoat stretched over beefy muscles, the sleeves tight on huge arms that ended in thick-fingered hands.

His face was not ugly, but a bit flat, his nose smaller than such a man should have. His eyes, set proportionally in his large face, were a pale hazel, discernible even in this dim light. His clothes were well made, sewn for him, at a guess—I could not imagine he'd have an easy time of it finding secondhand clothes to fit him. He gave me a look of grave suspicion but softened when he took in Marianne.

"Miss Simmons," he said, sounding relieved. "We was expecting you."

He opened the door wider, almost deferentially, to let Marianne inside. When he looked at me again, all his suspicions returned.

"Where is she, Mr. Coleman?" Marianne asked.

Coleman moved his bulk around Marianne and into the darkened hall. "Doing the mending. I'll take you in, so she knows it's you."

Marianne saw nothing odd in his phrasing, but I was curious. She followed Coleman down a narrow hall, and I came behind, my walking stick quietly tapping the floor.

While the entity that was the Drury Lane theatre had stood on this spot for a very long time, the building we walked through was itself not very old. The previous manifestation of the theatre had burned down in 1809 then risen again in 1812. The new building was modern and fairly comfortable — that is, if you were fortunate enough to afford its luxurious boxes. Behind the stage, the actors had to make do with narrow corridors and small dressing rooms. But it was relatively warm back here, with stoves rather than the old hearths that had put out very little heat.

Coleman stopped in front of a door, knocked firmly, and pushed it open. We entered a large room filled with open wardrobes, trunks, shelves, and tables. All the furniture overflowed with pieces of clothing, but everything was folded neatly, stacked into manageable piles. Someone had made order of the chaos.

A woman sat on a low chair among the clothing, needle in her hands. She was middle-aged turning to elderly, a once-plump body thinning, hair going gray under a cap. She pushed the needle into a bodice she was mending in one smooth movement, fingers graceful as she pulled the thread through. She didn't look at the fabric or even at us but somewhere in the middle distance.

"Mrs. Wolff," Coleman said in a loud voice. "They're here. Miss Simmons and her gent . . . er . . ."

"Captain Lacey," I said, moving forward and holding out my hand.

Mrs. Wolff didn't turn to us. I understood why when I saw the opaque film over her wide pupils. She wasn't being rude. She was blind.

"Do you trust him, Miss Simmons?" Mrs. Wolff asked, still stitching. Her head cocked, as though she listened for the answer. Her voice was faintly laced with Cockney, but she spoke as one who'd practiced until she'd taken the back streets out of her speech.

"I do," Marianne said. "Captain Lacey, may I introduce Mrs. Hannah Wolff?"

I gave a startled exclamation, and Mrs. Wolff chuckled. "They all do that. Yes, my dear, I am Hannah Wolff, the celebrated actress. If you're old enough, you'll have seen my Lady Macbeth. If you're *truly* old enough, you'll have seen my Juliet."

"I saw you as Gertrude," I said, almost reverently. Hannah Wolff had breathed life into the role, as she had every role, but that night as Gertrude she'd been magnificent. Her performance had all but obscured the other actors on the stage. *Hamlet* hadn't been Hamlet's play that night; it had been hers.

"You're old enough then," she said. "I didn't want Marianne fetching some young officer back from the army with nothing to do. He wouldn't care."

"Captain Lacey is not young," Marianne said. Very flattering—I was a little over forty. "But young enough. He's lame, but he walks around quite easily. He's also getting married in the next few days and so is a bit impatient."

"My felicitations," Mrs. Wolff said. "But if you're getting married, you won't be interested in our problem."

I was growing a bit tired of people telling me what did and did not interest me. I found a chair that was free of clothing, drew it close to Mrs. Wolff, and sat down, planting my hands on my cane. "I am interested. Forgive me for sitting. The cold makes my leg ache."

"Please, be comfortable, Captain," Hannah said. "Well then, Marianne must have told you a little about it. Abigail Collins is a dear friend of mine. When I got run down by a dray and two heavy horses and lost my sight some years ago, I wasn't good for walking around the stage no more. Abby made sure I kept my place in the company, coaching other ladies on their parts. If someone hands me the right pieces of clothing, I can sew them together or help the ladies into them. I am very good at fitting clothes now—the hands can see what the eyes don't. I became Abigail's dresser. She has a voice like a cathedral bell. She says a word on a stage, and she's heard in the back row, with all the emotion dripping from it. The punters love her."

"I've seen her perform," I said. "I agree, she is astonishing. As you were."

"Too kind, Captain. But this summer, Abigail up and went, and I ain't heard a word from her since. She's not written—Coleman or my sister read all my letters out to me. But they say she's not sent anything for a long while."

"Did she stop to say good-bye when she left?"

"She did," Hannah said. "It were nothing unusual. She was off to the seaside—Brighton—

where she goes every summer for her health, then on to Bath for more water. A great one for bathing, is Abby. She always comes back before the season starts, though, to have Christmas with me and my sister and husband and practice her parts for the coming plays. My sister used to act as well, though she gave it up for soft living, and never looked back." Hannah stopped and sighed. "But this year, Abby never arrived."

"Perhaps she lingered in Brighton or Bath to do a few plays," I suggested. The great actors and actresses sometimes spent time with provincial companies, to help them pull an audience, or simply for the enjoyment of it.

"I'd have heard, wouldn't I?" Hannah said. "She'd have written, or Coleman would have seen notices in the newspapers. Abby doesn't write many letters, but she's good about imparting news or telling us she's delayed."

Coleman broke in from his place by the door. "Tell him about the box."

Hannah pushed the needle into the fabric and left it there, her fingers remaining on it. "The box puts a different complexion on it, you see. Terrible thing, it was."

"A box?" I asked when she paused to shake her head. "Something in a box here at the theatre?"

"No, a parcel," Marianne broke in. "Delivered to Abigail before she went."

"From?"

"Well, that's the thing," Hannah said. "We don't know. They tell me it came from a reputable London delivery firm."

"Aye," Coleman said in his gravelly voice. "Fuller

and Hamilton's. Package done up the same as any. The delivery man was nervous, said the gent what dropped it off was laughing and saying the delivery man should be very, very careful not to shake it."

Hannah reached out her hand and patted the air, as though trying to comfort Coleman.

"Coleman saved us all, he did," Hannah said. "He takes the parcel away from Abby and opens it himself. Inside is a wooden box, very pretty, he says, like from a shop. Coleman, he was in the war, and he sniffs it and says he smells gunpowder. He dropped the box into a tub of water and opened it slowly. What do you think, Captain? The sides were done up so that a spark when the box was opened would ignite packed gunpowder. Coleman said there'd been enough powder and bits inside to blow off poor Abigail's face."

"Good Lord," I said, blinking. I looked at Coleman, who gave me a slow nod. "Thank God for Coleman's quick thinking."

"Aye," Hannah said. "I was glad he was on hand. But Abby was shaken, I can tell you."

"I do not blame her," I said. Using gunpowder to fight in war was one thing; delivering a package of it to kill an innocent woman was something else altogether. "Did anyone go round to the delivery company and ask who sent the parcel?"

"I did, sir," Coleman said. "No one there had seen the man before. They described him as medium height, about the same as any gent, a bit spindly. Dressed well enough, they said, and paid the fee."

A good description, but it could fit many men in London. I turned back to Hannah.

"Do you know of any other threats or attempts to

hurt Mrs. Collins?"

Hannah shook her head. "That was the main one. I know Abby got bad letters, but she never showed them to me or talked about them. I knew because of the way she acted, all brisk and bright, when you could tell she was scared senseless."

Marianne said, "And that's why I asked you to look into it, Lacey. Because it's more than an actress taking some time for herself, isn't it? We want to know if whoever was trying to kill her succeeded. Surely you can spare us ten minutes for that."

Chapter Two

Hannah was correct — the incident did put a different complexion on the situation.

"Why did you not say so at once?" I asked her. "And why did you not mention this six months ago when it happened?"

Marianne shrugged in her maddening way. "I did not think you'd believe me. I only grew worried when Abby didn't return and didn't write, and Hannah asked me to help. You were busy running off to Norfolk, planning your wedding . . . I wanted you to hear the story from Hannah and Coleman before you judged. You have the habit of dismissing what comes out of my mouth."

I started to disagree then fell silent. She was not wrong. I might have brushed off Marianne's tale as exaggeration or embellished to gain my interest if I had not heard of the incident from Hannah.

Hannah could not tell us much more, however. The extent of what she knew was Abigail Collins had received letters that upset her and then the frightening package.

Everyone in this room believed Abigail to be in real danger. I'd not have been let into this private sanctum otherwise, I realized.

I wished I could reassure them, but I could not. Obviously Mrs. Collins had an enemy, perhaps more than one. No one decided to send a person a box of gunpowder if they did not mean to cause real harm. A rival actress, perhaps? From stories Marianne had told me, I knew actors could be cruel to one another as they competed for roles or places in a company.

Actresses also sometimes took lovers, and those lovers might be married. Perhaps an angry wife had sought revenge. Or perhaps someone from Mrs. Collins' past was threatening her. I had not much to go on.

Hannah had drooped a bit after she delivered her last speech. Marianne rose and shot me a look, and I got to my feet. I made Hannah a bow, though I knew she couldn't see me, and I complimented her again on the roles I'd seen her play.

She dismissed me as a base flatterer before she picked up her mending, but I could tell she was pleased. I did not exaggerate—Hannah Wolff had truly had the gift. The accident that had robbed her of her career was tragic indeed.

"Where do you think Mrs. Collins is, Coleman?" I asked as the man led us back through the hallways to the stage door.

"Don't know. But I don't like thinking she ain't safe." The large man sent me a worried look. "Miss

Simmons says you can find anybody. She right, sir?"

Miss Simmons stood next to me looking innocent. I gave Coleman a nod. "I will certainly try. I do not like the story I've heard tonight."

"Thank you, sir." Coleman sounded relieved as he opened the door and let us out into the cold. "We're all so very worried."

I put on my hat as I stepped out into the dark passage. I was worried myself, and not happy that Marianne had chosen to tell me about Abigail's disappearance so late in the proceedings. Many things could have happened to her between leaving in the summer and now.

Coleman seemed ready to be rid of us at the moment. He said a truncated good night and closed the door quickly behind us, shutting out the light and warmth.

"Well?" Marianne asked as she put her hand on my arm as we walked back to Russel Street. The short afternoon had drawn to a close as we'd talked to Hannah, and now the lane was nearly black, a fog seeping up from the river to chill us.

"Well?" I asked in return.

"Will you be leaving for Brighton, or maybe Bath?"

"Neither at the moment," I said. "I will be going to Oxfordshire, to get married."

"Your wedding's not for two days. Surely you can stop at Bath before you run to your nuptials, and see if Abby's there."

I was about to snap that Marianne was sanguine about the time it took to journey around England, but I closed my mouth. She was truly frightened.

"I promise I will do what I can," I said. "Both

before I leave and after I return."

And I would. Abigail Collins was in danger, no doubt of that. She might have decided she was safer hidden in Brighton or Bath—I hoped with friends she could trust. On the other hand, her enemy might have found her and done something irreversible. That I did not like to contemplate, but I'd seen too much evil in my life to dismiss what Mrs. Collins could face.

"I can begin inquiries at least," I said. "Discreet ones—I give you my word I won't put Abigail into any danger if she's being hunted. I'll talk to the delivery firm. They might remember something about the sender, though I have little hope of turning up new information. And Grenville must know people in Bath and in Brighton who might be able to help. But I really cannot postpone my trip to Oxfordshire."

Marianne gave me a dark look. She knew I could not, but she would continue to be displeased about it.

Fog grew thicker by the minute as we walked along Russel Street toward Covent Garden and Grimpen Lane. Marianne shrank to me, not only for warmth but also for protection against pickpockets or robbers who might use the fog for concealment.

I believed someone followed us, but they kept to the shadows, stopping when I turned to look. A predator? Or one of Grenville's servants, assigned to keep an eye on Marianne. More probably, it was a man or men belonging to James Denis, sent to watch me.

We reached the turnoff to Grimpen Lane without incident. Marianne signaled a landau—Grenville's—waiting in Russel Street in the direction of Covent

Garden. The coachman saw her, nudged the horses forward, and made his way toward us.

"Will you let me know what you've found before you rush off to your wedding?" Marianne asked as the coach stopped next to her.

"Of course. Though I doubt I will have a chance to discover much before I leave."

"As you like." Marianne accepted my hand to help her inside, and I shut the door for her. She put her head out the open window. "Thank you, Lacey," she said sincerely.

I stepped back from the landau, the coachman started the team, and the carriage rolled off into the fog. I settled my coat and walked into the dark mouth of Grimpen Lane.

Fingers landed on my arm. I grabbed the wrist the hand was attached to, swung around, and brought up my walking stick.

A soft gasp came out of the fog. I stopped, startled, and stepped back, looking down into the face of a young woman I knew. She looked back up at me, alarm in her dark eyes.

"Felicity," I said in surprise, releasing her. "Where did you—"

My words were cut off by a heavy blow between my shoulders. Not from Felicity, but from someone behind me, ready to rob me while the lovely Felicity distracted me.

I swung around with my stick, but the darkness and fog made me as blind as Hannah. A cudgel from a second attacker smacked me in the side, in my ribs. I struck out again, this time contacting a body with my stick, drawing forth a grunt.

Another blow landed on my back and then on my

injured knee. I cursed as lightning pain lashed through me, and I fell.

"Don't kill him, for God's sake," I heard Felicity say.

Kind of her. I swung my stick again, trained to go on fighting no matter how much I hurt. On the battlefield, fighting meant survival.

On the streets of London, it meant my attackers increased their assault. I took another blow to the ribs and then one to the head. White spots danced before my eyes. I managed to get my sword out of the cane, and I stabbed upward. I heard someone yell, and then another blow to my head made everything darker than the surrounding fog.

*** *** ***

I awoke cold, wet, hungry, and very, very angry.

The light in the room was weak, but it stabbed through my eyes when I opened them, increasing the fierce pain in my head. I let out a groan between dry, cracked lips.

A glass landed against my mouth, and fiery liquid trickled inside. Gin. Foul stuff. But at the moment, the only thing that wet my tongue. I swallowed, feeling the gin burn all the way down to my stomach.

"Thank the Lord," a woman's voice said. "I thought they'd gone and hit you too hard."

"Felicity." At least, I tried to say the word. My tongue blocked my mouth, and very little came out.

"They made me." She sounded angry. "I didn't want to do it, Captain, but he said they'd kill you, and me too, if I didn't bring you along."

"*He* who?"

She didn't enlighten me, or perhaps my words came out an incoherent jumble. The light in the room was feeble, a rush light that did little to illuminate.

I concentrated on staying awake, though the gin engulfed me with waves of sleepiness. I'd seen enough head wounds on the battlefield to know that going to sleep could be deadly. I reached out, surprised when my hand worked, and managed to touch Felicity.

"Why?" I asked.

Felicity bent over me, her hair hanging down in a straight black swath. "I didn't ask him."

She might be lying, and she might not. Felicity was a game girl, but she had intelligence and was a little more observant than the other girls of the streets. She hadn't picked up the Cockney or other London dialects of her colleagues, speaking with more care and less slang.

From what I understood, Felicity's mother had been a slave brought here from Jamaica; Felicity's father English or European. Her mother, freed in England, had become a housemaid, raising Felicity to be the same.

Felicity hadn't fared well in service. She'd told me the man of the house at her last place had taken plenty of liberties with her, threatening her with dismissal and ruin if she denied him. She'd decided that, if men wanted such things, she might as well make some profit from it, instead of spending her days hiding from her employer. Her dark skin, smooth black hair, and large brown eyes made her sought after on the streets, though of late, she'd taken up with my old sergeant, Pomeroy, now a Bow Street Runner. I did not think Pomeroy would approve of her helping to snatch his former captain away in the fog, however.

"I'm getting married, damn it."

Felicity leaned closer. "Don't try to talk. You're hurting, but it will soon be over."

With what? My death?

I'd spent the last two years angering dangerous people—easy for me with my hot temper, my stringent views of right and wrong, and my tendency to poke into things that were none of my business. I'd annoyed Bow Street and its magistrates as well as high-placed gentlemen in army regiments, lordships, underworld criminals, the headmaster of a prestigious school, a powerful woman who ran brothels, and various other men about town.

I also knew many secrets of one very dangerous man, James Denis. Perhaps he'd decided I knew too much about what he'd done in Norfolk.

"Denis," I said.

Felicity understood. "I told them. I told them what would happen if Mr. Denis got word. But they wouldn't listen."

Hmm, perhaps not Denis then. Upon reflection, the abduction was all wrong for him. Denis had captured me once before but known I'd get away. I'd come to understand that if Denis wanted me dead, he'd kill me before I realized it had happened.

I found if I took my time and had patience, I could form words that were somewhat discernible. "Who has brought me here?"

The trouble was, time had lost meaning for me. I paused so long between words that minutes went by before I could form the complete sentence.

Felicity didn't answer. The rush light burned out, the straw of it crumpling into nothing, and I was in darkness.

Much later, after more hunger and thirst, another light made me open my eyes again. This light was made by a tallow candle—I smelled it—and its glare illuminated the eyes, nose, and mouth of a man. *Only* his eyes, nose, and mouth, a disembodied face in the darkness.

The sight was so terrifying I began to laugh. I could hear Lady Breckenridge's cool voice, admonishing me for being late to my own wedding— *You were waylaid by a bulbous nose, bleary eyes, and slash of mouth? Really, Gabriel, why did you not simply lay him out and climb out the window?*

I had no idea who the face belonged to. I did not recognize him from my wanderings about London, or as a friend of my many acquaintances. He was, as far as I knew, a complete stranger.

"Why were you at the theatre?" he asked me.

The question brought the buried laughter to my lips. Two eyebrows joined the rest of the face as they came down over his nose, which made me laugh harder.

A kick to my ribs made me cough, but I couldn't stop laughing. "Why were you at the theatre?" he repeated.

"Seeing a play," I managed to gasp out. Why else did one go to the theatre?

"I meant today. Drury Lane. Through the back. No performances tonight."

With effort I drew a breath and forced my laughter to quiet. I raised a weak hand and beckoned him closer, coughing a little, which wasn't feigned. My mouth was dry, and the kick to my ribs had radiated pain.

The man bent down. Now I could see wiry side-whiskers growing on his cheeks, shaved off before they reached his upper lip.

I opened my mouth and shouted as hard as I could, "None of your business."

The answer got me a blow across the face. The man swung on Felicity. "Get it out of him. Any way you can."

He walked away. The glow of the candle illuminated a compact figure, the man not tall. Strong, though. My face and side ached.

He disappeared, taking the candle with him. While I lay still, trying to quiet the waves of pain, I assessed what I'd learned of the man in the short moments. His speech and accent put him as middle-class or even a gentleman, not a ruffian from the gutter. I hadn't seen his clothes, but he'd smelled of soap and clean wool. His side-whiskers had been carefully trimmed, as had been his thinning hair.

I still had no idea who he was or why he was interested in me or Drury Lane theatre. Had I just met the man who'd put together the incendiary device meant to kill Abigail Collins?

Felicity rummaged in the darkness, struck a spark, and lit another rush light.

I hated rush lights. The smell of them reminded me of my miser of a father who'd refused to pay the tax on either wax or tallow candles. Not that he wouldn't turn about and spend a fortune on his mistresses or gaming, but the rest of the family lived under the sputtering gloom of rush lights. Good lighting and his family had not been as important to my father as women or cards.

Felicity sat down on the cot with me and smoothed her hand over my chest. The gesture, as light as it was, hurt. I'd likely broken a rib.

"Tell me," I said to her.

"Well, I don't really know, do I?" Felicity settled in beside me as though she were a lady come to take tea. "He thought you fancied me and would come when I beckoned. I told him he was wrong about that, but he doesn't like to listen."

"Why is he interested in the theatre?"

Felicity opened her brown eyes wide. She was a striking woman, the bone structure in her face and the color of her skin displaying both her African and European ancestry. "I told you, I don't know. He snatched me too."

"You were walking about freely on the street," I said, anger allowing my words to flow past the pain. "I struggle to believe you'd be obedient to a man you didn't know."

"I obey him because I'm trying to *avoid* chains," Felicity said. "If I don't help him, he said he'll sell me onto the first ship to Jamaica. Not why would I want to go there? After all the trouble my mum took to get away from there in the first place?"

She spoke lightly, but I read fear in her eyes. Laws now prevented the slave trade in England, but the unscrupulous still sold human beings onto ships that would take them to the Indies or Americas, where slavery was still legal, and slaves were in abundance. Felicity would be bought and sold like chattel, and I did not need to be very imaginative to understand what she'd be bought for. She sold her own body on the London streets, true, but that was her choice, and she collected and kept the money. She was owned by no one.

If Felicity disappeared into slavery, her life would

be impossibly harsh, and likely short. She was intelligent and wily, so perhaps she could convince an owner to treat her better, but the odds were not good. In the end, she would have no rights, no redress, nothing to prevent her captors using her as they wished and disposing of her when they were finished.

My voice was still weak, but my convictions were strong. "I won't let that happen, Felicity. Never."

Instead of falling into a swoon and declaring me her savior, Felicity laughed in true mirth. "Fine words from a man tied to a pallet. You couldn't run a step."

"Fetch me my swordstick, and we'll see."

"Can't. Left it in the street."

"In the street?" I half rose, anguished. The walking stick with the sword inside it had been a gift from my lady, bought to replace another stick I'd lost in dire circumstances. The new walking stick had a gold head, engraved. *Captain G. Lacey. 1817.*

I treasured it. The stick would be long gone by now, stolen by the denizens of Covent Garden.

"I left it there," Felicity repeated, winking at me. "Where it might be found by a friend."

"Where it might be picked up and sold at the nearest pawnbrokers."

Felicity shrugged. "That's a risk."

"Blast you."

"You're sounding better. Want more gin?"

"No." I did not feel better—my head pounded, my ribs ached, and my leg hurt like fire. "If you help me, Felicity, I'll make sure you're all right."

She cocked her head and regarded me with intelligent eyes. "Gentlemen have made me such promises before. Men richer and stronger than you. They always lie. Or at least, they forget all about it when the time comes that I need their help."

"Because those gentlemen aren't me." I reached for her again and gripped her hand. "I will keep you safe. I would whether you helped me now or not. I give you my word."

Felicity paused, but I knew her hesitation did not mean she debated whether to trust me. Trust had been burned out of her long ago. She would decide, but not because of any pretty promises from me.

I drifted away on pain and the dregs of gin for a moment, and when the moment passed, I found Felicity's soft body on top of mine, she busily kissing my lips.

I couldn't struggle as she swept her tongue inside my mouth. I could not have tasted very good, and I didn't respond, both from choice and because I could barely move. Felicity kissed me thoroughly, and she was quite good at it. If I were not anxious to wed another or lying in a wash of pain, I might take her offer. As it was, I rested my hand by my side and waited until she finished and sat up.

I did not ask for help again; I lay quietly and let her decide. Felicity studied me as she traced my lips with her fingertips.

"You'll take me somewhere this Perry bloke won't find me?"

"Is that his name? Perry?"

Felicity lifted her fingers away. "What's your answer?"

"Yes."

"You're marrying a rich lady. You can give me plenty of money, can't you?"

I could not answer to what Lady Breckenridge might agree to pay for my safe return, so I had to shrug—a movement that hurt. "I will do what I can."

Felicity didn't think much of my answer. "When you marry, her money goes to you. That's English law. Then you can do with it what you want."

"Not if the money is in trust. The estate and its wealth go to her son. My wife has only a jointure and whatever her parents put into trust for her. Money under English law can be complicated."

"Then why are you marrying her?"

I tried a smile. "I like her."

Felicity gave me a pitying look. "That's no reason to marry a woman. You marry for money. If you like a woman, you take her as your lover."

I knew I was a bit unfashionable in my desire to marry Donata simply because I esteemed her. I'd married for passion the first time as well. This time, I hoped I was a little older and wiser in my choice, but I admit, it was still passion that drove me.

"If you can't give me money, what else can you offer?" Felicity asked. "A night with you?"

"Not that either. I am about to troth myself to another."

"So, you can give me neither money nor your attentions. You ask me to help you, and in return, I receive only your promise that Perry won't sell me off. That's it? That's your bargain?"

"I am afraid so."

Felicity leaned down and kissed me again, her lips warm and soft. She must have dazzled her clientele, and she must dazzle poor Pomeroy.

"All right then," she said.

Chapter Three

Felicity had to help me stand. As soon as I got to my feet, I fell to the floor, my head spinning. I lay there in a heap of pain, wanting to expire.

Felicity gave me no mercy. She put a digging hand on my shoulder and dragged me up again. "We have to hurry. If he comes back and catches us, we're done for."

I wanted to know more about this man who thought nothing of kidnapping a viscountess' betrothed off the street and threatening slavery to a young woman if she didn't help him. But breathing and moving took all my energy; nothing remained for more speech.

Felicity ducked under my arm, half carrying me to the door. The room turned out to be very small, the door not many steps from the bed. The door also appeared to be unlocked. Felicity opened it easily and led me out to a small landing at the top of a flight of stairs.

No lock or bolt? Either her fear had been strong enough to keep her in place, or Felicity had not been honest with me.

She helped me down the stairs and out a door at the bottom, which didn't seem to be guarded. Again, too easy.

We emerged into a narrow passage that smelled strongly of slops. The night was still black and shrouded in fog. I had no way of knowing where we were or even what time or day it was. Was this the same night I'd been kidnapped? Or had more time passed?

Felicity ducked out from under my arm and pinned me back against a cold wall. My weakness alarmed me. A slim woman, even one as fit and strong as Felicity, should not have been able to shove me about.

"All right, Captain. You make good on your promise. Get me away from here. Somewhere safe."

I tried to nod, but my head hurt too much. "I'll need a hackney."

"I'll get one. But we need to hurry. No telling when Perry will be back."

I gave up on the next nod as well. Felicity left me leaning against the wall, the only thing holding me upright. My legs kept trying to bend, and in fact, did so without my awareness. When Felicity returned, she found me sitting on the noisome cobbles, my knees around my head.

"Captain, we have to *go*."

She pulled me up too fast, and I nearly fell again. Felicity managed to hold me upright, my arm slung around her shoulders, and we stumbled from the passage to the street. I thought we were in the environs of Drury Lane, somewhat north of the theatre, closer to High Holborn, but I couldn't be certain.

A hackney waited not far away, the driver looking about him uneasily in the thick darkness. He jumped down from his perch when we approached and helped Felicity lift me inside.

I groaned as the coachman's touch pressed my hurt ribs, but his look held no compassion. Likely he thought me drunk, and I could not blame him his assessment. I reeked of the passage I'd collapsed in and the gin Felicity had poured down my throat.

"Where to?" the coachman asked.

"Curzon Street," I managed to say as Felicity crammed herself against me in the small seat. "Number 45."

"Right you are."

The hackney listed sickeningly as the coachman climbed back to his box, and I nearly brought up all the gin.

When I dared open my eyes again, the coach was moving and Felicity glared at me. "We can't go *there.*"

"Can you name a safer place?" I asked, my voice weak. "My lodgings are unguarded. If Mr. Perry finds us gone, he will go first to Grimpen Lane to look for me. The friends I'd turn to for help are not in London." All my London friends were gone, in fact— either at country homes celebrating Christmas or in Oxfordshire waiting for my wedding.

"We might be safe from Perry, maybe," Felicity said. "But are we safe from *him*?"

"Jump out if you don't like it. Run back to your

lodgings and bolt the door."

"Those *were* my lodgings. Perry will be back any moment."

"Then go to Pomeroy."

Felicity let out a snort. "He's a dear one, inn't he? If he knew what I'd done tonight, he'd slap me in a cell, never mind I've shared his bed."

I could not disagree with her. Pomeroy was unforgiving when it came to crime. He'd attempted to arrest me more than once, and I could easily imagine him arresting Felicity without a twinge of remorse.

"Then it seems you have no choice," I said.

Felicity gave me an unhappy look but collapsed against the seats in silence.

I drifted in and out of consciousness as we moved through the shrouded city. I hoped Marianne had not met with misfortune on her way home. Perry had asked me about Drury Lane, knowing I'd been there. Because I'd given him no answers, he might turn to Marianne for them—it had been his ruffians and Felicity who'd followed us in the dark, so Perry would know Marianne had accompanied me. At least she'd gotten into Grenville's coach and had been taken to the safety of the house he kept for her.

Then again, Perry might decide to walk to the theatre itself and find the blind Hannah vulnerable there. I thought of Coleman, huge and strong, and felt a little better. Coleman seemed to care about Mrs. Wolff and would look after her.

It could not be coincidence that Perry had abducted me just after Marianne asked me to make inquiries about Mrs. Collins. After I married—if Donata would accept a beaten up, tardy groom as a husband—I would return to London, find Mr. Perry, and shake some answers out of him.

Number 45 Curzon Street was a plain Georgian house with less pretension than most of its neighbors. The house had a black painted door, a thick brass doorknocker, sash windows with black shutters, and solid brick walls.

The coachman descended, and the horse cocked one back foot to rest its leg. Before the coachman could lift the doorknocker, a large, beefy man yanked open the door and peered out into the fog in suspicion, much as Coleman had at the theatre.

I clutched the hackney's windowsill and pulled myself forward, so the man would see who I was. His look turned to faint surprise, but the suspicion remained. He called to someone behind him and stepped out of the house.

He and another equally large man—I knew both had once been prizefighters—carried me between them into the warm, lighted house. I had no chance to see whether Felicity followed, because the two men carried me all the way up three flights of stairs and into a bedchamber before I could look for her. The bed here was made up, as though the owner of the house had been expecting a guest, although no fire burned in the grate.

While I sank onto the soft bed, one of the lackeys laid a fire and the other lit candles. Real wax candles, the scent of them soothing. No rush lights for Mr. Denis.

I hoped to drift to sleep, but a third man, this one spare and small with gray hair, joined the first two. Denis's former pugilists quickly and competently stripped off my clothes, and the third man, apparently a surgeon, wrapped up my ribs and tended to my other wounds. A sip of laudanum went past my lips, and I slept.

I woke, blinking, to daylight, in an elegant room decorated in hues of ivory and Wedgwood green. Plaster medallions depicting women in classical Greek dress adorned the walls, and above the fireplace hung the painting of a young lad bending forward to blow a spark to life on a spill. Blackness surrounded the boy, but the spark threw a bright light upward, illuminating him in brilliance. The painting was a masterwork, no doubt old, no doubt pilfered, and no doubt priceless.

A man I hadn't met before entered the room. He was younger and more slender than the other lackeys, and he started laying out shaving gear with expressionless competence.

He helped me out of bed, bathed me, shaved me, and dressed me in clean clothes—my own. The lackeys must have gone back to my flat for my things.

My ribs still hurt but were bearable now that they'd been wrapped. Touching them gingerly, I surmised they had not been broken but perhaps severely wrenched. I'd live.

I missed my walking stick, but I made my way downstairs the best I could without one to a private dining room in which I'd breakfasted before. A place had been set for me at one end of the table.

At the other end sat James Denis, a man who thought nothing of hanging priceless stolen paintings in his guest rooms. My life had become tangled with his in a complex mesh, and here I was again, at his mercy.

I'd always supposed a criminal mastermind would be aged and bent with a lifetime of dissipation, as novelists and playwrights would have us believe. Mr. Denis, in contrast, was a little past thirty, had dark hair cut short, a clean-shaven face, a slender build, and dark blue eyes that missed nothing.

His eyes also held a cold cruelty, an intelligence that weighed everything and assessed it in terms of how it might be of use to him. I'd only once seen Denis grow emotional about anything—a few months ago, in fact—and that emotion had led to disaster.

Denis looked up as I seated myself, but he didn't greet me, going back to eating his meal in silence. Another lackey went to the sideboard, spooned out a complicated dish involving eggs, sausage, and fish from a silver covered tray, and set the plate in front of me.

I didn't speak. There wasn't much point. Any conventional politeness would be lost on Denis. He'd know what I truly thought, and I knew what he thought. So we ate in silence.

Not until the meal was complete and the footmen cleared the plates, did Denis turn his attention to me. His butler set down a cup of coffee, exactly centered in front of Denis, then brought a cup to me and slid out of the room.

·I drank gratefully. I did not know where Denis obtained his coffee, but it was rich and good, better than any I could buy for myself.

Denis began as I sipped. "I do not like street girls," he said. "They are like mongrel dogs, too apt to attack the hand stretched out to them, even if it contains their bread for the day. I have no dealings with them. You installed one in my house." His cold eyes met mine, as he waited for me to explain my audacity.

"I promised her protection," I said. "I could think of nowhere else to take her."

"Mr. Grenville has several large houses at his disposal, as does your wife-to-be. You also are acquainted with gentlemen in this city who enjoy reforming prostitutes. And yet, you bring her to my doorstep."

He was angry with me. Denis's expression was cool, but I saw the deep irritation behind it. The anger surprised me. Was he put out because I'd brought a street girl here or at my audacity in thinking of his home as a refuge?

"My friends are in Oxfordshire," I said. "Awaiting me, in fact. My reforming friends, the Derwents, are at their seat in Derbyshire for Christmas and New Year's. Mrs. Brandon is likewise spending the winter out of London. I cannot be certain the skeleton staff left behind in either household would admit Felicity or protect her from this man she fears. I can't risk that they won't toss her out as soon as I depart. I know she can be wearying."

"I've not met this woman before, but my men tell me that, yes, she is troublesome. I have put her in an attic room, but if she does not wish to stay there, I'll not stop her leaving."

"She might stay put. She's more afraid of being sold back to Jamaica than she is even of you. I must ask you to give me your word you'll not give her to slavers or to the man who is pursuing her."

His chill stare froze me. I'd finally found a way to

outrage Denis, but I still wasn't certain how I'd done it.

"I have no interest in buying and selling human beings," he said. "I tolerated her arrival last night only because my man failed in preventing your abduction. He saw it happen but lost you in the fog."

Denis had put men to watching me and my street long ago, after he'd learned of my existence during the affair in Hanover Square. Everything I did in my life was now noted and reported to Mr. Denis. The lackey's failure to prevent my abduction must have been punished. Denis's men had beaten me senseless before, but I could have pity on the ones who had to face his wrath.

"Perry is the name of the man who took me," I told him. "He questioned me about my visit to Drury Lane theatre, where I'd gone to inquire about an actress who might be missing."

"Perry. I don't know a man of that name."

He surprised me, because Denis knew so much about everyone in London. I described my abductor with the large nose and side-whiskers, giving my conviction that he was not working class.

Whether this interested Denis, he made no sign. I hadn't expected it to—Denis dealt in far darker crimes that involved a great deal of money. An actress fleeing a jealous rival and a middle-class man who'd beaten me wasn't in his usual sphere of concern.

I also told him about the incendiary device, which interested him more. He did not say so, of course, but listened to the description of the device and its delivery without changing expression.

Before I finished my coffee, another of Denis's

pugilist footmen entered the room and leaned to murmur something into his ear. Denis looked at me again.

"Her ladyship's carriage is here, Captain," Denis said. "I imagine you'd better get into it."

I masked surprise that Lady Breckenridge's coachman had known to come here. But of course, the man Denis had stationed in Grimpen Lane would tell the coachman that I'd removed here for the night.

Denis rose, took a last sip of his coffee, and left the table. He paused at the door and looked at me with his usual unreadable expression. "Felicitations upon your nuptials."

I had no idea if he meant it, or mocked me, or simply mouthed the convention. I gave him a nod, thanked him, and went back to drinking every drop of the delicious coffee.

I wanted to talk to Felicity before I descended to the coach. The footman I waylaid to fetch her for me thought it amusing I felt it inappropriate to ascend to her bedchamber myself. He ran up the stairs, telling me he'd bring her down to the ground floor reception room.

I didn't wait long there, after sending word to Lady Breckenridge's impatient coachman that I would be ready soon. While I waited for Felicity, I asked for pen, ink, and paper, and composed a note to Marianne, telling her briefly what had happened to me and warning her to take care when she went out.

I gave the note to the lackey who brought in Felicity. He didn't much like being my errand boy but promised to give the note to Denis, who would see it was delivered.

Felicity followed the lackey into the reception room, behaving as though she were a great lady, the footman a common servant. She'd availed herself of the plentiful soap and water in this house—her face was scrubbed clean, her blue-black hair combed until it shone. She had no change of dress, but her high-waisted frock of brown broadcloth was neither soiled nor torn.

Felicity dropped the gracious lady persona as soon as the half-amused, half-disgusted footman closed the door. "Lacey, let me leave."

"You're safe here," I said. "He gave me his word."

"You'd trust a word of one like Denis?" Felicity lowered her voice to a near whisper, as though fearing he had someone listening, which he likely did. "You've gone soft if you think he won't play you wrong. I can't stay in this house."

"Mr. Perry will never dare try to harm you while you are here," I said. "Mr. Denis has told me you are free to leave at any time. But he also said that, if you choose to go, his protection will not extend beyond this house."

"Then take me with you."

Her desperation was true. She was afraid, but I could hardly have her accompany me. "I doubt my bride would be happy to see me arrive with you in tow."

"You mean with a black whore in tow." Felicity scowled. "Pretend I'm a servant, a maid of all work, or some such. I don't care. I can't stay here."

"Felicity . . ."

"How can I make you understand? You're a man, a gentleman born, and no one will ever do anything bad to you because of that. But I have all counts against me, don't I? If you think people out there aren't above going around the law to do whatever they want to me, you're wrong. If not Mr. Perry, then someone else."

I did have compassion for her, but I'd come to know Felicity since she helped me during the terrible time of the Covent Garden abductions. She was ruthless, hard, smart, and determined. "You are an intelligent and resourceful young woman. You've managed very well for yourself thus far."

"Doesn't mean I'm safe now. Just tuck me on the top of the coach and pretend I'm a maid you hired. Her ladyship never need know."

Her ladyship always knew everything, so that was not a consideration. What changed my mind was Felicity's terror. I'd not seen her this deeply afraid before.

I made my decision. "Very well, but you'll ride with the coachman, and you'll behave yourself when you're in her ladyship's house. I aim to marry, and I'll let nothing stand in the way of that."

"Right you are," Felicity said in obvious relief. "I'll not interfere, Captain, I promise." She sent me her more usual smile. "And when you tired of married life, we can speak again. Every man does tire of it, you know. How do you think I make a living?"

I told her not to be impertinent, swallowed my misgivings, and left the room to make my way out of the house to the waiting coach.

Chapter Four

I'd grown to like Oxfordshire. I'd spent my boyhood in Norfolk, near the North Sea, flat lands under wide skies. The demarcation between land and sea hadn't always been clear—the gray-green marsh grasses blended with the gray-green of the water. When the tide was out, the land stretched for miles; when it was in, we were surrounded by ocean.

The lands around Oxford could have been in a different country altogether. Gentle hills lined with woods surrounded farms, pastureland, and meadows; hidden villages were tucked along roads that bent around beckoning corners. In the midst of it all, the Thames rolled along, here a calm river that spoke of serenity rather than the industrial waterway of London. The city of Oxford, with the spires of its university threading the sky, could stir me with its beauty, never mind that I was a Cambridge man through and through.

The roads that wound through all this beauty led to spreads of magnificent estates, and the coach took me to one of those now.

A thin dusting of snow coated the ground to either side of the wide, mile-long drive to Pembroke Court. The drive ended in front of the large manor, its bricks golden even in the weak winter sunshine. The house had been built—or rebuilt—in the early eighteenth century, and was a Palladian mansion with plenty of many-paned windows, arched pediments, and classic columns. A rotunda had been built onto the front part of the house, the main doors opening into it.

When I'd visited last summer, this house had been a haven of peace. The gardens had been in full bloom, my afternoons spent walking their paths or eating ices with Donata and her mother on the terrace. My evenings had passed in quiet conversation with Donata's father, Earl Pembroke, the nights after supper filled with music, games, and interesting discussions between the four of us. The mornings had been for riding and reading the reams of newspapers delivered to the earl at breakfast. My visit here had been tranquil, a balm to my soul.

On this winter's day, the atmosphere was much different. Two footmen and a butler came out to greet me and help me from the landau, but they were harried and rushed. The butler, a tall man with stately gray hair, tried to be as cool as usual, but I saw that he wished himself elsewhere. Even the bridegroom's arrival was not as important as whatever events were taking place inside, his demeanor said. But the servants were polite as always, the butler taking in my swollen eye, bruised face, and the bulk of bandages under my clothes without a blink.

Felicity, true to her word, kept to the top of the coach, riding it around to the back with the coachman after my luggage and I disembarked. I walked alone into the house to find it transformed.

Instead of the calm quiet I'd come to think of as embodying Pembroke Court, I found chaos. The whole of the house's staff hurried up or down the stairs, hanging garlands, carrying furniture, nailing up streaming ribbons, some barking orders, others racing to follow them. I'd observed a construction team tear down and rebuild a house near mine with much less noise and anxiety.

Several ladies, including my betrothed, supervised, gave orders, and even helped with the manual labor. Lady Breckenridge saw me and broke away, leaning over the stair railing to take in my sorry state. "Gabriel, what the devil has happened to you?"

"Tedious story," I said, but I knew I wouldn't put her off.

As she started down the stairs to me, I paused a moment to drink her in. Lady Breckenridge, the only daughter of Earl Pembroke, matched the elegance that was Pembroke Court, her childhood home. She was now thirty, had a weight of dark hair that today was knotted up out of her way, a sharp nose in a comely face, and shrewd blue eyes that noticed everything. At eighteen she'd married Viscount Breckenridge, who took her to live on his vast estate in Hampshire. Breckenridge had been a cavalry officer, a boor, and a womanizer, and Donata had shed no tears when he'd died. Her six-year-old son,

Peter, was the current Lord Breckenridge, and the huge manor house in Hampshire and its lands now belonged to him.

Breckenridge might have broken a lesser woman with his brutality, but Donata had gritted her teeth, swatted back at him with his own game, and survived. The survival had made her acerbic and unlikely to hold back her opinions, but I'd come to admire her spirit and intelligence.

This afternoon she wore a dress of moss green cotton embroidered with gold stitching at its cuffs and hem, with tiny embroidered flowers and gold stems flowing up the bodice to embrace her bosom. A white fichu made the gown modest but exposed her long neck. I thought her a vision in finery, but I knew she'd consider this a plain day dress, appropriate for supervising the decorating.

"Weary me with the tale then," Donata said. She frowned at a footman who'd squashed a flower while trying to weave a garland around the banisters, then stepped off the last stair to meet me.

She put her hands in mine, rose on tiptoe, and kissed my cheek, a subdued greeting, though we'd long since become lovers. But her father's household staff surrounded us, and she would behave nothing but respectably in front of them.

Donata pulled me away from the activity into the drawing room. "Mama and Papa are somewhere about, as is Grenville. I apologize for none of us greeting your carriage, but we had no idea when you were to arrive."

She looked pointedly at my injuries, which would mar my face when I stood up with her tomorrow.

"I was waylaid." I told her the story then, leaving

nothing out, including bringing Felicity with me. Donata listened to everything I said with steely calm.

Her first comment was, "As usual, you've landed yourself in something dire. I am familiar with rivalries — society hostesses I know wake in the morning planning how they will best their enemies that day. The way they scheme would make your generals against Napoleon look feeble. But the fact that Mrs. Collins was sent an explosive device hints at more danger than a mere jealous rival, do you not think? I do not blame the poor woman for running away. Are you supposing Mr. Perry sent the device?"

We'd moved to a sofa by then, a long couch made of rich satinwood with gold cushions, and Donata rested her hand on mine.

"The possibility occurred to me. Mr. Perry never told me why he was interested in my journey to the theatre, but he might be looking for Mrs. Collins so he can try again. Who he is and why he wants her are questions that need answering, but I'm more concerned with the whereabouts of Mrs. Collins herself."

"You will find her," Donata said with every confidence. "Grenville will help; you know that, and I will as well."

The idea of Donata being caught and questioned by Perry and the ruffians who'd blackened my ribs made me cold. She'd been put into danger before because of me poking into gentlemen's affairs.

"Is Gabriella well?" I asked, firmly changing the subject.

Donata's eyes flickered, knowing full well I was trying to put her off. She let me, though I knew we'd return to it.

"She is upstairs," Donata said. "Having a last-minute fitting to her gown. She is a robust young lady, not liking to sit still for long."

I couldn't stop my smile. "She is a Lacey."

"I must tell you that she is a bit nervous about meeting you again."

My own nervousness was rising, but I strove to hide it. "Why should she be? She must know by now I'm not a monster. Or at least, not much of one."

Donata touched my cheek, her fingers cool on my hurts. "Discovering after so many years she has a second father has been unnerving for her. Half a year has not been that much time to grow used to it."

The revelation had been shattering for us all. I'd believed for fifteen years that my only child was dead and gone, and to come upon her one morning in Covent Garden market, buying peaches of all things, had stunned me senseless. To find that Gabriella's mother had never told her I'd fathered her had stunned me further, and angered me beyond imagining.

I swallowed a hard lump in my throat. "I want to see her."

Donata got to her feet with me. "Let me warn her you've arrived. And that you look like a pugilist who's lost his final match."

I caught sight of myself in a mirror with a heavily gilded frame. I did look bad — bruises on my face and my cheek puffy.

I did not want to frighten Gabriella, but the need to see my daughter, to hold her hand, erased all worries about my appearance. Donata said nothing more, only walked away from me and out of the room, her green skirts making an agreeable rustling.

I followed her, not one who enjoyed waiting tamely in overly ornate reception rooms while others decided whether or not to fetch me.

In the hall I caught sight of Bartholomew, my valet who'd once been Grenville's footman, and his brother, Matthias. The two were lending their strong frames to helping the Pembroke servants shift furniture. At the moment, the two lads were carrying a heavy table across the large rotunda. They saw me, gave a collective stare to my beaten face, and went back to their task. I knew I'd be relating the tale all over again to Grenville soon.

I went on up the staircase, which wound around the rotunda, watching Donata's green skirt as it rippled softly around her leather slippers. Her ankles in white stockings were fine and slender.

Donata stepped off the staircase two floors from the bottom of the house and turned down a hall that was a series of rooms rather than a single corridor, one room leading into the next. Each antechamber was small but sumptuously furnished with paintings and ornate furniture, little jewel boxes leading to the main rooms at the end. I imagined Pembrokes of the previous centuries in their silks and powdered wigs rustling through these stately rooms, on their way to meet about important government business or for private assignations.

The fifth room's double doors were closed. Donata knocked once on them and turned the handle. "At least let me make certain she's dressed," she said, then slipped inside the room and closed the door in my face.

I waited in the outer room, which had a window with heavy brocade drapes framing a view of the park. In spite of the snow and the fading afternoon, the manicured gardens held their structured symmetry, evergreen shrubs encircling flowerbeds barren for winter. Beyond the gardens were trees and flowing hills, delightful country for riding. The difference between these elegant grounds and the coal-stained streets of London I'd left early this morning struck me anew.

This was Donata's home. I was a visitor here, and I always would be. Likewise I would be at the Breckenridge estate and the townhouse on South Audley Street in Mayfair. I ought to be annoyed by that—I would technically be the head of Donata's household and yet always be an outsider.

But I wasn't. I had a house of my own in Norfolk, which Donata was alarmingly determined to make something of, though the estate would never bring in any income.

Also, I had witnessed heads of households, including my own father, be utter bastards to their families until it was a relief to all when he finally dropped dead. Donata's first husband had been such a man, and I did not want to follow in either gentleman's footsteps. Give me a good friend, a warm woman, and a comfortable place to lay my head, and I was happy. Perhaps the army in me made me enjoy the simple things in life; I had no idea. In any case, I was content to be Donata's husband and had no interest in trying to seize any power from her and her son.

The door opened behind me, and I turned, my thoughts scattering like the light snowflakes on the winter breeze.

My daughter had grown a little taller since I'd

seen her in the summer—at least, I thought she had. She'd also grown more beautiful.

Gabriella had been taken away from me when she'd been a toddler, barely able to say my name. Now she was a young woman, poised to enter the world and make it fall at her feet. Gabriella was a Lacey, all right—her dark brown hair and brown eyes attested to that. I also saw my mother in the tilt of her nose and lift of her chin. Gabriella was garbed in a plain brown and cream striped day gown, the dress of a country girl, and she was regarding me critically, any shyness I feared absent.

I was the one who was awkward. I loved Gabriella with every breath I took and had missed her as hard.

I noticed Donata had stayed behind in the inner room, giving us privacy. I blessed her astuteness and tact.

"Gabriella," I said. The name stuck a little in my throat.

Gabriella gave me a polite curtsey. "How do you do, sir?"

She wasn't as demure as the correct words made her out to be. She studied me with frank curiosity, which was an improvement over the shock and confusion with which she'd regarded me when she'd first discovered I was her true father. Today Gabriella's look said she wanted to know all about me, including how I'd acquired such a spectacular set of bruises.

"I do well," I said. "Considering. Your journey from France was good?"

"We were a bit tossed on the crossing, but Lord Pembroke's carriage met us in Dover, and we were as comfortable as could be from there to here."

"And your mother and . . . Major Auberge? They do well?"

"Mama is fine, as is Papa." Gabriella said without embarrassment. Major Auberge, who'd stolen my wife and daughter more than fifteen years ago, had been the only father she'd ever known.

I had to stop and take breath. "And you?"

"Very well, sir. My health is good, as usual."

The Laceys had always been robust. I started to answer with another politeness, but I couldn't pretend any longer.

"Please don't call me *sir*, Gabriella. It's too bloody formal. My father made me call him that."

Gabriella's brows rose a little. "You mean . . . my grandfather?"

"Yes, and he was a selfish tyrant. I strive every day not to be like him, so please do not address me so."

"Then what shall I call you? I have no wish to be impolite, but I cannot call you *Papa*, sir—I mean, Captain. And *Captain* is too formal as well, is it not? I will have to think of something else that would not offend either my papa or you. *Father*, perhaps?"

My heart, which had been banging and drubbing during the little speech, slowed a bit. "Father. Yes, I like that." I nodded and hoped I wasn't babbling. "Father will do very nicely."

"I have thought a lot about it since we talked last summer," she said. "I must admit that discovering I had two fathers was very confusing at first, but I have decided after much contemplation on the matter to let it be comforting. I rather like knowing I have a father in France and a father in England. To be honest, sir . . . *Father* . . . the most difficult thing for me to face is that I am not French—that both my true parents are English. I'd been so proud of being French, you see."

Her downcast look made me smile. "Then I will do my best to show you how wonderful it is to be English."

Gabriella's obvious doubt made my smile turn to a laugh. I pushed my fears aside, put my hands on her shoulders, and kissed her cheek. "I'll make you fond of the damp and of boiled food." I paused. "No, I won't. I admit I preferred life in Spain and Portugal. I've often wanted to return there and sit in the sunshine."

"Perhaps you will," Gabriella said. "Perhaps when I come for another visit, we may go. I'd like to see it too."

Something tight inside me eased. I'd feared Gabriella would want nothing to do with me, that she'd come here for my wedding because her parents had pressed the obligation onto her. But she looked at me in eagerness now, as though determined to explore the possibilities of having a new friend in me.

Lady Breckenridge came out of the bedroom beyond, interrupting any foolish sentimentality I might have uttered at this moment. "If you've finished with your greetings, Gabriella, you need to resume your fitting, or they'll never have the changes made in time. Gabriel, Barnstable is upstairs—he'll tend to your injuries. At a wedding, guests should be gazing at the bride, not at a groom who looks to have been brawling with pugilists. We'll have a meal at eight, but we're in such sixes and sevens, it won't be much more than a cold repast. And don't you dare run off with Grenville before you have your face tended to."

So saying, my beloved fiancée whisked my daughter back inside the room. Gabriella shot me a look of amused sympathy before the door slammed shut, leaving me outside it.

I needn't have worried. All was well here.

*** *** ***

Lady Breckenridge's butler, a black-haired man called Barnstable, had doctored my injuries before. His homemade remedies had brought me more relief than had any physician's potions.

This time Barnstable cleaned my face and applied one of his ointments to my cuts. The mixture stung a bit, but I tolerated it, knowing it would help. He checked the ribs Denis's physician had wrapped, rubbed more ointment there, and rewrapped them.

"Takes down the swelling beautiful, sir," Barnstable said. "And how is the knee?"

My torn knee had seen his ministrations before, to its benefit. "It escaped great injury this time," I said. My abductors had kicked it to render me helpless, but they'd done little more than bruise it.

Barnstable tutted and gave me another ointment to be rubbed into it. He'd found me a spare walking stick and left me to change my clothes and rest. He too was helping with the wedding preparations, he told me, and could not linger. I, the groom, was superfluous.

Not that I minded putting on a clean shirt and breeches and lounging on the soft bed in the large guest room. I'd slept in this chamber before, in its wide, brocade-hung bed under a high ceiling painted a soothing white, with pictures of landscapes and horses hanging on the walls. This room had a different sort of elegance from Denis's extremely tasteful spare chamber with its one exquisite painting. This chamber was warmer, more homelike, welcoming.

I closed my eyes, hoping for sleep, but what I saw was Hannah Wolff, aging and blind, her head up while she spoke with worry for her friend. I also saw Perry leaning to me out of the darkness, his side-whiskers, nose, and brows outlined by the wavering rush light.

I heard a faint rustle *not* part of the dreams and woke in a hurry. I'd trained myself long ago to come instantly awake and to take hold of whatever intruder had come for me. I closed my hand around a thin wrist and opened my eyes to see Felicity standing next to my bed.

I released her the next instant, thankful I hadn't undressed for my nap. "Good Lord, how did you get in here?"

"Servants' corridors run behind the walls," Felicity said calmly. She left my side to flop into one of the chairs and put her feet up over its arm. "I can't stay downstairs. They want me to fetch and carry — did as soon as I walked in. The majordomo is a tyrant, and I'm no one's slavey."

"Well, you cannot be in my bedchamber," I said, rising and brushing off my clothes. "Her ladyship's tolerance is only so great."

Felicity expression held vast indifference. "I need a place to sit calmly and not be expected to carry about loaded trays and bins that pull my arms out of my sockets. The majordomo never so much as offered me coin for helping. I did my years in service, thank you, and I won't do it again."

Those below stairs would of course have put her to work immediately, if she styled herself as a maid. Staff in large houses always needed the extra help, especially with many guests arriving for an event. "I will ask her ladyship to provide you a room," I said.

"Don't bestir yourself. I'll sit right here until it's time to go back to London. Tomorrow night you'll be with your lady anyway. You won't be needing this bed."

"Felicity . . . "

"I see you have two choices," she answered without moving. "Lift me over your shoulder and carry me away elsewhere, or ignore me and let me stay here. Less embarrassing than her ladyship having to explain to the housekeeper that the servant you brought isn't really a servant and needs a room of her own. What will they all think?"

I had no doubt that Donata would put whomever she pleased into whatever room she pleased, and damn them all, but Felicity was right that I'd want to spare her any awkwardness. The late unlamented Lord Breckenridge had brought his mistresses into his house even when Donata was there, expecting her to look the other way. I did not wish the staff of this house to believe I was cut from the same cloth.

Before I could answer, someone knocked on my door. Instead of jumping up and hiding herself, Felicity remained where she was, yawning and settling deeper into the chair.

I limped to the door, opening it to reveal Lucius Grenville. He was as impeccably dressed as ever—he must have asked his tailor to make him a coat and breeches suitable for a gentleman in the country keeping himself out of the way the day before a wedding.

"Lacey . . ." He began, then saw Felicity.

"Hello, Mr. Grenville." Felicity gave him a wide and sultry smile. "How nice to see you."

Grenville stared at her then me, his animated dark gaze assessing. "Lacey, why have you got an impertinent London street girl in your bedchamber on the eve of your nuptials? And why do you look as though you've gone back to the wars? Mathias warned me of your appearance, and I knew I had to come and dig out the story."

Nothing for it that I invited him in, let him seat himself—far from Felicity—and tell my tale again. Felicity punctuated the most dramatic moments and emphasized that I would still be under my captor's power had she not rescued me.

"A nice problem," Grenville said when I'd finished. "Trust you to have interesting adventures the moment I turn my back. But no matter. I'm in them now. Where do we begin?"

Chapter Five

We could not begin right away; I needed to get married.

Grenville at last convinced Felicity she could not sleep in my bedchamber and took her off to find better accommodations. Where, I did not know, but I trusted Grenville's discretion.

Thankfully, I passed an uninterrupted night with much-needed sleep and woke to find that the swelling in my face and the pain in my ribs had gone down a bit.

Bartholomew came for my morning ablutions as usual. He prepared a bath for me, then shaved me, being careful of my cuts and bruises, and helped me into my regimentals. Grenville had offered to purchase a new tailored suit for me for the occasion, but I'd declined. Not from pride at his charity, but because these regimentals—cavalry, Thirty-Fifth Light Dragoons—were who I was. Lady

Breckenridge understood.

Bartholomew brushed the dark blue coat and its silver braid, which he kept in good repair, and settled the epaulets on my shoulders. I regarded myself in the mirror, a tall, upright man with unruly brown hair, a bad knee bent a little with my injury, and dark brown eyes that had seen much. My face, which never was able to lose its shadow of whiskers, was now decorated with dull red cuts and purpling bruises.

But while I could long for the handsomeness of my former commander, Colonel Brandon, or the charm of Grenville, I had learned that I could only ever be myself. Donata knew what she was marrying—no illusions. Her own experiences had stripped any romantic notions from her. She knew me for what I was, and I knew her.

I gave a final nod to Bartholomew, who at last stepped back from settling, brushing, and smoothing my coat and let me go.

I descended, my shako beneath my arm, through the splendor of the decorated house to the gold drawing room, where the ceremony would take place. The influence and money of Earl Pembroke had obtained a special license, so we could be married at Donata's home rather than in a church, and a bishop had come to perform the ceremony. It was nine in the morning, fresh winter sunlight filling a cloudless sky.

The gold drawing room had been so named because of the amount of golden satinwood and gilt furniture that filled it. The room itself was vast, the length of it exactly double its width. The high coffered ceiling was of polished wood, its grain reflecting sunlight that poured through the multitude of arched windows. The predominance of gold in the fabric, the wood, and the gilt was contrasted by reds in cushions, colorful landscape paintings, and scarlet and white hothouse flowers.

For the wedding ceremony, the sofas, chairs, and tables had been pushed to the sides of the room, and guests filled in where the furniture had been. Lady Breckenridge's mother, Countess Pembroke, had been correct about the warmth of the chamber when she'd suggested it the day I'd proposed to Donata. The room was heated by three fireplaces, two on either end and one in the middle of the inside wall.

The guest list contained only family members and a few close friends, but the room was plenty crowded. Though Donata was an only child, she came from a large family; Earl Pembroke had two younger brothers and a sister who'd each married and born issue. Several of the grown children of these had already born issue themselves. Pembroke's uncle and *his* substantial family had also come, as had Lady Pembroke's brother — another earl — and his family. Donata's close friends and the friends of her parents filled out the room.

I was represented by Grenville, my daughter, and my daughter's French step-uncle and aunt. The uncle, Quentin Auberge, was the brother of the man who'd eloped with my wife and stolen my daughter. The tone of Major Auberge's letter, when he'd written to me that his brother would accompany Gabriella across the Channel, had implied that he didn't think it appropriate for himself or Carlotta, my former wife, to attend my wedding. I'd quite agreed.

Though Quentin Auberge and his wife spoke little

English and were country gentry rather than aristocrats, they'd had no trouble getting along with Earl and Lady Pembroke, who both spoke fluent French and shared interests with the Auberges. At least I'd not had to worry about entertaining them.

Gabriella wore the gown she must have been fitted for yesterday, a thin white muslin over a cream-colored slip, the muslin embroidered in bright colors at the cuffs, neckline, and hem. Her hair was done up in a fashionable knot, exposing her white neck. Gabriella would be eighteen soon, a young lady ready for the world.

My heart squeezed with something akin to pain. To me, she'd always be the little mite who'd clung to my boot while I walked about camp, or rode on my shoulders as we visited my comrades in arms. My fellow soldiers had laughed at me and called me Lieutenant Nanny, and I hadn't cared one whit.

Gabriella smiled at me, serene, protected by her aunt and uncle, nothing troubling her young heart at the moment. I longed to change the world so nothing ever would.

I'd entered the room on its far side to stand near one of the large fireplaces with Grenville and the bishop. Grenville gave me a look of approval, hard won from him. But Bartholomew had done a fine job on me, cleaning and brushing the uniform, polishing my boots until I could see my face in them. I'd bathed so long my skin felt soft and wrinkled, but Bartholomew hadn't let me out of the bath until I'd gleamed like my boots.

Grenville was as natty as ever, but I noted that he'd not tried to out-dress every gentleman in the room this morning. He kept himself subdued in his monochrome suit, letting me have my day.

No, not *my* day. The crowd quieted as the double doors on the other end of the chamber opened to reveal Donata poised on the threshold, her hand on her father's arm.

The beating of my heart drowned out all other sound. I knew the women of my acquaintance— Louisa Brandon, Lady Aline Carrington, and my landlady Mrs. Beltan—would demand from me the details of Donata's wedding finery. I also knew I'd never be able to tell them.

I saw only Donata's fine-boned face and the way the light played upon her dark hair, how blue her eyes were as her gaze fixed on me. She seemed to be in shimmering silver, though later I realized that her gown was a glistening net over a more solid dress. But I couldn't have told if the gown fastened in front or back or what sort of sleeves it had, wouldn't remember the intricate pattern of blue ribbon across her bodice. I only knew, when Donata stopped beside me and gave me a sharp look, that the ribbon matched the color of her eyes.

We'd be a misalliance, as plenty of impolite people had pointed out—she an earl's daughter, me the son of a country gentleman, pretty much a nobody as far as London was concerned. But Donata was a widow, her first marriage having given her a son who was now a wealthy viscount. Her second choice in husband would not be as socially crucial. She had money, she had standing, family, and respectability. And now she had me.

My first marriage had been hastily performed by a country vicar via special license, I having stolen my bride from her family with the help of Colonel

Brandon. He had procured the license for me so we wouldn't have to flee to Gretna Green as did so many other illicit couples. I scarcely remembered the ceremony except my triumph as I signed the register, Carlotta, my bride, nearly collapsing in nerves.

This ceremony was much different. Slow, stately, and performed with all the pomp that could be managed, the wedding to Donata would not be forgotten. Her father put her hand in mine, and her warmth came to me through her touch.

And thereto I plight thee my troth.

My truth, my fidelity. I to her, and she to me. As I slid the gold band onto her finger, I repeated the words for the second time in my life. *With this ring, I thee wed; with my body, I thee worship; and with all my worldly goods, I thee endow.*

I didn't have many worldly goods, but I would gladly give her everything I was. My heart was in the kiss I pressed lightly to her lips. This lady with the sharp tongue, shrewd stare, and decided opinions had saved me from emptiness.

And so, I was married.

*** *** ***

The wedding breakfast commenced in the sumptuous dining room, the table full of Donata's family. My daughter sat next to me, her manners as polished as anyone's—she'd do no shame to her family. Donata had told me her plans for bringing Gabriella out this Season, to dress her in muslin and feathers and parade her about ballrooms in order to find her a good match. When Gabriella had come to London the first time, her stepfather had told me about a young man in France who'd been sweet on Gabriella, but apparently nothing had come of it.

This summer, when I'd mentioned him, Gabriella had looked surprised and told me the young man had married. Therefore, according to the world, Gabriella was free for the plucking. My feelings about that were in flux.

For now I had laughter, flowers, feasting, toasts to the bride and jokes that bordered on the crude about the groom. Ladies and gentlemen alike laughed at me, but I could only feel triumph.

Donata took it all in her stride, sending barbs back to her friends that set them laughing. We were a merry lot, though I did catch dark looks from two gentlemen—Cecil Pembroke, Donata's third cousin, son of her father's uncle; and her first cousin Edwin Phillips, the son of her father's sister. Donata had told me both had hoped to make her their own, thus growing closer to more Pembroke money and becoming stepfather to a viscount.

She had related this to me with some glee. She disliked both gentlemen and had vowed never to marry either. She'd arranged for them to stand close to the front at the ceremony so she could rub in the fact that she'd eluded them.

The wedding breakfast and extensive celebrations that followed continued without Cecil or Edwin shooting me, though they looked as though they'd be happy to. When the short winter day came to a close, we were cheered upstairs amid rather ribald remarks.

"Thank God that's over," Donata said as we closed the doors on our wedding suite.

We'd been given another guest chamber, this one entered via a short series of rooms like the one Gabriella and her aunt and uncle occupied. Our suite was in a corner of the house, far from the other guests, and very private. I was grateful to Lady Pembroke for her percipience.

I could not stay away from my wife. I slid my arms around her waist, finding warm woman under the smooth elegance of the dress. I pressed a kiss to her lips, this one holding more heat than had the kiss at the ceremony.

"Regrets, Mrs. Lacey?" I asked.

Her blue eyes flickered. "Too early to tell. Ask me in a year."

"I will be happy to," I said, and then we turned to other matters.

I rejoiced in my lady that night. Donata had warm skin which was smooth under my hands, a body that held no thinness of want, and an embrace that filled my heart.

She was never shy, my lady. She held me as I held her, rose to me as I came to her. We joined together, lovers in truth, both giving, both taking our pleasure.

I drowsed beside her later, aware of Donata scrutinizing me again.

At any other time I might ask her what she was thinking. But not tonight. Tomorrow we would renew our usual banter, and our arguments, and begin married life. Tonight I traced her cheek and pulled her close to bury myself again in the warmth of her.

*** *** ***

I'd half expected interruption in the night— Felicity arriving to demand to bed down in the suite's front room, or Cecil or Edwin barging in to challenge me to a duel.

Nothing so dramatic occurred. Not until I was

dressing in the late morning did Grenville, who had risen early to go riding, send word through Bartholomew that no one could find Felicity.

At the moment, I was not inclined to worry. For once I'd kept to Lady Breckenridge's habit of lying abed late instead of rising at my usual time before dawn to ride and breakfast. I had better things to do this morning than ride about the countryside or keep track of stray street girls.

"She might have gone back to London," Donata offered from where she lounged on the Sheraton sofa in our bedchamber. Bartholomew had come to dress me, and Donata had donned a yellow silk dressing gown to drink coffee and watch the proceedings. "This Felicity is not a feeble young woman, if I remember her aright."

"She might have done," I said. "But she was very frightened of Perry and begged to come here with me to keep away from him."

"Perhaps someone here frightened her more," Donata said.

Because my new wife was a perceptive woman, I gave her suggestion some consideration.

"Mr. Grenville said he looked for her while he rode," Bartholomew said. "But he didn't see no sign of her. She might be hiding in the house, but I ain't seen her, and neither has Matthias."

Concern began to rise through my languor. Lying against the pillows this morning with my bride in my arms had been a fine thing. I'd rested in a bubble of happiness, safe from the cares of the world.

But I knew that the world marched on outside our door, the bubble was temporary, and we'd go on living life with all its complications and dangers.

"I'd feel better if I could find her," I said. "A horseback ride to the village to look about would do me good."

"I'll have a look through the house myself," Donata said. "I know its hiding places, having hidden in most of them when I was a girl. Enraged my nanny and governesses to no end." She took a sip of coffee, smiling in memory.

I could not leave without giving Donata a lingering kiss on her lips, which Bartholomew watched with tolerant amusement.

"You may keep your remarks to yourself," I said to him as we descended the stairs.

"No remarks, sir. It's good to see you happy."

It was good to be happy. My bad knee and my ribs hurt me only a little as I went down, the euphoria of my night still clinging to me.

I met Grenville, who'd been in conversation with one of the many Pembrokes, and he agreed to join me. Outside was clear but very crisp. My breath hung heavily in the air, and steam rose from the horses the groom brought us from the stables.

"Do you truly think Felicity ran off somewhere into the countryside?" Grenville asked me as we rode away from the house. "She seemed happy with the empty bedchamber I found for her. It's a lovely day, but brutally cold."

I drew my greatcoat closer about me. "To be honest, I have no idea where she would go, or why. Felicity does as she pleases." I pointed out a path. "Let's try this way."

I turned down an overgrown, little used lane that led across a field and then under trees. The trees blocked the morning breeze at least.

Nowhere did we see a misplaced London game girl walking along, or being carried off, or any sign that anyone but us had come this way. We rode out of trees down to a canal, following the towpath. That canal led to the Thames, rolling quietly along between lightly snowy banks.

We went all the way to the village, through it, and around the other road back toward the house, seeing Felicity nowhere.

By the time we returned to the estate, I wasn't certain whether to be worried or not. Felicity could have caught the mail coach and returned to London without bothering to tell me. She could by lying low for reasons of her own. With Felicity, one never knew.

Donata had not found Felicity hiding in the house either, including in the guest room I'd occupied the day before. My concern increased. I made myself feel better by sending a message off to Denis in London, asking him to keep an eye out for her. The messenger left from the posting inn by fast horse, bolstered by the large tip I gave him and the promise of a larger one from Denis. He did not look happy, but he went.

I itched to begin my search for Abigail Collins, but I could not until my sojourn here was over. I already had obligations, including the grand New Years' ball Lady Pembroke had planned for tonight. Half the county would attend, and I was expected to be there for the full of it.

Fortunately, while the night's entertainment was lavish, and the guests did stare at me, they were at least polite. We rang in the New Year, I kissed my bride again in front of her family and friends, then we retired for the night.

I was enjoying married life so far. Once we were abed, I took from the bedside table a small box that contained Donata's New Year's gift. A pair of earrings, tiny and gold, agonizingly chosen with the help of Louisa Brandon.

I knew Donata possessed jewels of far greater cost and ostentation, and earlier this winter I'd presented her with a tiny miniature portrait of a young girl, painted several hundred years ago by Hans Holbein. But Donata's eyes softened when she saw the earrings, something truly from me. She handed me my gift, a watch, heavy and gold, inscribed: *To G. with much esteem, D., 1818.*

My way of thanking her lasted well into morning. We drowsed as the sun rose, bringing in a new year, a new day, a new life.

A tap on the outer door of the suite was followed by it opening and someone coming quietly into the sitting room. The inner doors to the bedchamber were closed, so I could not see who'd entered. The step was too light for Grenville, too secretive for a servant—in this house, they strode boldly about their business.

I rolled from the bed, donned a dressing gown laid out for me, thrust my feet into slippers, and went out.

It was my daughter. I closed the bedchamber doors behind me and ran hand through my mussed hair. Gabriella was in her dressing gown as well, her hair hanging down her back in a long braid.

"Good morning, Father," she said softly. "Happy New Year."

I went to her and took her hands. "Happy New Year to you, my dear. I have something for you."

I started to turn to fetch the bracelet I'd bought her, but Gabriella tightened her grip, stopping me.

"I came to tell you something. You were looking for the maid who came with you? I found her."

"Felicity? She's all right?"

"I should say so." Gabriella gave me a grim smile. "Come with me. I'll show you."

Chapter Six

Gabriella led me by the hand through the series of anterooms outside our suite and around a corner to a more modern part of the house. She put her finger to her lips and took me about halfway down a long corridor lined with ornately paneled doors.

We stopped in front of one of the doors, but Gabriella did not move to knock upon it. She gave me a little shake of her head to indicate we should wait.

For a few moments, nothing happened. Then I distinctly heard Felicity's low, throaty laughter. Oh, good God.

I pointed at the door. "Whose?" I mouthed.

Gabriella led me back down the corridor to its end. A niche between that hall and the older part of the house held a wide window with a window seat overlooking the grounds.

"I believe his name is Lord Bradford," Gabriella

told me. "An older gentleman, and married. His wife's room is a little way down the hall."

"Good Lord." I debated storming in and pulling out Felicity, but while I would not mind enraging Lord Bradford, it would embarrass Lady Bradford, not to mention my host and hostess. I studied Gabriella, whose eyes sparkled with amusement. "You do not look very shocked, Gabriella. Please do not tell me you approve."

"Of course I do not. I rather like Lady Bradford. But it is not uncommon, is it? For men to take lovers? At least among the wealthy classes. So says . . . my papa." Her tongue tripped a little as she made the distinction.

"No, it is not uncommon. But I'd not have spoken of such things to a child."

"In France it is spoken of more openly, even if we don't approve," Gabriella said, a little primly. "And I am not a child."

The stubborn words, spoken with a little push of her lips, reminded me strongly of the little girl she'd been. I sank to the window seat, pretending my leg hurt me, but in truth I could not breathe. January morning cold came through the window, but I had to sit still for a moment before the ache inside me eased.

I cleared my throat. "I suppose someone will inform Felicity when our coach is leaving for London."

"I will make certain. I must say, I am looking forward to London and staying with Lady Breckenridge . . . Mrs. Lacey, I mean. I want to see the city. Properly, this time."

Another qualm, this one of remembered terror when Gabriella, come to London last year with her mother, had gone missing. I took her hand and held it between mine.

"I am so sorry for what happened to you, Gabriella. The bastard is dead; you know that. He cannot hurt you anymore."

"I know." Remembered fear flickered through her eyes. "But I want to mend. I want to see the streets and the sights, find a London that is not frightening."

I tried a smile. "I'm not certain that's possible."

"This time, you will be with me. I know that if I'd listened to you before and trusted you, I'd have been safe."

"Do not blame yourself. It was my bloody fault."

"Do you think that?" Gabriella gave me a thoughtful look. "I have had a long time to contemplate this, sir . . . Father. I was confused and frightened, and young. I hope I am more sensible these days."

How long a time half a year was to the young! But I admired Gabriella for her determination and courage. She could have remained in France cowering in her stepfather's home instead of deciding to face life and conquer her fears.

"This time, you'll stay in a fine house in Mayfair and be perfectly safe," I said. "You'll have plenty of people to look after you—Donata, Mrs. Brandon, Lady Aline, the Derwents. I promise you this."

Gabriella wrinkled her nose. "Smothered, you mean. My parents have looked after me with embarrassing watchfulness. But do not worry, I am not so foolish as to run off on my own because too many people are concerned about me." She shivered. "Never again, in fact."

The man who'd abducted Gabriella had stolen her

sense of safety and the ease with which she moved about on her own. I hated him all over again. I rarely was glad when a human being died, but the man who'd hurt my Gabriella deserved what he'd gotten.

I squeezed her hand. The niche was cold, and by tacit agreement, we returned to the warmer confines of my suite to tell Donata what Gabriella had discovered. As I closed the doors against the chill, I wished I could likewise close the doors on all fear and pain my daughter could experience. I knew, though, that life would never be that simple.

*** *** ***

Felicity did appear when we were boarding coaches to return to London. She only looked at me when I growled at her, and languidly climbed to the landau's box.

"Such a fuss," she said. "I am not truly your servant, Captain, if you'll remember."

I could have lectured her about her promise to behave herself, but I gave up. Felicity had survived alone for years, using her charms to provide herself safety, money, food. She'd done what had come naturally to seek comfort, and probably gifts, while she hid.

I kept my frown in place as Felicity ascended, then I climbed with some difficulty into the coach, my ribs still aching, and settled next to my wife.

My wife. I could scarce believe it. Would I become old, very married, and dull, nodding to Donata down the table while I shoved my feet deeper into my slippers and absorbed myself in newspapers? I hoped so.

The fifty or so miles back to London was blissfully uneventful, and Donata's private landau kept up a good pace. Donata slept much of the way, the coach swaying slowly. Gabriella alternately rode with us and with her uncle and aunt in the coach lent by the Pembrokes behind us. Donata's son Peter alternated along with her, his nanny in the coach with the Auberges.

Donata expressed surprise that I was happy to have a six-year-old boy in the coach with me, but I wanted Peter to learn I would not shunt him aside now that I'd married his mother. He was a sturdy lad, already with the bullish look of his father. He was a bit awestruck with me—my great height and voice, I supposed. Plus, I had been told, to my distaste, that I at times resembled the late Lord Breckenridge.

Peter sat quietly on the seat when he rode with us, as though determined to prove he could behave. He seemed taken with Gabriella and talked with her readily. My new family was a bit pulled together, I reflected, but that ride to London was the best journey I'd taken in many years.

Grenville, despite the chill, had elected to ride horseback, changing horses at inns along the way. He did not explain his choice, but I knew he did it in deference to his motion sickness. The gentle ride that had me dozing with my head on Donata's shoulder would have had him quaking and ill in a trice.

Seeing the smoke and chimneys of London as we rode down the last hill told me my blissful journey was over. The idyll of being with Donata and the comfort of the Pembrokes' house was coming to an end.

Why returning to the metropolis should dishearten me, I did not know. I'd be living in

Donata's comfortable South Audley Street townhouse now, with her butler Barnstable bringing me coffee and remedies whenever I wanted them. But the sight of so many buildings packed together after the peace of the countryside in Oxfordshire made my high spirits dissolve. Perhaps it was my nature to sink when entering the gloom of black smoke and too many houses, to rise when riding alone in the openness of wilder lands.

Donata's coach pulled up, very late in the night, at the house in South Audley Street. Barnstable, having left Oxfordshire the previous day to arrive before us, led us inside to put us to bed.

The first impediment in my married life occurred then. Barnstable led me to a bedroom separate from Donata's.

"All gentlemen require their own chambers, sir," Barnstable said with some surprise when I objected. "As do ladies. I do not believe his lordship and her ladyship ever occupied the same bedchamber in all of their marriage."

"I will point out that I am not Lord Breckenridge," I said, weariness making me sharp. "Nor will I ever be. The current Lord Breckenridge is bunking down in a cot in the nursery. I am a simple army captain, who shares a bedchamber with his wife."

Barnstable had been taught not to argue with his employers, so he said nothing, only stood in the middle of the chamber looking put out.

Donata wandered in as though she noticed nothing amiss. "Very well-done, Barnstable. Thank you. Is the chamber not to your taste, Gabriel?" she asked once Barnstable had discreetly retreated. "I know you are partial to my guest room, but it is far too small for you, and this one has a dressing room through there." She pointed at a slender door in the middle of the wall.

When I'd been an overnight guest in her house ere this, I'd always stayed in a tiny but comfortable bedchamber, or in Donata's bed. The chamber currently in question was next to hers—Donata had the room in the front of the second floor, while this was in the back. Between the rooms was the narrow space of the dressing room.

The chamber was luxurious enough, the bed a solid piece of furniture with a brocade canopy, plenty warm for winter nights. A large table and chairs were arranged before a wide fireplace already flickering with warmth, as well as a wingback chair and cushioned footstool, ready for a man with a tired, war-injured knee.

It was sumptuous, but it bothered me. "This was Lord Breckenridge's chamber," I said.

Donata ran her hand along the back of the wing chair. "The finest in the house. Did you expect Breckenridge to take a fourth-floor room or the attic next to the nursery?"

"I'd expected we'd share a chamber. I did not marry you to keep my distance."

Donata shrugged and put on the indifferent air she did so well. "You have the run of the house now, Gabriel. Sleep where you like. This room is yours for any time you wish to be masculine and alone, far from feminine clutter."

I gave her a stiff bow. "My apologies. I do not mean to appear churlish, when you are going to such pains for me."

Another shrug. "It is your way to be churlish

when you are uncomfortable and annoyed. I know you'd be much happier sleeping in a hole in the cellar, but Barnstable would feel the sting of it. I put you in here for another reason." She dropped the indifferent air and gave me one of her pointed looks. "This was indeed my husband's chamber. I want to forget he ever occupied it. What better way than to cover it with much better memories of you?"

I stared at her. She returned the look without timidity.

My response to her sentiment would have highly embarrassed Barnstable if he'd chosen that moment to return. But he never interrupted, and Donata and I began then and there to layer fresh memories over this room.

*** *** ***

Felicity, who had spent the night in a maid's room in the attics, decided in the morning to be off. She'd meant to slip out without telling me, but Bartholomew alerted me, and I met her in the street when she emerged from the scullery. She said without rancor that she thanked me for my help, but she had a pal she could stay with, where she'd be safe. I reminded her how frightened she'd been of Mr. Perry, but she insisted she'd be perfectly fine with this friend — man or woman, she wouldn't say.

Her fear was still there, I saw, but she was adamant. I wondered if something had changed, and what she knew, but she closed against my questions.

What she couldn't do, Felicity said, was stay in a toff's house, where again, the staff expected her to work. She'd found her own way most of her life, and she would again. She thanked me for looking after her, and she went.

I watched her walk down the street, her head up as she met the stares of Mayfair servants who were about on errands at this early hour. I realized that trying to keep Felicity was like trying to cage a tropical bird who'd only known wildness. She was still afraid, but she had an even greater horror of shutting herself away from the world.

I would simply have to find Mr. Perry and make sure he never carried out his threats on Felicity. I was certain, at least, that Felicity would stay well out of his way.

Donata had made it clear she'd keep her usual hours of rising sometime after noon, and Gabriella and her aunt and uncle were still resting after their late arrival. Therefore, after breakfasting alone, I returned to my rooms in Grimpen Lane, intending to finish the-clear out interrupted by Marianne and my subsequent adventures, and to begin my search in earnest for Mrs. Collins.

I took a hackney to my destination, keeping a close eye out for any other ruffians wanting to break more of my ribs. I would not be caught so easily again.

The dingy street and smoke-stained houses of Grimpen Lane were a far cry from the wider avenues and mansions of Mayfair, but at the same time comfortingly familiar. One can grow used to anything.

It was early and cold, but the upstairs curtains in the house opposite mine were open their usual distance apart. Mrs. Carfax was the soul of frugality, saving on candles by having her companion, Miss Winston, open the curtains the moment she could discern dawn.

I nodded up at Mrs. Carfax's window, in case she or Miss Winston watched, took out my key, and opened the door that led to the dark stair alongside the still-shut bakeshop.

A burly man stepped out of the shadows beside the shop so suddenly I had to bite back a shout. I recognized one of Denis's men, sent, as always, to keep an eye on me.

"Bloody hell," I said when I recovered.

He remained impassive to my temper. "Bloke is up there waiting for you, sir."

Not many months ago, this man, a former pugilist, as were most of Denis's lackeys, had helped tear apart my old manor house in Norfolk. He'd made a very interesting discovery behind the kitchen fireplace and believed my response to that discovery shortsighted, tending toward the mad. His name, if I remembered aright, was Brewster.

"What bloke?" I asked. "Perry?"

"Naw. Wouldn't have let *him* go up, would I? I'd have hauled him back to Curzon Street. This cove picks the lock and walks in, sweet as you please."

"Picked the lock? Why didn't you stop him?"

"Wasn't about to, was I? He's a Runner."

"Pomeroy?" I'd take Pomeroy to task if so. The Bow Street magistrate's house was not many steps from Grimpen Lane. If my former sergeant had wanted to speak to me, he could have left a note at the door or in the bakeshop, or sent word to Lady Breckenridge's.

Brewster gave me another deprecating look. "Would have said Pomeroy if I'd meant him. No, some other Runner. New blood. Never seen him before."

Curiosity worked through my irritation. Why the devil should a Runner break into my rooms? If he searched for something there, he'd be disappointed. I hadn't much to find.

Nothing for it but to see what he wanted. I opened the door, still unlocked, and made my way up the stairs.

This staircase was steep, a more arduous climb than the stairs in Donata's house. I'd left the borrowed walking stick behind in Oxfordshire, planning today to obtain a new one, and now, with my still-aching ribs and throbbing knee, I had to hang on to both rails to drag myself up the stairs. The faded shepherds and shepherdesses on the walls smiled at me in greeting.

The door to my rooms was ajar. I walked in to find a large man with long red side-whiskers sitting in the wingchair in front of my cold fireplace. He was reading a notebook he'd taken out of one of the still-open crates, a notebook filled with my writing.

I'd begun, after my return from Norfolk, to chronicle the adventures I'd lived through in the last two years. Grenville's idea. He told me that such events would be fascinating reading for others — my children, at the very least, might want to read about what their aging father had got up to.

I was not the most articulate of writers, and I was not best pleased to find a complete stranger sitting in my rooms, reading my words.

I put one hand on the doorjamb to steady myself. "Who the devil are you?"

The man unfolded himself from my chair, cradling the journal in his hands. He was nearly as tall as I was, and he filled out his suit in the same way as did the pugilist Brewster downstairs. The suit was cheap—black wool, shiny with wear at cuffs and elbows, but neatly mended. His waistcoat was dull gray with a watch fob hanging across it.

The Runner had a square face with heavy red brows, light blue eyes, and thick, reddish-brown hair he'd tried to tame with pomade. His eyes held arrogance but also amusement, as though he enjoyed laughing at the slowness of others.

"Interesting reading," he said, holding up the book. "Quite clever how you worked out who truly did a murder during the chaos after a battle on the Peninsula. Reaching back into the past with no witnesses to solve a crime. Remarkable."

"That is a private journal," I said, my lips stiff. "And you did not answer my question."

"Left out in plain sight in the top of this crate." The Runner closed the book and returned it to the pile of the others. "I wasn't to know, was I?"

"A crate behind my locked flat door, not to mention the locked door at the bottom of the stairs. Forgive me if I thought my things safe. Now then sir, who *are* you?"

The man came to me, extending his hand. "Spendlove. Timothy Spendlove. I am new to the Bow Street house, but I've been patrolling from the Queen's Square house for some time. I've been needling Pomeroy to introduce me to you, but you know Pomeroy. If he doesn't want to do a thing, he's immovable as a mountain."

I didn't much want to shake the hand of a man who'd broken into my rooms without shame, but I did anyway. A man's handshake can tell much about him. Spendlove's was firm, the flesh of his palm hard, but he didn't try to squeeze or use undue pressure.

"Why did you want an introduction?" I asked, when we released the grip. "To discuss what is in my journals?"

"No, indeed. Though they are interesting." Spendlove patted the leather cover of the top one. "I am not here to discuss your past, Captain, but your present. In particular, why you are interested in the whereabouts of the actress Mrs. Abigail Collins and why Mr. John Perry is interested in *you*. And why, after your abduction by Mr. Perry, you ran at once to Mr. James Denis."

I closed my mouth over my retorts. I did not at all like that Spendlove knew everything that had happened to me in the last week, and where I'd been. He didn't mention Felicity, but if he knew about Mrs. Collins, Perry, and Denis, he'd know about her too.

Spendlove smiled at my reaction. "I should be clear. I am most interested in your connection with Mr. Denis. The others are superfluous. I'd like to know all about Denis, every single detail. I have made it my life's work, you see, to have James Denis arrested, tried, and hanged for his many, many crimes. Therefore, I will value anything you can tell me. Some of your activities involving him have been a bit, shall we say, questionable, and it's best that you relate everything I want to know. Do you understand me, Captain Lacey?"

Chapter Seven

My leg throbbed, and I had to sit down. The only open space was the upright wooden chair next to my table, so I made my painful way to it and sank to its unyielding surface.

I understood Mr. Spendlove quite well. Since I'd met Denis I'd tried to keep myself from being caught up in his world and its consequences, but here I was.

"What makes you think I can help you?" I asked. "I've been trying to stop Mr. Denis for two years."

"Have you now?" Spendlove looked down his large nose at me. "And yet, I've observed you assisting him to shut down one of his rivals, kill a few men, and sell on pieces of stolen artwork. Stopping him? I'd say you were assisting him."

"No." I clenched my jaw. "Denis uses people, like me, whether they wish to be used or not. He turns any event to his benefit. If you've been watching him, you will know this."

"I do know it. I also know he has magistrates looking the other way at his crimes—he doesn't pay *them*, you understand, they pay Mr. Denis to leave them be and hand them a criminal or two from time to time. But never mind about that. I came here today to give you a friendly warning."

I regarded him in irritation and did not respond. Spendlove's thin smile widened.

"A warning that I'll stop at nothing to get Denis," he said. "If *you* have to be hanged into the bargain, so be it. I don't much care how many magistrate friends you have, or if Sir Montague Harris or Thompson of the River Police praise your wit and ability. I won't let anything stop me, especially not a retired captain with too much time on his hands. So, stay out of my way. Leave off the inquiries about Mrs. Collins too, there's a good chap. We at Bow Street know all about her fleeing London after she received her mysterious package. Obviously such inquiries will be dangerous to you—already have been, haven't they? Bow Street can't be expected to dig you out of a scrape because you could not keep your nose away from what did not concern you."

"Let me worry about that." I made myself stand up again, though my leg had stiffened as I sat in the cold, and straightening it hurt. "I am uneasy about Mrs. Collins. There's nothing to stop me from inquiring after a friend."

"You'd never heard of the woman until a few days ago, except as an actress you watch with your viscountess and that idle Mayfair dandy." Spendlove tapped the top of my journal. "In here, I can see what you think about the slowness of Pomeroy and the rest of the patrollers and Runners. I agree with you somewhat about Pomeroy's wits, but he's the man to have by your side when a villain is trying to get away, believe me." He gave me a cold look, though his little smile never faded. "You are not the law, Captain Lacey. Leave it to those whose job it is."

"Every citizen in England is obliged to assist the Watch and the magistrates," I pointed out.

"*Assist,* not interfere. I'll find Mrs. Collins, don't you worry. *And* bring down Mr. Denis. Choose your battle, sir. And have a care which you choose. I'll bring you down with Denis if I have to. Don't matter to me that you just married into the upper crust. They answer to the law as does everyone else." Spendlove moved past me while I stood still, aching and not a little angered by his arrogance. "Good day, Captain. Heed my warnings, and we'll remain friends."

So saying, he grabbed a low-crowned hat from the shelf next to the door, gave me a nod, clapped on the hat, and walked down the stairs, whistling.

I remained in the middle of the room, unmoving, while I heard him go out the door to the street. More whistling sounded outside, a greeting of *Good day, madam,* to someone passing, then his clumping footsteps faded into the distance.

I stood still until a dart of pain shot through my leg again, and I had to sit back down on the hard chair.

Eventually anger overtook my pain and surprise. Spendlove had come here today to needle me and alarm me — picking the locks and entering my rooms had been calculated to demonstrate how much I should fear him. But Spendlove did not understand how difficult I was to intimidate.

Also, if Bow Street had been as diligent as Spendlove claimed about looking into Mrs. Collins' whereabouts, Marianne wouldn't have worried enough to ask me to search for her. Mrs. Wolff and Coleman likewise wouldn't be so troubled.

No, this was Spendlove's need to elbow his way into a new magistrate's house and take power for himself. I should dismiss him. Pomeroy at times grumbled that I got in his way, and didn't mind taking me to task over it, but I'd never let his bluster bother me.

However, as I climbed to my feet again and straightened my journals in the crate, Spendlove's words sank in and would not become dislodged. I was not frightened of him, but I knew he'd become a new ripple in the serenity I'd hoped I'd finally brought into my life.

*** *** ***

By the time I'd finished filling my crates and sent word to the company I'd hired to take the things to Donata's house, the morning had advanced, and the bakeshop was open. Two sturdy men arrived to carry the crates down the stairs and to a wagon waiting in Russel Street. They took everything, leaving behind only the furniture that had been in the flat when I'd arrived. The bits and pieces of furniture Grenville had given me or I'd purchased over the years had gone to South Audley Street before I'd left for the wedding.

I looked around the empty flat after the men made their final haul, strange feelings assailing me. So this was the end. The last of my memories of Grimpen Lane.

I'd lain in much pain in the bedchamber's huge

tester bed, recovering from both my war injury and my melancholia. There too, I'd curled around Donata and realized how much I loved her. In the sitting room, I'd argued with Marianne, discussed cases with Grenville, faced Denis and other men who'd tried to do me harm, lived through terror about my daughter's safety, and experienced impossible joy when she'd been found. These rooms had been both a haven and a hell, and I was startled how much I was loathe to leave them.

I had a thought. I went downstairs after I'd closed and locked the doors and sought Mrs. Beltan below. Her bakeshop was doing brisk business, as it did every morning, with plenty of housewives, maids, and errand boys queuing at her door for the day's freshly baked bread.

Though Mrs. Beltan and her assistants were busy shoveling bread into and out of ovens, Mrs. Beltan did pause for me while I asked my question.

She looked startled but pleased. "Well, if you want to continue paying on the rooms, I'll not object, Captain. You're a good tenant, for all your gruff ways. But I'd thought you'd be glad to be quit of this place, now that you're moved into fancier digs."

"The rooms would be handy for consulting in," I explained, "without bothering her ladyship. And I might now have the means to make some improvements to them."

Mrs. Beltan liked that, I could see. She was a fair woman, but frugal, never spending a penny when a farthing—or nothing at all—would do.

"Well, if you can provide a bit of paint and polish, so much the better. I'm choosy about my tenants, you know."

I did know. She'd let Marianne take rooms even with Mrs. Carfax's disapproval, but Marianne, for all her faults, had never brought gentlemen or unsavory guests back to her flat—she'd disappear with a gentleman who fancied her for a time instead.

I thanked Mrs. Beltan, bought a bun, and left the bakeshop.

Instead of returning with the cart to South Audley Street, I hobbled through the cold to begin my errands. Since Drury Lane theatre was nearby, I started there.

Covent Garden was open for the day, and a crush of humanity surged there to buy the freshest produce and other foodstuffs and household necessities the markets had to offer. I was kept safe from the danger of pickpockets and Mr. Perry by Denis's man Brewster, who followed me, not discreetly. I imagine Denis had chastised him thoroughly for letting Perry grab me.

I finished chewing the warm bun by the time I walked into the theatre's back passage. I knocked at the stage door, the sound echoing in the relative quiet. Silence met my vigilance, and I knocked again. As I was about to turn away, the door was yanked open then closed to a crack. "What?"

"Mr. Coleman," I said. "It's Captain Lacey. I came here a few days ago with Miss Simmons to speak about Mrs. Collins, remember?"

He gave me a nod. "You found her yet?"

Coleman's look told me he wondered why I'd return without doing so first. "No. That is why I would like to speak to Mrs. Wolff again."

Coleman peered past me in some suspicion. "Where's Miss Simmons?"

"I saw no reason to drag her out on a frosty morning. Is Mrs. Wolff about?"

"No, she ain't here. Mrs. Wolff don't come 'til it's warmer."

"Will you let me in, regardless? It's brisk."

Coleman looked me up and down as though thinking I should be able to stand a little winter breeze. But wind blew through the passage with Arctic chill, the temperature below freezing this morning. Coleman finally gave me another nod, jerked the door wider, and admitted me to the dark theatre.

The hall inside was not much better for warmth, but at least it was out of the wind. Coleman led me down the passage to the room with all the costumes, which was warmed by a stove, and stood still, waiting for me to speak.

"Do you know a Mr. Perry?" I asked him. "John Perry?"

The change in Coleman was instant. He stopped being impatient and effused a river of rage. "Why'd you want to know about *him*?"

"He gave me these bruises you are so curiously examining." I gestured to my face. "Or, at least, his friends did."

"Why?"

"I never did discover," I said. "He was interested in my visit here, but I did not remain with him long enough to find out what he wanted to know. Who is he?"

Coleman's angry gaze moved from my face with its healing bruises to my boots, polished by Bartholomew this morning but muddy from the streets. He took in my suit, well-made but one of my older ones, and the new hat under my arm.

He wasn't certain of me, but most people were not. I was a landed gentleman but not wealthy, from an old family that was not sought after for its connections. Finally Coleman gave another nod and answered. "Mr. Perry is Mrs. Wolff's husband."

My eyes widened. "Husband?" I thought about Perry and his thick face and wiry hair, and Mrs. Wolff, small, frail, blind, aged. "How can he be her husband?"

"The usual way," Coleman said without humor. "Banns, church, written in the parish register. She never did say why she did it, but some years ago, she did. They live apart now, and she won't go by his name. She's terrified of him, she is. I thought he'd gone north and stayed there."

"He was here three days ago and had me abducted and confined. Why? Is it he who's been frightening Mrs. Collins?"

Coleman shrugged his big shoulders. "He was likely wondering why you came here when none's here but Mrs. Wolff and me."

"Is Mrs. Wolff safe now? Where does she live? Not alone, I hope. If Perry is still about . . ."

"She lives with her sister and sister's husband, in a big old house off the Strand. She's safe enough there. Sister and her husband look after her. He's a clerk or some such in the City. I walk Mrs. Wolff home every night and drop 'round to walk her here every day. I'll keep Mr. Perry away from her."

"You might want to take more precautions than that. Perry had hired men pound me to the ground, and he won't hesitate to do it to you either. Blasted man lost me a walking stick."

Coleman listened to me without blinking. "Thank you for the warning. I'll find more to help me protect Mrs. Wolff while you find Mrs. Collins. Now, I must be getting on."

He seemed in a hurry for me to go away. He'd been much more cordial during our last meeting, but Marianne had been with me, and Mrs. Wolff had been there for him to worry about. I saw in him that he would protect Mrs. Wolff and resented any implication he would not.

I decided it best to leave for now. I thanked him and departed the room alone, Coleman having no intention of accompanying me.

The revelation of Perry as Mrs. Wolff's husband stunned me—I would not have guessed that. If Perry had coerced her into marrying him, it would be for a sinister reason. I wondered very much why she'd agreed.

Because Coleman had left me on my own, I took a wrong turn in the corridors behind the stage and ended up nearly walking onto the stage itself. I stopped when I realized my mistake, and looked out from the wings.

The theatre appeared very different from this angle. The stage was deep and wide, with plenty of room for elaborate sets, though today the boards were bare. Beyond the proscenium, the seating rose in a semicircle of stalls and boxes, stretching upward to a domed ceiling, which was decorated with pilasters and hung with chandeliers. It was lovely, like a most lavish ballroom.

Only one player was on the stage just now. A smallish man was walking about, back and forth, muttering to himself. As I watched, he turned to the nonexistent audience, rose to his full height, and bellowed out, "O cursed, cursed slave . . . Whip me, ye devils, from the possession of this heavenly sight!"

I realized I was watching none other than Edmund Kean, the great tragedian. I hadn't recognized him until he'd changed from the bent, muttering man to the lamenting Othello in one step. He'd *become* Othello in the space of that moment, war-weary, believing the woman he loved was betraying him.

Kean turned and saw me. Abruptly, Othello faded, and Kean, now only an irritated gentleman, limped toward me. "You there. What are you doing?"

I made the best bow I could. "I beg your pardon, sir; I did not mean to intrude. My name is Captain Lacey. I was asked here by Mrs. Wolff and Miss Simmons to look into the disappearance of Abigail Collins."

As Mr. Kean did me the courtesy of listening, his intense, dramatic gestures disappeared, and he looked at me in ordinary worry. "It was a bad business, that." He shook his head. "I was not here the day the package came, but I heard the entire story from Coleman. Poor Mrs. Collins. The gunpowder could have marred her for life, killed her even. I do not blame her for fleeing, even if it is playing merry hell with the schedule. If you're off to find her, do persuade her we will do everything to protect her when she returns. We need her."

"You believe she is staying away of her own accord?"

Kean shrugged. "What else? She is a strong

woman and a brilliant actress, but badly frightened. I have no idea who is tormenting her. No doubt a rival, who took it too far."

"I'd say the package shows much more evil than simple rivalry. The gunpowder might have killed not only Mrs. Collins, but perhaps Coleman, or Mrs. Wolff—or you—if it had been opened without thought."

Kean shuddered, a flash of his dramatic self escalating the shiver, before he shook his head again and returned to being a mere mortal. "It is obvious you know nothing of the world of the theatre . . . Captain, is it? I've elbowed my way into plenty of theatre companies and roles, although it never would occur to me to kill or maim for them. Humiliation of a rival, however, I am not above." He gave me a brilliant smile, and this man two-thirds my height again looked taller and more robust.

I could see his talent in these flashes, when he became a different person entirely. I'd watched him play Richard III in this very theatre and would have sworn he was in truth a pathetic hunchback consumed with the desperation to hold on to his crown.

"Who are Mrs. Collins' rivals in particular?" I asked him.

"My dear Captain, I could name a hundred. Begin with the other actresses in this company, then move to those of Covent Garden, Haymarket, and others. Dramatic actresses only, I would think. When Mrs. Collins speaks as Portia or Cleopatra, she *is* them, her voice rich and beguiling. I've seen her render the entire theatre into a mass of weeping. But she has no talent in song—cannot carry a tune, poor woman.

Thus, I would eliminate sopranos and any women in musical productions."

I saw his concern behind his words, which I sensed weren't spoken in humor. He was outlining to me what he considered the greatest possibilities.

"What about male rivals?" I asked. "Or spurned lovers, that sort of thing?"

"Mrs. Collins has no spurned lovers. She's had lovers, of course, but she always manages to part with them without fuss. Her husband, an actor of not much consequence, died of fever long ago. That is why I believe in this rival. Sift through them, find the prankster, and bring Mrs. Collins back to us. Tell her to hurry it up, there's a good fellow."

Kean spoke as though I could rush away, lay hands on Mrs. Collins, and be finished by nightfall. I suppose that was what he wanted me to do.

Finished with me, Mr. Kean gave me a vague, "Nice to have met you," and turned away, walking back across the stage. He returned to muttering under his breath, ignoring me completely.

I left him to it. I had to make my way back to the corridor and search for the door again, but I eventually found the passage that led me out to the tiny lane behind the theatre.

As I walked to Russel Street, I had the feeling of leaving one world behind for another. Inside the walls of the theatre, the magic of the stage and actors like Kean existed in a sort of soap bubble, the rivalries, jealousies, threats, and little joys pushed together and distorting the world outside. Outside the walls, we went about our lives, tending to our needs, taking care of business, and looking forward to the few hours we could spend in the magical world of the theatre.

I put aside my whimsical fancies once I joined the swarming populace of London in Russel Street, and continued with my errands.

I wanted to visit the delivery company who'd sent the package and then to speak with Marianne, but I faced the fact that first, I needed a new walking stick. Nothing for it. My leg was hurting in the cold, and if I were to rush about London, I would need the prop.

Shops in the Strand would sell walking sticks. Grenville might chide me for not patronizing the most fashionable haberdashery in Bond Street, but at the moment I simply needed something to help me stand.

I hired a hackney to take me the few streets south where I began to roam the shops. I wondered if I were anywhere near where Hannah Wolff lived with her sister, but I had no way of knowing in which of the many lanes around the Strand she dwelled. Coleman had shoved me away before I could ask, and I doubt he'd have told me, in any case. Another detail I would have to pry from Marianne.

I had to look into a few shops before I found a stick that suited me. It didn't have the excellent sword my other had hidden inside it, but I hadn't much choice at the moment. The one I purchased was of stout oak, well polished, its brass handle formed into the bill of a goose, similar to the head of the one I'd lost.

After my purchase, I made my way to Fuller and Hamilton Deliveries, also on the Strand. The firm had rooms in a respectable-enough looking building opposite Somerset House, near St. Mary's le Strand. When the head clerk understood that I was not, in fact, hiring them to deliver a package, he dropped his polite manner and wanted nothing to do with me. Bow Street, he said, had upset them enough, trying to blame them for the package, wanting to go through and open every parcel in their offices. What customers would trust them, once galumphing Bow Street Runners had torn open all the goods?

I had to talk quickly before I could convince him I had nothing to do with Bow Street, and was in fact the friend of a friend of Mrs. Collins. The man was inclined to toss me out, but at the last moment, he agreed I could speak to the clerk who'd taken the delivery order. He wanted my promise I'd go away after that, and not to Bow Street.

I gave my word I would keep whatever they told me in confidence and use it only to help Mrs. Collins, which was the truth. I had no intention of assisting Spendlove.

The clerk who appeared was a younger man, in his twenties, I surmised, his face still a little spotty with youth. He had very dark hair and a pale complexion, his smallish eyes darting about nervously. He had not been the same since the incident with the package, he told me, and had asked to work in the back of the shop, and not with the customers.

"I wouldn't say the chap was spindly exactly," the clerk said when I asked him about the man who'd dropped off the package. "Thin, yes, I think. Difficult to say. But his suit was fine. A respectable gent. Except he kept laughing. Big teeth. Quite an admirer of Mrs. Collins, he said, which was why he wanted to send her a gift. Too timid to take it to her in person. Best way, he said. His hands weren't small, I noticed, but rather big. Unusual, I thought, because chaps with big hands are usually tall."

"But he was not tall?"

"Oh, no. Not like you, sir. About my height, I'd say. I could look across right into his eyes."

The clerk stood about halfway between five and six feet. I'd met many men in London of similar height, Grenville included. The description did not advance me much, but it took away the possibility of Coleman. Coleman was unmistakably huge.

The young clerk still looked shaken by the incident. "Not your fault," I said. "You weren't to know."

"I wasn't, was I? The package looked all right, didn't weigh much, didn't rattle." The clerk's forehead shone with sweat. "Good thing I didn't open it up to look inside, wasn't it?"

"No one was hurt by it," I said. "That is what you must remind yourself. The man at the theatre realized the danger in time and knew what to do."

"Thank God for that, is all I can say. Gave me a turn when I heard, and then the Runners came and asked me all sorts of questions, as though I'd made the thing myself."

"It is their way," I said, thinking of Pomeroy and his zeal. "But you are not to blame. They know that."

The clerk did not look reassured. Likely it would be a long while before he felt calm again.

The head clerk wanted me out, that was obvious. I gave each man a half crown for his trouble, which made the head clerk a trifle more polite, and I took my leave.

I found another hackney and traveled west, ending up rolling along Piccadilly. I debated who to visit first, Marianne or Denis. The early hour decided for me. Marianne these days kept the same hours of rising as Donata.

I directed the coach to take me to Curzon Street. I had no appointment with Denis, but I'd long since decided that if he were to use me to carry out tasks for him, he'd have to put up with me coming and going when I pleased.

When I arrived at the house I was taken upstairs right away, to my surprise, and ushered into Denis's sparse but tastefully decorated study.

Chapter Eight

Denis's desk was bare as it often was, the usual pugilists standing near the door and window to guard him. No, not the usual. The man, Cooper, who'd been a fixture in this room, was gone.

Denis saw my gaze drift to where Cooper used to stand, and the look he gave me was hard. I returned it with a neutral one of my own and sat in the offered chair.

"The incendiary device," I began, both of us forgoing polite greetings. "Would you have any idea who could make this sort of thing? I'd like to ask him who hired him to construct it."

Denis steepled his long fingers before he answered in his cool, careful manner. "I have already put together a list of possibilities. When I find the man I will let you know. Or the woman."

I blinked. "You cannot think a woman made that terrible thing, can you?"

Denis gave me a thin smile. "You are a romantic, Captain. I assure you, the female sex is capable of committing ruthless and violent acts. You wish to believe all women are mild and kind, but you see only the veil of manners society creates for them to hide behind. Your own wife is anything but mild."

"True, but I do not believe she would build a box to blast gunpowder into a person's face. Whoever made this knew what it would do, and yet crafted it anyway."

"And I have a few in mind who would do it. I will cull the list and send word when I have found him."

"Or I could help in the search." I felt a great desire to put my hands on this person as quickly as possible.

Denis gave me a small shake of his head. "This is a task I must do myself. These are extremely dangerous people who would kill you before you reached them. You have come to me for my expertise in this matter; now you must rely upon it."

I had to concede his point. I told him what I'd discovered at the delivery office, which I did not think much, but he nodded as though making a note of it.

When I mentioned Spendlove and his crusade against Denis, Denis revealed he already knew all about him, which did not surprise me.

"He is another problem to leave to my expertise," Denis said. "Mr. Spendlove will not trouble me for long."

Alarm touched me. "I hope you are not thinking of having him killed. The magistrates will not look the other way if you murder a Runner."

"Your thoughts stray to violence so quickly,

Captain. There are other ways of controlling a man."

"Such as giving him something he needs and could never obtain for himself," I said. "And asking him to run unsavory errands for you in return."

Denis met my mild expression with one of his own. "I believe you and I have gone beyond simple debt and repayment. Far beyond."

I did not like the assertion, but again I had to concede the point. In Norfolk I'd become caught up in the drama of his life, and I'd openly helped him commit crimes. My fate and his were tied, and Mr. Spendlove knew that.

"Perhaps," I said.

"More than perhaps." Denis sat back in his chair, making the small gesture that meant he was finished with me for now. "I will send word when I have found the maker of the device. If you gain more information that might help, by all means, pass it on to me." He did not rise when I did, only regarded me across his empty desk, his narrow-fingered hands flat on it. "But do not look for these men yourself. It would be the end of you."

"I would think you relieved to be rid of me," I said.

His gaze met mine for a moment, whatever emotion in it unreadable. "You would be mistaken. Good day, Captain."

I gave him a polite nod, moved to the door, which one of the pugilists opened for me, and went out.

I mused over what Denis had said as I descended and went out into the cold again. I wondered if his last declaration contained any sentiment, or if that again was my romantic view of the world. I was cynical enough to tell myself that Denis meant the words exactly as he'd said them, no more. I was useful to him. He'd dared form a bond of friendship with one other man in his life, and that bond had cost him dearly.

I decided to walk to Clarges Street, which was not far. I did not want to wait any longer to ask Marianne more about Mrs. Collins; I still had very little information about the woman. If Marianne was not yet awake, I'd rest in her luxurious downstairs drawing room and wait. The day had truly turned cold, but any house Grenville paid for would be warm and comfortable.

Marianne's footman opened the door to my knock and told me, to my surprise, that Marianne was both at home and out of bed. A maid led me upstairs to her private sitting room, but when I entered the room, I found Marianne in dishabille and Grenville with her. I was interrupting a tête-à-tête.

Grenville lounged in a chair of the Louis XV style, which was all gilt and embroidered cloth. He wore a dressing gown over a loose shirt and ankle-hugging pantaloons, his feet encased in slippers rather than shoes. He sipped from a glass of claret and had one lock of hair out of place.

Marianne, in a peignoir, her hair caught in a simple knot, greeted me without an ounce of embarrassment. Grenville's face was a bit flushed as he nodded at my "good morning," but he strove to maintain his sangfroid as always. I wondered why the devil Marianne had agreed to let me upstairs, but I behaved as though nothing was out of the ordinary.

"How goes married life?" Grenville asked, languidly lifting his claret again. The maid brought me a glass of the blood-red wine and retreated, leaving the three of us alone.

"I have no complaints about my *married* life," I said, sitting down and sipping the claret. Smooth, rich, excellent. "The other bits of my life are more complex." I told them both about my visit to the theatre and the delivery company, Kean's advice for me to talk to Abigail Collins' rivals, and my encounter with Spendlove.

"Have a care," Grenville said. "You get away with much, because you have won the respect of Runners and magistrates. I should not like to see this Spendlove make things difficult for you."

Before I could answer, Marianne said, "Lacey makes life difficult for himself, all on his own."

"That I cannot debate," I said, savoring another sip of claret. "But I've come to ask you more about Mrs. Collins. If you can cease mocking my character and tell me about her and anyone who might wish to see her hurt, it would help."

Marianne shrugged, unworried about my irritation. "There is not much to tell. I have not seen much of Abby lately, very little since we started at Drury Lane six years ago, in fact, though we used to be great friends. But she's a principal, and I, never more than chorus. There is a chasm between the two, you know. When one of the chorus crosses to the lofty pinnacle of principal, her life changes, and she has no more time for her old friends."

Marianne spoke nonchalantly, as though none of it mattered, but I saw a sadness in her eyes.

"Is that what happened with Mrs. Collins?" I asked. "She used to be chorus, and left others behind?"

Marianne nodded. "Abby was chorus in the old

days, when we were in a company of strolling
players together. When we came to London to try
our luck, she became an understudy after a year or
so, which can be death, or it can blossom. For Abby,
it blossomed. One day she's playing a maid in the
great hall, the next, she's walking onstage as
Gertrude. Main actress broke her leg. End of her
career, beginning of Abby's."

Grenville broke in. "Which must have led to
resentment?" He'd left behind his embarrassment
and listened with his usual curiosity.

"Well, of course. The trouble with the theatre,
gentlemen, is that there are many aspiring actresses
and few roles, especially for women. Shakespeare is
the favorite in all dramatic theatres, but he only
wrote a few great roles for women, didn't he? — Lady
Mac, Cleopatra, Viola, maybe Cordelia, though she's
such a milksop. Her evil sisters are more fun to play.
The moderns have a bit more for women, but
audiences love Shakespeare. When I started,
companies would let us buy our way into roles. Lady
Mackers was the most expensive, though I managed
to scrape enough together to buy Ophelia once. But if
the audience doesn't like you, the company manager
won't let you buy in again."

"Did Mrs. Collins buy her way in?" I asked.

"Of course she did. She was a few years older
than me, so Gertrude and Lady Mac were her roles of
choice. Abby was well liked right off. Got in a lot of
practice. But when we joined the professional
strolling players, the lead actresses didn't want
anyone taking their plum roles. So Abby was chorus,
with me. After a few years, we decided there was
nothing for it but we should come to London, where

we'd be famous." Marianne laughed, a sincere laugh. "Every actress' dream, isn't it? I discovered fairly quickly I'd never move higher than the chorus. It didn't matter. Acting was a job to me, a way to make a few coins, not what I wanted to do forever. But for Abby, acting was in her blood. The theatre was her life. She worked hard. And she got what she deserved." Marianne spoke without rancor, nothing but admiration in her voice.

"What about other actresses at Drury Lane when Mrs. Collins was elevated?" I asked. "Were they angry?"

"I'd say so. Quite a few mutters that she grew so popular only through a stroke of luck, or that she took the right lovers to get herself to the top of the company. But the truth was, Abby was that good. The committee didn't have to think hard about giving her lead roles."

"Would any of these ladies have been angry enough to send Mrs. Collins the incendiary device?" I asked.

"I wouldn't think so." Marianne let out a sigh. "But I admit I have no idea. Only an understudy can be certain of taking over an actress' role if the actress is hurt or ill, as Abby did, but that understudy might only be able to continue for that play. The theatre's committee would decide who to hire to take over all Abby's parts, and they might entice someone away from another company. There's no guarantee someone from the Drury Lane chorus would get the roles in the end. Anyway, Abby didn't receive the letters or package until the very end of the season. Why would the understudy wait that long? Mrs. Wolff told me an understudy hasn't been appointed yet for this season, so no one stands to gain by keeping her away at the moment." She let out another sigh. "Besides, if I'd thought any of the actresses at Drury Lane responsible, I'd have confronted them with it outright. I'm at my wits' end, which is why I asked you for help. Now that you are safely married, will you go out and find Abby? Please?"

The *please* was delivered with an edge to her voice, but I saw in Marianne's eyes that the plea was real.

"I am trying to gather information before I rush about England," I said. I took another sip of the fine claret and thought about what would help me. "Tell me about her husband, Mr. Collins."

Marianne started. "Collins? What the devil for? He's dead, isn't he?"

But jealousy and a need for vengeance could last a long time. I shrugged. "Indulge me."

Marianne continued to glare at me as though she had no intention of answering. Then she snatched up the teapot on the table beside her and poured herself a cup of tea. The tea smelled exotic, probably the best the markets had to offer. Marianne took a sip, making no reaction to it, and scowled as she set down the cup.

"Very well, if you must know the story— Frederick Collins was an actor in the traveling company we joined. Abby fell for him pretty quickly, and they married after only three months of courtship. He was younger than Abby by several years. Well, they were lovebirds for a time, until Abby wanted to go to London with me. Collins wanted to stay in the poky country, settle down, and have a family. But as I say, Abigail had the theatre in her blood. She didn't want to settle. She wanted to play at Drury Lane or Covent Garden. They quarreled over it constantly. Finally Collins agreed to come with Abby and me." Marianne lifted her teacup again, her fingers unsteady. "It was the end of him, poor man. Not two weeks after we arrived in London he caught cold in the awful boardinghouse we lodged in, and died. Abby grieved—she'd truly loved him—but then she threw herself into acting heart and soul. And the rest is as I've told you."

Grenville listened to all this with interest, and I knew he, like me, had never heard these tales of her past.

"What made *you* decide to become an actress?" I asked her. "If theatre isn't in your blood as it is for Mrs. Collins?"

Marianna dropped her frown and beamed a smile at me, one of her coy, maddening smiles. "Now that question has nothing to do with Abby or her going missing. It's pure sordid curiosity."

Grenville said, "It might have some bearing on why Mrs. Collins went missing. Else Lacey wouldn't ask."

"Well, Lacey can take my word for it. You are not investigating *me*, gentlemen."

The affable Grenville was growing impatient. I forestalled his next remark by asking, "What about other principal actresses at Drury Lane? Would they be likely to want to frighten Mrs. Collins? I met another of the actresses once. Mrs. Carter."

When Grenville and I had traveled to Kent to investigate murders that had happened in an army regiment, the gentlemen there had played an appalling came, dealing out cards that represented the ladies among us gentlemen. Mrs. Carter had been one of the ladies so dealt.

The game was how I'd met Lady Breckenridge. I'd drawn the card that indicated I should escort her about, among other things. She'd assumed me a boor, like her husband, and I hadn't thought much of her.

"I wouldn't think so," Marianne said. "Mrs. Carter is famous enough in her own right and doesn't need to consider Mrs. Collins her rival. But you never know with actors. Rivalries can be vicious, and the tricks actors play on each other mean. Coal dust mixed into face powder, costumes loosened or made uncomfortably tight, crucial props going missing at the last minute, the way to the actor's entrance mysteriously barred. A rival might do anything to make an actor look incompetent to an audience, or a manager."

"Including sending devices that could kill?"

"I promise you, no one I know would go that far," Marianne said. "Although, perhaps the person only thought the device would mar Abby's looks, give her scars. Abby is pretty—not a stunning beauty, but you'd never know it when she throws herself into the parts. But with a face too scarred even for makeup to cover, she'd be done, wouldn't she? It would break her. I'm frightened for her, Lacey. Abby's been a good friend to me."

"I promise I will do all I can," I said. "Now, what about this man, Perry? Do you know why he is married to Hannah Wolff?"

Marianne shook her head. "As to that, I never learned. Puzzling, isn't it? I thought perhaps Mrs.

Wolff needed his money, now that her career is over, but her sister's husband, Mr. Holt, is a cit, and makes decent coin. They're happy to look after her. Perry must have had some sort of hold on her. It's the only explanation."

"Coleman seems to watch over her."

"Coleman's potty about Mrs. Wolff." Marianne smiled. "He worships her, always has. After she lost her sight, he became her watchdog. Doesn't let her stir a step without him. She doesn't mind. He'll take care of her, don't you worry. But I can try to find out what Perry has on her."

Grenville reached over and clasped Marianne's hand where it lay in her lap. "Not you. I want you to stay as far from Mr. Perry as you can. If he's not above having gentlemen beaten and abducted, I don't want you near him. Or even near the theatre."

Marianne looked annoyed but didn't jerk from Grenville's grasp. "What did your other mistresses do when you locked them away all day?" she asked him. "Embroider?"

"I am not locking you away. I told you—come and go as you please. I only want you to stay far from harm."

"I've faced gentlemen and situations far more frightening than John Perry in my life, I'll have you know," Marianne said. "Believe in my resilience."

"You *are* resilient," Grenville said. "That doesn't mean I want you to have to face such things ever again. What is my wealth and position for if I can't use them to protect what I care about?"

I saw Marianne's expression soften. Not for long, but the tightness at the corners of her eyes went away. I pretended to focus my attention elsewhere while they watched each other.

I took a discreet leave after that, and the two of them didn't seem to mind me going.

*** *** ***

I walked the relatively short distance to South Audley Street, noticing that Brewster, whom I'd spotted resting against a bollard near Marianne's house, followed me all the way.

When I entered Lady Breckenridge's townhouse, I found it a hive of activity. Luncheon had come and gone, the afternoon advancing, and I was hungry.

Me missing the meal seemed not to be a cause for consternation. Barnstable merely asked if I'd dined when Bartholomew pushed past him to take my coat, and when I replied in the negative, said he'd send a repast up to my rooms, or her ladyship's, as I preferred. Her ladyship was awake now, and taking coffee in her boudoir.

The Auberges and Gabriella were up and had eaten, and now were preparing to go shopping.

"Hello," Gabriella greeted me distractedly as she and her aunt and uncle bundled up against the cold. "We are going on a quest. We're to visit Egyptian House and then book shops. I want to buy English books, though Mrs. Lacey says I must have more clothes." She made a face, telling me that the wonders of Egyptian tombs and the contents of books were more important to her than the latest fashions. "Will you join us, Father?"

The manner in which she asked suggested Gabriella had debated a long time whether to include me and had decided it would be polite to do so. Her invitation was given with clear words and a smile, but because she'd told herself it was the right thing to do.

With reluctance, I shook my head. "I have been on too many errands this morning, and must plan many more. I will take you to Grenville's tomorrow and show you his Egyptian collection. I believe it trumps most museums, except that they have larger pieces. You will like his house — one of the most interesting places in London."

Gabriella looked relieved, though she tried to mask it. I kissed her cheek, letting a surge of tenderness erase my current frustrations and worry. She kissed me back on both cheeks, French fashion, and followed her uncle and aunt out to the waiting landau.

I saw them off, Gabriella waving to me through the carriage's window.

Brewster lingered near the railings that separated the scullery stairs from the street. I beckoned him over and asked him to follow the carriage. He tried to argue that Denis had paid him to watch *me*, but I told him that if Perry or anyone else harmed my daughter or the Auberges, I'd hold him responsible. Brewster gave me a sharp look, but finally he nodded, turned away, and jogged after the slow-moving landau.

I went upstairs to Donata's private sitting room. My wife lounged full-length on a Roman couch, a bandeau woven through her dark hair, her peignoir flowing over her legs. She read correspondence that was scattered on her lap, a thin black cigarillo clasped loosely between her fingers.

"There you are, Gabriel," she said without looking up. "Do you always rise so painfully early?"

"Always." I leaned down and kissed her forehead.

She looked at me then, her brows drawing together. "What has happened? You look worried. Tell me. Perhaps I can help."

I sat down next to her where she made room for me on the couch and rested my hand on her slim ankle. My first wife had never been the remotest bit interested in anything I did. It was refreshing to pour out the events of the morning while Donata listened and made comments with her usual perceptiveness, smoke from the cigarillo slowly curling about the two of us.

"I do not like the sound of this Spendlove fellow," she said when I'd finished. "He must not be encouraged to believe he can simply step into your life and cause you trouble. I have solicitors, you know, who are now at your disposal."

Well I knew. The Breckenridges and Pembrokes both had plenty of solicitors and men of business to deal with their properties, financial holdings, and other legal matters. I'd already faced a barrage of them over the marriage settlements that ensured I didn't rob Donata of all she had.

"I dislike to employ them to keep me out of Newgate," I said.

"Well, I do not dislike it. I went to much trouble and patience to get you to propose to me, and I'll not lose you to a trumped-up Watchman."

I tried a smile. "You contrived to make me propose?"

"Of course I did. You sparked my interest during that billiards game at Astley Close, when you were so disgusted with me. I at first wanted to punish you for your rudeness, and then I began to like you and wanted you to like me."

"Then my falling in love with you was according to your plan?"

"Indeed."

Her feigned nonchalance warmed my heart. "Perhaps your schemes worked too well. Now you have a husband who is excellent at tweaking the noses of those in authority, and who is always perilously close to trouble."

Donata took a pull from her cigarillo and let smoke trickle out with her words. "I know you are. You cannot help being the man you are, which is why I have such affection for you. But I will not have my husband spending the night locked away in Bow Street for trying to help people. You will find Mrs. Collins and get Mr. Perry arrested for what he has done to you, and to the devil with Mr. Spendlove."

Now we came to why I had such affection for *her*. Her spiritedness, her caring, her interest in life beyond her own circle. I caressed her ankle. "I was not prepared to drop my search, in any case."

"Good." The word was delivered with emphasis. "How will you commence? The best thing would be to ascertain Mrs. Collins' safety. If she is in someone's clutches, we must get her out of them."

"I do intend to find her," I said. "And keep her safe if I can."

"I have been thinking this through while you were out. A journey to Bath might be the thing—we can look for Mrs. Collins and plan for your daughter's future at the same time. She must learn a little polish, but that will be simple, as she has an unspoiled, natural manner. Bath is a bit plebian, but Gabriella will enjoy it. She will meet the right sort of young men there, which might bring us luck when I bring her out later in the Season."

My worry about Perry, Spendlove, and Mrs. Collins evaporated on a wash of confused emotions. "She's a girl still. Why are you so quick to marry her off?" I must have sounded resentful, because Donata gave me a look of surprise.

"Gabriella is nearly eighteen. Better for her to settle soon into a match—the engagement can last as long as anybody wishes. A betrothal to a good gentleman prevents her eloping with a slippery-tongued blackguard or accepting an offer in desperation from an old French farmer who needs a nursemaid."

All good arguments, but we were talking about my little girl. "You had an early marriage," I pointed out, making my voice gentle. "Arranged by your family."

"If you mean I should give up looking for a good match for Gabriella because my first marriage was a disaster, you will fail to convince me. The match was perfectly fine, as a matter of fact. My parents and I were much deceived in Breckenridge's character, is all. But my widow's portion is more than adequate, I have use of this house for my lifetime and a place at the Hampshire estate until my son marries, the dower house after that. And Peter's future is assured."

True, Breckenridge at least had not kept his wife in penury, but he'd been crude, disgusting, and openly promiscuous.

Donata continued, not in the least bothered by Breckenridge now. "A perfect excuse all around to allow you to look for your missing actress. We'll let Gabriella enjoy London for a few days—I do need to get her fitted for a wardrobe—and then be off to see the sights. Bath first, then we'll take Gabriella to Brighton to see the Pavilion. Grenville might even finagle an invitation inside." It was just like Lady Breckenridge to sit, unflappable, and propose a solution, planned to the last detail.

"Won't leaving London upset your schedule for the Season?" I asked. Donata was famous for her musicales and soirees, which were attended by everyone who was anyone.

"Not at all. The height of the Season isn't for a few months, and the more important balls and events won't happen until then. An unexpected journey is just the thing to keep life from becoming tedious. I will send a message to my man of business and tell him to hire a house for us in Bath."

"In which we will share a bedchamber," I said firmly.

"Of course," Donata answered without blinking. "Bath's townhouses are tiresomely small."

Chapter Nine

Marianne was still not pleased I hadn't produced Mrs. Collins out of the air in the few days I'd been inquiring about her, but she was happy she would accompany us to Bath. Grenville had promised to set her up in a fine house with plenty to do, and Marianne almost softened to me.

We took Peter and his nanny as well, though his tutors tried most stringently to persuade Donata to leave the lad behind, so he would have no break in his education. Donata denied all requests. His tutors could join us on our sojourn if they wished, or she could hire new tutors once she arrived in Bath. The tutors, when given this ultimatum, went quiet and complied.

"They like an easy life in London," Donata said as she directed her maids in packing her trunk. "But they do not want to risk me severing their connection to Peter completely. I learned very early on how gentlemen would attempt to ingratiate themselves to my son, so they might be rewarded when he comes into his majority. I must be very careful about who is around him. The manner in which gentlemen try to exploit a six-year-old is rather disgusting."

I found it so too, and knew that many speculated I'd married Donata in order to have influence over the very young, very rich viscount. The fact that Donata did not share their opinion was gratifying.

The Auberges chose to stay in London, in Donata's house, when offered the opportunity, the fiftyish couple a bit tired from all the traveling they'd been doing. Now that Lady Breckenridge and I were safely married, they considered us adequate chaperones for Gabriella, and, after all, I was her true father. By law, Gabriella was mine, and mine alone. I'd agreed she could continue living with her mother only because of my compassion for Gabriella. I'd decided after painful contemplation that I wanted her to be happy more than I wanted to possess her.

The final travel arrangements were a bit awkward. Marianne would ride alone in a chaise provided by Grenville, while Donata, Gabriella, Peter and his nanny, and I would cram together in a hired landau. None but me and Gabriella were surprised by this. Donata explained patiently that, in the eyes of the world, Grenville's actress-mistress was hardly fitting company for a young miss like Gabriella. We had to pretend Marianne was not part of our party, which I thought absurd, but Marianne surprisingly agreed.

"I'll not have it put about that Gabriella was ruined because of me," she said. "The newspapers can print whatever drivel they wish of Grenville and his second-rate actress, but Gabriella will not be a part of that, not if I can help it."

And so it was decided. We set off for Bath the next morning, planning to break the journey at Reading and again at Chippenham. Had I been alone, I would have pushed through in a very long day, but my lady wife was not inclined to arrive in Bath winded and exhausted like a post horse, as she put it. Grenville, who staved off his motion sickness by riding horseback again, would need to change horses often as well.

Our journey took us through the heart of Berkshire, a cold land in this season, but the weather continued crisp and clear. As we neared Hungerford, Grenville informed us that Marianne wanted to stop for a time.

I understood why, and acquiesced. Donata was not adverse to stopping either—a quiet meal in the parlor of an inn was just the thing, and Peter could have a nap.

The innkeeper in the high street in Hungerford gave us his best rooms. He remembered me from my brief stay at the nearby Sudbury School, but was a bit more deferential to me now that I'd arrived with such a grand party. Donata retired with Gabriella and Peter to the upstairs parlor, and Marianne informed Grenville and me, in the common room below, that she was setting off on her visit.

"I want Lacey to go with me," Marianne announced as she tied her bonnet. "Not you, please," she said to Grenville.

Grenville drew a breath but let it out again. In another circumstance, he might grow angry, but I saw him rein in his temper. "Why not me?" he asked in a quiet voice.

"Because he's not afraid of Lacey," Marianne said.

Grenville flushed but again I watched him dampen his anger. He understood, even if he didn't like it.

"Very well," he said, trying to make his tone light as we entered the hall. "I and the new Mrs. Lacey will sit upstairs, peer out of windows, and laugh at the quaint customs of the natives."

"Why would you do that, Mr. Grenville?" my daughter asked, walking down the stairs. She'd been instructed to stay at Donata's side, but I'd discovered she was not one to blindly obey. "Laugh at the villagers, I mean? I live in a village."

Grenville's cheeks reddened. "I beg your pardon, my dear. I said it in jest. I am a dandy. It is a requirement that I wear the best clothes, squint at people through my quizzing glass, and make rude remarks."

"Why?" Gabriella asked in perfect candor.

Marianne laughed. "She sounds like you, Lacey. Shall we go?"

"Might I come with you?" Gabriella asked. "I feel cramped from the carriage. I'd love a good stretch."

"It is a long way," I said. "Another five or so miles. And Mrs. Lacey likes your company."

"I am robust," Gabriella said, looking stubborn. "And she and Mr. Grenville get on well. They talk about things I don't understand, such as how it is correct to be rude to people."

Grenville looked half amused, half discomfited. I enjoyed my daughter's company, but I hesitated. Marianne's errand was highly private, and it was not my business to say who could learn her secrets.

Marianne herself answered. "Of course you may come, Gabriella. But no more than you and Lacey."

I agreed, and we prepared to set off. I went upstairs to explain to Donata, who was already settling in with newspapers, coffee, and cigarillos, that Gabriella would accompany us. Grenville joined Donata, pretending to be so weary from the journey he had to sink into a chair and not move for several hours.

I hired riding horses for us. Gabriella might call herself robust, but I had no wish for her to walk five miles out and five miles back in this cold. We had to go by horseback rather than the coach, as the last mile or so was off any good road. I was happy to see that Gabriella rode competently—Major Auberge clearly had taught her well.

The Kennet and Avon canal, which ran alongside the town of Hungerford, was icy though not frozen over. Ice and snow clung to the canal's banks, and the air was frosty. We traveled along the towpath, trees cutting the rather sharp breeze that blew across the fields. After Froxfield, we left the canal and rode across country to the small house Marianne had led me to once before, nearly a year ago.

I noticed changes in the cottage immediately. The roof had been repaired. The woodwork looked more sturdy, and the stone walls had been refreshed with whitewash. While the garden was now covered with snow, I saw vegetable beds readied for spring. Smoke rose from the wide chimney, and the front door was firmly closed.

When Marianne had revealed her secret to me, I'd realized why she'd been stealing my candles and the remains of my suppers—she'd sent as much money as she could to this place, and filching from me let her provide even more coin. Grenville, once he'd learned about the house, had proved his generosity, as the repairs indicated. He gave Marianne as much money as she demanded, and Marianne, to her credit, sent it all here.

The door opened as we dismounted, the plump woman I'd been introduced to only as Maddie looking out at us.

"Oh, miss, I'm glad you've finally come. He's been in such a state, wondering if you'd ever arrive, saying you'd been killed on the road."

"Not at all," Marianne said, speaking loudly so her voice could be heard inside. "It's a bit snowy, and the horses had to go slowly. But we're here now."

Marianne went inside. I paused in the doorway, indicating Gabriella should wait as well.

"Marianne's son," I said in a quiet voice to Gabriella. "He is . . ."

I couldn't finish, because I did not know what to say about David. Different? Unusual? Perhaps mad?

Marianne called back to us. "You may come in now."

I ushered Gabriella into the house. The ground floor was a wide kitchen, warm against the winter day, a stair in the corner leading above. The flagstones were clean, the fire high, signs of dinner preparations on the long table. Marianne sat on the wooden settle near the hearth, her son David on her lap.

David was about eight, but he clung to Marianne as a much younger boy might. His body was plump, his legs long, his chubby face emphasizing his too-close eyes, large forehead, and slack mouth. He said, "Mummy," again and again as Marianne rocked him.

Gabriella's first surprise when she saw him turned to understanding. She moved to Marianne, unafraid, and sat down next to her. "Poor boy," she said.

David, hearing a new voice, looked up, his face red and tear-streaked. Gabriella smiled at him. "I'm Gabriella. How do you do?"

David wiped his nose with his hand, smearing mucus on his faintly dirty face, and did not answer.

"This is David," Marianne said. "My son." She spoke fiercely, as though daring anyone to debate the fact.

"How is he?" I asked Maddie, who was his caretaker.

"Oh, full of mischief most days, but we rub along. Don't we, Davy? He's been asking and asking about his mum. He don't like to be too much without her."

"I come as often as I can," Marianne said in a hard voice. "And I send the money."

."Bless you, child, I know that," Maddie said. "We're ever so grateful. I bought Davy new boots. He wore right through the others."

"Where is his father?" Gabriella asked Marianne in a gentle voice.

"Dead and gone," Marianne said without inflection. She'd never told me who David's father had been, only that he was dead.

"So you have taken care of him?" Gabriella said. "That was awfully good of you. And Maddie too."

"Not much choice, was there?" Marianne asked, her tone still sharp.

Gabriella shrugged. "You could have left him in a hospital, given him to another family, abandoned him in the street. People do, you know."

Marianne gave her a startled look then transferred her gaze to me. "Lacey, your daughter is a mite too worldly for her young age."

"Things happen, even in the provinces," Gabriella said. "One of my cousins was born like David. We look after him. Some of the villagers say he was cursed by God, but that's nonsense. He's a sweet boy. No, it happens when the child is growing in the womb, doctors say. No one knows quite what or why, but it's to do with anatomy, not curses."

Marianne pulled David close. "I tried to keep him with me. But others said stupid things, like he was bad luck, and they threatened to sling me out. So I found a home for him with Maddie. She was an actress in my company, but tired of it all."

"Ready to put up me feet," Maddie said good-naturedly. She'd returned to the table and began shelling peas into a bowl. "Marianne said I could have a house and allowance and look after David. Restful out here in the country."

"Did you know Abigail Collins?" I asked her.

"Abby? Of course, I did. Everyone knows Abby. What a talent she has. I gather she's done well for herself at Drury Lane."

"She's gone missing," Marianne said.

Maddie's eyes widened. "Oh, aye? How can she be missing? Season hasn't started yet, has it? She always goes to the seaside and Bath, don't she?"

"Perhaps not this time," Marianne said then quickly told Maddie the tale of Abigail's fright and departure.

"Do you know who would be cruel enough to try to harm her?" I asked Maddie.

Maddie went on shelling the peas, her movements slowing while she considered. "It's been a long while since I had a conversation with anyone in the theatre. I left the traveling players—never went to London. There were those who were jealous of her, of course. Abby had talent, she did. But that was a long time ago. I wouldn't know who would have it in for her now."

"What about a place she'd hide if need be?" I asked. "A special place she liked to go?"

"Well, now, these days she'd have plenty of blunt to go anywhere she liked. Paris even. But in the old days, she had a couple of places. A little boardinghouse in Bath, in a passage called Cook's Lane near the Old Bridge. She could put her feet up and watch the world go by, she said, and no one would know. Also in Brighton, in Hove, actually, in a little house. She wouldn't tell no one where that was, not even me, and we were such mates. Now that she's famous, she can afford a nice townhouse in Bath and likely one in Brighton itself. But I ain't seen her in years."

I mentally made note to check all these places regardless of cost. A frightened woman would seek refuge where she felt safe.

We remained a little longer, Marianne holding David until he grew restless and wanted to play. Gabriella, who I could see was good with children, let him pull her outside with Marianne. There she and David threw snowballs at each other, Marianne helping David form them. I saw Marianne let down her tight façade for a brief time, laughing out loud as she watched her son romp in the snow.

Marianne looked a bit older when she relaxed her

cynical countenance, but her natural prettiness also shone through. I wondered if she'd ever allowed Grenville to see this side of her. I'd tried to persuade her to be more open with Grenville, but Marianne found it difficult to trust.

Marianne clung to David for a time before we took our leave. When we walked back to our grazing horses, Marianne's face was wet. I pretended not to notice as I turned to boost Gabriella to her saddle.

"You like children," I said to her.

Gabriella smiled down at me, my daughter, my treasure. "There are so many at home that I must be fond of children or flee. There are my four brothers and sisters, all younger than I, and my Auberge cousins, some of whom are now starting to have children themselves. We're a large family."

She spoke offhandedly as she voiced what I'd longed for all my life. Carlotta had given Auberge the family I'd wanted, while she'd been too terrified of me to share my bed.

We rode away, Marianne in silence, me regretful, Gabriella the only cheerful one among us. When we reached the inn, Marianne had composed herself, and said she'd sip an ale downstairs until we were ready to leave.

Grenville and Donata had managed between them to turn the inn's rather spare parlor into their own den of comfort. Gabriella and I entered to find Donata ensconced on cushions, her feet up on more cushions, smoking a cigarillo and reading a newspaper. Grenville lounged in a deep chair, his feet up as well, a rug across his knees, a thick dressing gown over his clothes, and a sporting magazine in his hand. Matthias waited nearby, alert to top up coffee or claret.

"Ah, there you are," Donata said. "You were a long time. We might have to put up here for the night."

"Chippenham isn't far," I said. I seated my daughter then took the remaining chair in the room, which had no cushions at all. "And then an easy ride to Bath in the morning."

"You do like to rush about." Donata turned the page of her newspaper. The look she gave me over the paper wasn't admonishing, though. She seemed elated about something.

"What is it?" I asked. I glanced at Grenville, who was watching me with an oddly satisfied expression. "You two are conspiring."

"Not I," Donata said. "Grenville, rather."

Grenville gave a practiced yawn. "Can't think what you mean, dear lady. I've merely been keeping my feet warm."

Donata tossed down her newspaper, sat up in her chair, and patted the arm of it for Gabriella to come to her. Matthias brought Gabriella a cup of tea as she abandoned her chair and went to Donata.

"We haven't spun away the time idly while you were gallivanting," Donata said. "Keeping our feet warm, indeed. Grenville wanted to give you the impression that we have been lazy because he hates to be caught out being industrious. We've been looking at houses to lease, or perhaps to purchase. We believe we have found two or three in the area that might suit."

I looked at her in surprise. "You wish to live in Hungerford?"

"Good Lord, no. It's not for me. It's for Grenville."

I understood. "For Marianne, you mean. So she can be close to her son."

Grenville shrugged, striving to maintain his façade of ennui. "Saves her the bother of traveling all the way from Mayfair. She won't hear of moving David, so why not have her stay nearby? I could do with a little country place. Good for walks, dogs, hunting. A quiet retreat."

Grenville wasn't much for quiet retreats, well I knew. Walking about the country with dogs he could do, but he tired of it quickly.

Before I could remark on his generosity, Gabriella laughed. "You won't be able to poke fun at the natives then, Mr. Grenville. You'll be one of them."

"Too true, my dear." Looking slightly embarrassed, Grenville resumed his magazine.

"Tell Marianne," I said to Grenville.

"Hmm?" The magazine lowered. "I'll have to, won't I? She'll notice when I bring her to whatever house I settle on."

"I mean, tell her now. I imagine it will make our remaining journey that much more comfortable for you."

Grenville made another grumbling noise. He gave me an impatient look, then heaved an aggrieved sigh, set down his magazine, and called for Matthias to bring him his shoes and coat. He took his time, making a show of straightening and readying himself. The great Grenville could not be seen outside a private room with any sign of dishabille, not even to visit his mistress in the common room of a pub.

Chapter Ten

I had never been to Bath. I'd lived in Norfolk all my young life, with occasional jaunts to London until I attended university at Cambridge, not far from home. The fens, rivers, and flat lands of eastern England had been my bailiwick, until I'd joined Brandon and the army, and traveled the world.

I'd never seen John Wood's elegant Crescent, or the Pump Rooms, or the Upper and Lower assembly rooms. Bath was all about its Season, its gatherings, about seeing and being seen. The spa town had experienced the height of its social power in the eighteenth century, but its streets still spoke of wealth, elegance, respect, refinement.

At the end of the three-day carriage ride, I longed for an ordinary public house with a large glass of ale and a warm fire, but I was now married to a dowager viscountess, and such comforts would have to wait. The house we'd let, which Donata insisted on calling *small*, stood tall near one end of the Crescent. We made no secret of arriving and moving in — the entire street saw the cart loaded with baggage that pulled up behind our carriage. They'd also have seen the men Donata had hired beforehand carrying new furniture inside the house. When one went to Bath, one made a show of it.

Grenville made his own show in a house a few doors down. He would live there by himself with his valet and staff, with Marianne's abode a few streets away.

It was odd but pleasant to explore the grand house with Donata and Gabriella, deciding whose room was whose, discovering which sitting nooks would be perfect for Donata's newspapers or Gabriella's sewing. My wife and I were moving into this house together, a new undertaking for both of us. I had never settled into a domestic arrangement like this before — my first marriage had been conducted inside army tents, boarding houses, or at best, rooms in another officer's house. This townhouse, albeit leased, would be wholly for Donata and me.

The front windows of the first three floors looked along the Crescent and across to a green sward, a bit barren now but free of snow. A few hardy people, bundled against the cold, strolled there even now.

A long staircase with a polished balustrade rose through the house on its right side as one entered the front door. The main rooms were on the left side of the house, one in front, one to the rear. A third room on each floor rested in the back. The ground floor held a fashionable drawing room, dining room, and reception room for guests; a more private sitting room, library, and morning room were on the next.

Donata and I took the front bedchamber two floors above the ground floor, Gabriella in the bedroom in the rear, leaving the attics free for a nursery and the staff. All in all, a fine house, decorated throughout in restful cream, yellow, and black.

"A bit fusty," Donata said, looking about. "Old fashioned. But what can you expect from Bath?"

Her look held approval, however. She was pleased, but long habit made her disdain to show it.

Gabriella was fascinated by the house, but she, like me, was eager to see the sights of the town. Donata conceded that while the staff put the house to rights we would have time to walk about, acclimate ourselves, and do some shopping.

The weather was clear if chilly, the wind a bit brisk. We walked the length of the Crescent and along to the Circus, the three of us nodding to passersby or stopping to greet those Donata knew. Donata introduced Gabriella to one and all, and her acquaintances were eager to admire her. They had no time for me, a mere husband—a young girl about to make her come-out was far more interesting.

"I'm not sure I want bringing out," Gabriella said privately to me as she and I wandered along, while Donata paused to look into shops. "I'm a child still."

"Not a child. You're a young lady already." My heart squeezed. "I have missed so much of your life."

Gabriella shook her head. "I was quite a handful when I was younger, I'm sorry to say. My mother constantly told me, in exasperation, that I was just like my papa. I thought she meant my French papa, but now I see she meant you."

"It was not a compliment, I am afraid."

Gabriella looked me up and down with her natural frankness. "The more I come to know you, the more I shall take it as one." She glanced behind us, so she did not see the sudden moisture in my eyes. "Mrs. Lacey looks as though she'll be quite some time. What's that large place over there?"

I calculated from having studied the plan of Bath Grenville had leant me that Gabriella had spied the Upper Assembly Rooms. It was a square building just off the Circus, with tall columns supporting a Greek-looking portico and rather plain sash windows. People moved in and out of the building, taking their time, enjoying their afternoon walks. We left the new Mrs. Lacey and her already box-laden maid to their shopping and strolled to it.

"Can we enter?" Gabriella asked when we reached the doors.

I saw no reason why not. We were as respectably dressed as the ladies and gentlemen who walked in and out, and the building seemed open to all. Card play was offered here all days but Sundays, I'd read. I would have to pay a subscription to join the games, but surely there would be no harm if we simply walked in to see the rooms.

Before we ducked out of the morning light to the interior, I spied a man across the road, who was watching us intently. I at first suspected Denis had sent Brewster or one of his other lackeys all the way to Bath to look after me, but on second glance, I decided not. While Denis's men wore clothes of fine cloth, they always managed to look like the ruffians they were. This man had the bearing of a gentleman—his large greatcoat was well made and the hat he pulled down to his eyes fine. He stared at us without hiding the fact until the Upper Room doors were opened for us, and I quickly ushered Gabriella inside.

Gabriella had noticed nothing amiss. Her eyes were only for the rooms we found ourselves in. We followed others from the foyer to a giant room in the shape of an octagon, with wide, tall windows high on the walls and ornate fireplaces flickering with warmth. Massive, glittering chandeliers seemed to float overhead. The chandeliers were unlit—so much sunlight came pouring through the windows that no candles were needed.

Others were meeting here and parading about, so I escorted Gabriella along the polished floor. Ladies and gentlemen greeted one another and talked among their parties, but I knew no one, and so we passed quietly along. There was an air of perpetual holiday about the place I wasn't used to—I felt as though I watched from a long way off. I was among them but not part of them.

"It is very lovely," Gabriella said as we made our second perambulation. "We have nothing like it near our village, though I suppose Paris would have rooms like this."

"This is a spa town," I said. "People come from all over England to take the waters, and also to wander about in elegance. If you have an ailment, the Pump Rooms will provide a cure, or so it is claimed."

"I'm rather healthy," Gabriella said. "Do you think Mr. Grenville would join us? He could promenade to show off his new suits."

I did not hide my amusement. "At this early hour?" We'd risen long before dawn and had made

Bath before luncheon. "We'll not see Grenville until six o'clock at least. *If* he deigns to come out on his first night in town."

"Why does he do such things?" Gabriella asked in genuine curiosity. "Pretend to be so disdainful, I mean? Mr. Grenville is an intelligent gentleman, from what I can see. He speaks to me in fluent French with hardly any accent, and he knows so many things. Yet he hides away and lets people talk about him, while he makes fun of everyone else. He is two different people sometimes."

I'd long thought the same myself. "He lets the world see only one of his personas—the haughty dandy. The other his great friends alone see. To allow us a glimpse of his true self is a sign of Grenville's affection for us."

"I still find it odd. And there is nothing wrong with Miss Simmons. It is silly that I cannot speak to her in public, or even be seen with her."

"I agree, but such are the rules in England, I am told. I suppose in France, young misses and actresses run about together all the time?"

Gabriella returned my dry tone with a smile. "Well, perhaps not. Young misses are well guarded, especially by fathers like my papa." She rolled her eyes, then remembered who she spoke to, and flushed.

"I am glad to hear it." I held out my arm to walk her the other way. "Now, shall we return and join Mrs. Lacey for a repast? I am sure she will tell us what we will do for the rest of the day and into the night."

Gabriella flashed me another smile, this one of comradeship. I saw in it the little girl who'd clung to my boot as I walked and begged me to lift her onto my shoulders.

I schooled my expression as we strolled together again through the octagonal room and the long foyer and back out into the sunny afternoon. Donata and her maid were making their way toward the Upper Rooms, the landau following slowly.

I lifted my hand in greeting to her, but when traffic cleared a bit, I spied the same gentleman in the greatcoat across the street, still watching us. Determined, I sent Gabriella toward Donata, who had almost reached us, made an abrupt about-face, and strode toward the gentleman.

Alarmed, my follower darted into a side passage. I walked quickly after him, leaving sunshine and my family for a close street of smaller houses. This street emerged into another, much quieter than the main thoroughfares. I heard the man's footsteps ringing as he hurried away from me, and he slipped around another corner.

I did not have the advantage of knowing Bath as I knew London, despite my study of the street plan as we'd traveled. I could only follow the man, who led me into older and still narrower streets. Though my ribs had healed enough for me to walk along without trouble, they pained me a bit, and I kept up with the man only through force of will.

At last my quarry had to slow for a cluster of people who were wandering about, clearly not knowing the town any better than I did. "Sir," one of the gentlemen said to the man I chased. "Can you tell us the way to the Pump Rooms?"

The tall man pushed past them, not answering. The inquiring gentleman, a red-faced, plump cylinder in his greatcoat, stared after him. "Good heavens, how rude." He turned to me. "Sir?"

"Back that way." I pointed behind me, hoping the direction was correct. "Excuse me."

I tipped my hat and kept moving, my walking stick tapping rapidly on the uneven pavement. I heard the gentleman continue his exasperation behind me.

I was sorry not to have assisted him, but I had more pressing matters. The man I pursued had turned another corner. I was breathing hard from the chase, and told myself I'd been living too soft since returning from Norfolk.

The encounter with the tourists had slowed my man as well, and I at last closed the distance between us. I was on his heels as he rounded a corner into a tiny, deserted passage. There I seized a handful of his flapping greatcoat and jerked him to a halt.

The man's hat fell to the cobbles, and he swung around, ready with a practiced punch. But I was practiced as well. I deflected the blow and gave him one of my own.

As we fought, I reflected that he must have learned boxing in the controlled atmosphere of a place such as Gentleman Jackson's or other instruction rooms. His blows were precise but predictable. I had learned fighting on the battlefields, where gentlemanly rules didn't apply. I ducked under his reach as he swung at me, shoved my elbow into his gut, and hit him hard in the face when he doubled over. As he gasped and groaned, I grabbed him by the lapels with one hand and lifted him against a brick wall, jamming the handle of my new and strong walking stick to his throat.

"Who the devil are you, and what do you want?"

Instead of looking fearful, the man eyed me in anger. He had light brown eyes, somewhat protruding, and a sharp face that hadn't been shaved in a day. He answered through thin lips. "It will not go well for you, Captain, if you do not release me."

I pinned him harder. "No threats. Tell me why you are following me."

"Paid to, aren't I?" His flat accent came through, a man from the west country, not London.

"By whom? Mr. Denis?"

"By that filth? I'm a patroller, you fool. I'll haul you to the magistrate if you do not let go of me."

"A patroller." He seemed quite well dressed for a foot patroller or a constable. In spite of the shadow of beard on his face, his dark hair was neatly trimmed and pomaded. Not quite a gentleman but not of the working classes either. "For Bath?"

"For Bow Street. For Mr. Spendlove."

I tightened my grip, my famous temper rising. "Spendlove is having me followed? I am here on holiday, with my family. I do not want him, or you, or anyone else, near *my family*."

"I'm not concerned with your lady wife or your daughter. I'm told to watch that you do nothing but escort your ladies about and keep away from trouble."

"And if I choose not to keep away from trouble?"

"Then I am to arrest you and take you to Mr. Spendlove."

His face was turning dark purple under my cane. I eased off a bit, but I had to resist the urge to punch him again along his unshaven jaw.

"I do not like being followed," I said. "For any

reason. Go back to Spendlove and tell him that."

He gave me a nasty smile. "Can't do that, sir. As long as you're in Bath, I watch you. I work for the magistrates. You go to your Pump Rooms and assembly rooms with your wife and daughter, and we'll rub along fine."

My anger didn't abate. Denis always had men watching me, which irritated me, but I'd grown used to it. Denis did as he pleased. But for a Bow Street Runner to hire someone to follow me about as though I were a common criminal infuriated me. Abigail Collins was missing, her life threatened, and Bow Street chose to watch *me*.

"Very well then," I said as I took a step back. "Follow me. Be poised to arrest me. Meanwhile, I will get up to what I like. When you come to take me, better bring more men than yourself."

Disgusted and in fury, I swung away from him and strode off, my walking stick beating the cobbles to punctuate my anger. I heard the man breathing loudly behind me, but I noted that this time he did not follow.

I was a while discovering the way back to the main streets of Bath and the Crescent. When I emerged to the elegant curve of houses and the park beyond it, the beauty and grace of the setting had turned gray and very much colder.

Chapter Eleven

Spendlove's man watching me every moment meant I could not put plans in motion; at least, not how I envisioned executing those plans. In the morning, I told Bartholomew as he poured me coffee in the dining room that I'd need his help.

Society in Bath favored more daylight hours than did life in upper-class London, I'd learned — breakfast in the Lower Assembly Rooms either before or after drinking the waters or bathing in the Pump Rooms, then to the Upper Assembly Rooms for tea or cards. In the evening, to the theatre or whichever of the assembly rooms was hosting a ball or concert that night, and then home and to bed.

Donata had explained the schedule to me before she'd fallen asleep the night before, murmuring last thing that she rarely observed it. I woke at my usual hour, my nose in her back, inhaling her lovely scent. I basked a moment in the warmth of her, then kissed her cheek, rose from the nest of our bed, and left her to her sleep.

I went downstairs to find the dining room sideboard loaded with silver dishes, holding everything from simple toasted bread to slabs of ham to a whole fish pie. The cook had expected a crowd, it seemed. Or perhaps she believed army captains ate this much every morning. She might have been correct, because I loaded my plate.

Bartholomew entered to pour me coffee, and I drank deeply of it as I ate the good food. I'd noted that Bartholomew's usual cheerful exuberance had deserted him this morning, but he brightened a trifle when I told him I'd need his help.

"Ah, good, sir," he said, topping up my cup for the third time. "I wondered when you'd ask."

"Is that what has you long faced? I always welcome your assistance in my investigations."

"No, sir, not that. It's the staff here. Had to nearly wrestle the first footman to wait on you at table this morning. For dinner and supper it's the butler's show, I understand, but I'm your valet, sir. Your man. I take care of you in the mornings." He looked put out and angry.

Domestic troubles, something new to me. The entire staff of this house had been hired through one of Donata's agents and had been in place before we arrived. "I know very little about all that, Bartholomew. Her ladyship will have to tutor me on the niceties."

"Trust me, sir. A gentleman's gentleman should be near to him until he first leaves the house in the morning."

"I see you won the wrestling match," I said,

sipping more coffee. "Any casualties?"

"No, but a footman came nigh to a bloody nose." He gave the absent footman a dark scowl. "What is this task you have for me, sir?"

"I need you to find a small boardinghouse on Cook's Lane, which is near to the Old Bridge somewhere. The trouble is, I'm not sure exactly which boardinghouse, so we'll have to narrow it down. I want to discover if Mrs. Collins is there, or has been there recently."

"I can do that, sir." Bartholomew's eagerness returned, and he set down the silver pot. "Shall I go right away?"

"Not yet. I will be going out this morning. When I do, I want you to watch out the window without anyone seeing you. A man should follow me—he will likely be wearing a two-caped greatcoat and tall hat. Wait until he's followed me out of the Crescent. Watch after that to see if anyone else comes after or remains to observe the house. Only when you are certain no one will see you should you pursue the errand. Return home a roundabout way and speak to no one about what you've discovered. I should be home again in time for Mrs. Lacey's rising."

Bartholomew listened to all carefully. He was an intelligent lad, and he'd follow my instructions to the letter.

I finished my breakfast, realizing that if I did eat to the cook's expectations, I would need to hire that horse for a hard ride very soon. Bartholomew saw me out the door, handing me a new hat and leather gloves as I departed the house.

I pretended to ignore Spendlove's man when I spied him and walked away with determination in my stride. As I'd hoped, he left his post and followed me. I passed the house Grenville had taken, assuming he intended to remain firmly in bed until the afternoon, and made my way several streets south to the smaller house Grenville had hired for Marianne.

Marianne was up, though not dressed, but she readily accepted my invitation. In a very short time, she came downstairs in a dark blue ensemble fit for walking about Bath in the winter. The maid handed her an umbrella in deference to the clouds building in the sky, and we walked from her house arm-in-arm.

"Thank heavens you came," Marianne said as we strolled in the direction of the Pump Rooms. Under the bonnet lined with blue that matched her eyes, her expression was sour. "I wondered if I'd wait through a morning of tediousness before *he* deigned to rise from his bed and remember he'd brought me with him. But are you certain you want to be seen walking with me? Everyone knows I am that notorious actress the great Grenville is squiring about."

"I am counting on that. We will search Bath together for Mrs. Collins — everywhere except where I suspect her to be, that is. There is a gentleman from Bow Street following me."

Marianne's expression cleared. "Ah, you are being underhanded."

"Exactly."

"I take it the gentleman in the rather ugly greatcoat is the Runner in question?"

"He's a patroller, working for a Runner who has taken an interest in me. I have been ordered not to search for Mrs. Collins. But because I take orders poorly, and I am not certain that Mr. Spendlove's motives are pure, I'd rather find her myself."

"Good of you. Though now you have me even more worried."

I walked with Marianne purposefully along a few streets, making certain we moved in a direction completely opposite to the one in which I'd sent Bartholomew. We crossed a bridge over the Avon, which flowed icily beneath us, then climbed a hill to a fine view of the town. Bath lay below us, only a few miles long and lesser wide, its layout a pretty symmetry beyond the mist of the river.

"Bath doesn't have many permanent residents," I reflected. Most of the Crescent was to let for anyone who could afford it. "How would someone as prominent as Mrs. Collins hide herself here?"

Marianne's look told me she thought me a simpleton. "She's an actress. If she wishes to play the part of a housemaid or cook's assistant putting up her feet for a time, no one would look twice. She's not gentry-born, and she can slide back in with her own class quite easily when she chooses. On a stage, she's wearing powder and costumes, and how many people see her close to? Believe me, hiding in plain sight is easier than simply not being seen."

"Is that what you are doing?" I asked. "Hiding in plain sight?"

Marianne looked swiftly up at me. The street leading to the hill was quiet this early, and no one was near. "Why on earth should you say that, Lacey?"

I regarded her for a time, taking in her carefully dressed hair, the blue wool spencer with puffed sleeves over her walking dress, the expensive bonnet with its blue silk trim. "I've known you for nearly four years now," I said. "I've noted that you are not the same as the other actresses I've met—you admitted that acting is more a way for you to earn a coin than a true calling. You don't come from a working-class background. More middle-class, I'd say, even gentry perhaps. Your accent is neutral, meaning you've learned to use one that will hide your origins, and you are not from London. You don't much like the country, so I assume you come from a fairly large town, such as this one or something farther away. Bristol possibly, or even Leeds, though I wouldn't have pegged you as from the north."

Marianne jerked her hand from my arm. "Aren't you the fine Bow Street Runner? My life and where I come from are hardly your business. I had no idea you were watching me so closely."

"Not watching. Observing. You fit no pattern, and that always makes me curious."

"Well, you will have to continue to be curious then."

"We are friends, Marianne," I said. "I'd hardly betray your confidence."

"Friends, perhaps, but you are also great friends with his worship, Mr. Grenville, upon whom I now depend for my daily bread. I shouldn't want you to have to wrestle with your conscience whether you should tell him all about me. You would win out on his side, because gentlemen always club together."

"Not always. I told him nothing about David, remember? Until you asked me to, that is. I attempt to keep my patience with you, but you try the patience of the best of men, and I am not the best of men."

Marianne's snort was her only answer. She tried to walk on, but I latched my fingers around her wool-clad arm and pulled her back.

"Tell Grenville," I said. "That way, I won't wrestle with my conscience, and you won't constantly wonder whether you can trust me."

"Tell him?" Marianne laughed, but it held no humor. "My dear Lacey, remember I said he was my bread and butter? Shall I have him sling me out? Who will feed me then? You and your fine lady wife?"

"You thought he would toss you out about David. Instead, he gave you plenty of money to repair David's little house, and he adheres to your wishes not to move him from it. That speaks of a generous man who cares for you."

I hoped to see contrition, but Marianne showed none. "Yes, I know you and he are the best of chums. Live and die for each other, wouldn't you?"

"How long will the poor man have to work to gain your trust? You're putting him through a hell of a trial. One day, he will lose *his* patience, not for anything you've done, but because you refuse to give yourself to him. Your whole self."

"Ah." Marianne looked both sad and triumphant at the same time. "That way lies disaster." She looked down the hill at carriages heading for the Pump Room so their inhabitants could take their morning cure. "We ought to be getting back now. I would not want wagging tongues to ruin things with your new wife."

I released her and gestured for her to walk on, then offered my arm again after we'd gone a few paces. "My wife is highly intelligent," I said. "As you are. The difference between you two is that Mrs. Lacey keeps no secrets. She has no closed doors about her past, even the most sordid bits of it."

"But Mrs. Lacey is an earl's daughter, and she always will be, no matter what gentleman she marries. Though people might question her taste in husbands, she will remain on her lofty pillar above the squalid masses forever. I do not have that luxury. Therefore, my secrets remain my own."

I shrugged, though the more she spoke, the more curious I became. "My advice stands. Tell Grenville. Trust *him*."

"So simple you make everything sound. *I* will decide what to do, if ever."

"Very well. However, I believe Mr. Spendlove's man needs more exercise. Let us walk the long way around the Crescent and then back to your lodgings, shall we?"

*** *** ***

I arrived home after seeing Marianne to her house to find that Bartholomew had already been on his errand and returned.

"She ain't there, sir."

I believed him, but I couldn't help asking, "You're certain?"

"*Certain* is pushing it a bit." He rubbed his short, pale hair. "There were two boardinghouses on that street, one of them with a bit of a damp problem. The other was the one where your quarry liked to stay, but they ain't seen her. I asked to have a look at the rooms anyway, but they were empty except for a few bits of furniture. The rooms were cold and smelled musty, like no one had opened the windows in a while. I asked, to see what the landlady would say, if I could take the rooms myself, but she said she always held them for Mrs. Collins the actress, had for years. She boasted of it. I said I supposed Mrs. Collins paid up for the whole year then, so they'd be available whenever she arrived. Yes, the landlady said. That's what usually happened. Except this year, Mrs. Collins sent an agent to pay it for her, in October, instead of coming herself. Most unusual, the landlady said."

"And did the talkative landlady describe this agent?"

Bartholomew turned his face to the ceiling as though seeking inspiration in the plasterwork. "Tall man, thick side-whiskers, bulbous nose, bushy brows, ugly sort."

"Good Lord. Mr. Perry." I had to rise and pace. "There cannot be two such men. But why would he pay Mrs. Collins' rent? Did he come here to find her and then needed an excuse for asking at her rooms of her? Rather expensive excuse, I'd think. Or perhaps he wanted to maintain the fiction that she is living here, when she is, in fact, dead? Or instead of being a villain, perhaps *he* is hiding her, paying the rent for her to keep everything seeming as usual." I shook my head, still pacing. "No, he must be a villain in this. He exploited Felicity and had me beaten. I refuse to look upon Mr. Perry as any sort of benefactor."

"Not to mention he lost you your walking stick," Bartholomew said.

"And for that, of course, I shall never forgive him."

Bartholomew peered at me to see whether I was

joking. I wasn't, really—my fury at Perry had not abated.

"Would you like me to go back and ask more questions, sir?"

"No." My leg began to twinge, and I sat down again. "I do not want Spendlove's man or anyone else getting wind of our inquiries. Thank you, Bartholomew. You have been most helpful."

Bartholomew looked much more cheerful than he had this morning. "You're welcome, sir. Now then, her ladyship instructed me to have you take a light luncheon and a bath before your afternoon. She said she had a long day and evening planned."

I tried not to grimace as I went upstairs, but truth to be told, I enjoyed bathing. Hot water on a cold day felt good to my limbs. I remembered the days, not so long ago, when I'd go for weeks to months without immersing myself. Such a thing was not practical in the army. But while I'd been sweating in India and again on the Peninsula, Mr. George Brummell and Mr. Lucius Grenville had made cleanliness fashionable. All gentlemen must now separate themselves from the great unwashed with large quantities of soap and water.

Bartholomew prepared my bath in the dressing room near the fireplace there, and by the time I was as clean as could be, Donata was out of bed and dressed, ready to begin the social whirl of Bath. We'd begin in the Upper Assembly Rooms, she informed me.

"We aren't likely to find many we know here," she said as Bartholomew put the finishing touches on my toilette. "Bath is hopelessly outdated these days, though my set does make its way down here for the quiet. But not usually until later in the Season. Never mind, we shall walk about and be stared at."

An activity not to my taste. But it would look odd, Donata said, if we kept ourselves to ourselves and never went out. People would remark upon it. In order to attract the least amount of attention, it seemed, we must proceed to show ourselves as much as possible.

Grenville joined us for the outing. We all rode together to the assembly rooms in Donata's hired landau, and all and sundry did indeed stare when we descended. Donata took it in stride, used to being watched, as did Grenville. Gabriella was too interested to notice the scrutiny, but I was painfully aware of heads turning when we passed, the murmurs that began behind hands.

I especially did not like how they stared at Gabriella. Donata declared that because Gabriella was not out yet, she would not attend any of the grand balls in the evening, though taking tea with us and visiting the sights of Bath would be fine. However, I disliked the curious stares turned her way, some of which bore rude speculation.

"Best we let everyone know she is under my wing," Donata said in her practical manner. "I adore quashing gossip. Leave it to me." Donata sailed off with Gabriella to the tea room, Gabriella giving me a rueful look behind her.

"Do you regret your rush to the altar now?" Grenville asked as he and I moved through the Octagon Room toward the card room.

"Not a rush. Took too long for my liking."

"You could have remained as lovers in plenty of comfort, you know." He gave me an amused look.

"No need at all for matrimony."

"I disagree. My rooms were devilish *un*comfortable, and I didn't wish to embarrass Donata any longer trying to discreetly leave her house in the early hours of the morning."

Grenville shook his head. "Your attitude is deplorable, Lacey. All gentlemen are supposed to bewail putting their head in the noose. You will make the rest of us look shabby."

I chose not to answer his teasing. Waking up next to Donata this morning had been a fine experience. I'd let myself be surrounded by her warmth, thinking of nothing else, a thing I hadn't been able to do in a long time.

"Other gentlemen should choose their wives more carefully then," I said. As we strolled, I told him in a low voice what Bartholomew had discovered at Mrs. Collins' rooms this morning.

"Bad, that," Grenville said when I'd finished. "We must find this Mr. Perry and have a few words with him."

"Yes, indeed." I touched my temple, where the bruises Perry's ruffians had given me were still healing.

"You should put Felicity to the question. She knows more than she is telling."

"Perhaps."

Grenville's eyes narrowed at my abrupt answer. "You are too soft on her, Lacey. You have sympathy for her, as do I, but Felicity is a hard and ruthless young woman."

"Not her fault. Her life has made her so."

"True, but that does not make her less ruthless. Be careful of her."

I knew Grenville was correct. He was also correct that my soft heart for waifs and strays could lead me to trouble, and had more than once in the past.

We left the Octagon Room for the wide card room, which was located at the very end of the building. Quite a few gentlemen had already gathered here to play whist and other games. Some players focused with vast concentration on their cards; others merely held them while they talked to other gentlemen.

Grenville and I joined a game of whist. The gentlemen at the table were a bit taken aback to have such a famous personage as Grenville sit down with them, but when Grenville wished, he could put others much at their ease. He had little difficulty introducing the topic of the theatre. He and the other two gentlemen discussed favorite plays, then actors and actresses, while I played cards in silence and listened.

Kean was much admired at this table, and so was Mrs. Collins. "My wife loves the woman," the gentleman on my right said. "We must see all her plays. She's quite comely still. Mrs. Collins, that is." He guffawed. "And my wife, I should hasten to add, since she is in the next room and liable to hear of it."

Grenville gave his joke an appreciative smile. "Does Mrs. Collins come to Bath?" he asked. "Or has she grown too lofty for anything but London?"

"She played here last year, early in the spring, a few performances only," the same gentleman answered. "But I haven't seen her name advertised anywhere this year. My lady wife would inform me, I assure you."

The other gentleman at the table wasn't as interested in the theatre, but he too agreed that Mrs.

Collins had appeared in no production here since the previous year.

We played whist with other gentlemen after the first two, and then Grenville and I split to play piquet, a one-on-one game, with others, but we'd learned nothing further by the end of the afternoon.

"Conclusion," Grenville said, disgruntled. "She isn't here. We made the trip for nothing."

"Finding nothing is part of an answer," I said. "And Gabriella and Marianne are enjoying themselves."

Grenville shot me a look. "Married life has positively cheered you, Lacey. Do not let it ruin that fine pessimism you've cultivated."

"I have plenty of pessimism, my friend. I am becoming more and more convinced that Abigail Collins is dead."

I broke off, rather rudely, but I'd spied a gentleman staring at me—one who'd been watching me all afternoon in the card room and pretending not to. He looked too respectable to be connected with Spendlove or Bow Street, or even Denis. He was the epitome of respectability, in fact.

Not as tall as I, the gentleman was thin but not spare and wore finely tailored clothes. His hands were well kept, his hair dark, his voice moderated. He'd played quietly and counted out coins when he'd lost without making a show of it. Not a gentleman to stand out in a crowd; I'd hardly have noticed him if he hadn't been trying so determinedly to study me.

He was watching me now. I decided to confront him, but when I started toward him, he abruptly turned and exited into a courtyard.

I chose not to chase him. If society in Bath at this time was as sparse as Donata claimed, I'd no doubt see him again.

Grenville looked puzzled, but I decided not to enlighten him. I might be mistaken—the man hadn't the look of a patroller, who would likely not have been admitted into the assembly rooms anyway. I'd keep my eye out.

We walked back to the foyer at the time we'd agreed upon to meet Donata and Gabriella. Gabriella had been quite delighted by the tea and the company, and she chattered about it as we strolled together to gather our things.

As we neared the front doors, I saw my gentleman again. He touched the arm of a woman whose back was to me, her figure hidden by a long pelisse, her high-crowned bonnet keeping me from seeing her face.

But her stance and manner were familiar. When she turned her head slightly to listen to her gentleman, the curve of her cheek was more familiar still.

I missed a step, catching myself on the walking stick before I stumbled. Donata put her hand on my arm in concern, then she saw me staring and turned her head to see what held my attention. But several people had moved between us and the couple by then, and when the crowd cleared, they were gone.

"Gabriel?" Donata asked. "Are you well?"

I nodded. "Of course. I am still a bit clumsy on this new stick." I made a show of adjusting it. "What is next on our exhaustive tour of Bath?"

Chapter Twelve

Several evenings into our Bath journey, having learned nothing at all, I started to feel my old melancholia creep in. Donata was receiving callers below, but I had excused myself to write letters in the nook of our bedchamber, or at least to pretend to write them.

Melancholia touched me whenever I felt ineffectual. I had started out looking for Mrs. Collins as a favor to Marianne, and I had learned nothing other than what Mrs. Wolff, Marianne, and Maddie had told me. I'd been beaten on the street and confined, followed about by a Bow Street Runner, and had traveled a hundred or so miles to Bath with little to show for it.

If Abigail Collins had come to Bath anytime since she'd left London, someone would have remarked upon it. I planned to ask again at the ball we attended tonight, but I was not optimistic. Three possibilities existed: Mrs. Collins was here and hiding very well; she was not here at all and never had come here this winter; or she was dead.

I wrote a letter to Sir Montague Harris, a London magistrate I knew and trusted. I asked him to look for one Mr. John Perry and described him, stating all he'd done. I now had the means to prosecute him for assault and abduction, if I could convince Felicity to be a witness for me.

There was a rub—Felicity. I had no way of knowing where she'd gone or even whether she'd stayed in London. Or perhaps she'd been in cahoots with Perry all along, though why she'd help me escape if so was beyond me. But Felicity was a complicated young woman, and I had no way of knowing what her motives were.

If Abigail Collins was alive, she was still in danger, and I couldn't find her. I longed to stride through the town searching for her, but Spendlove's man followed us everywhere, and I had to be cautious.

I finished my letter and sealed it then remained at the desk, staring in front of me. The daylight outside faded, until I sat in the dark, the flicker of fire on the hearth the only light.

A pair of arms came around me, and a clean scent enveloped me. I closed my eyes as my wife surrounded me with her warmth.

"The cook is having a light supper prepared," she said. "Before the ball."

I didn't move. Having to dress to go out into the light and noise seemed too much effort.

Donata's lips brushed my cheek. "We have a little time before then."

I turned, put my arms around her, and pulled her down into my lap. My melancholia dissolved as we became man and woman, nothing more. The bed was not far, and the next hour was spent in much more pleasant contemplation.

*** *** ***

The subscription ball this night was in the Lower Assembly Rooms. We arrived in style in Donata's landau, which pulled up near the end of the Parades to let us out. Donata's overly high feathered headdress had nearly crushed against the coach's roof and tossed about in the wind as she descended. But feathers must be worn, she'd said, and as we entered the rooms, I saw that most of the ladies of Bath agreed with her. We were in a sea of plumage so vast I pitied the peacocks and other birds that had been plucked to grace the ladies' heads.

Donata's acquaintances swept her away quickly, and I retreated to find the card rooms. Gentlemen and their wives, it seemed, spent almost no time together at these gatherings. The practice made me wonder why they bothered to marry at all, but I well knew that most society marriages were arranged to keep money and property intact. Gentlemen tolerated their wives, as Felicity had posited, taking mistresses if they wanted a woman's company. When a gentleman was in love with his wife, it was remarked upon, and said gentleman teased. I'd grown up with these practices but always thought them daft.

The ballroom of the Lower Assembly Rooms was very long—nearly ninety feet, I'd read in the literature. It had a row of large windows, dark now, looking out toward the river, and enormous crystal chandeliers soaring overhead. The room glittered and glowed, light falling on the ladies' jewels and the shimmering rainbow of their gowns.

I headed for the game rooms, where I could find cards, backgammon, or chess, as I liked. But I was already tiring of the fashionable life, where a man did little more than imbibe brandy and wager all his money at games, while his wife dressed in feathers and floated about out of his sight. Too dull for me, but I'd always preferred action to the sedentary life.

I had nearly reached the card room, when I glimpsed the lady I'd seen in the Upper Rooms on our first afternoon. Tonight she was in a silver gray ball gown that hung low on her shoulders and wore a waving feathered headdress similar to Donata's. Again her back was to me, but when she turned her head to speak to the young woman next to her, I knew her.

I was about ten feet behind her when I halted. I prayed she and her daughter would walk on and never notice me, but it was not to be. When the lady turned all the way around to answer another greeting, she saw me.

Words died on her lips, and her eyes widened, but she quickly mastered herself. She finished the greeting, kissing a woman on the cheek, shaking a gentleman's hand, smiling all the while. Then her acquaintances moved off, and Lydia Westin faced me again.

I had not seen her in a year and a half, not since the hot summer when I'd helped her discover who had murdered her husband, a colonel in a cavalry regiment. She'd left London as the year cooled, heading for the Continent with her daughter. I had assumed she'd remain there.

Lydia couldn't look away from me, nor I from her. The younger woman with her glanced at me then Lydia, her brows coming together in puzzlement.

Lydia, who'd always been attuned to social niceties, seemed to realize she couldn't cut me dead in the middle of the Lower Assembly Rooms, not without causing an enormous ripple of gossip. She pasted on a smile and closed the few steps between us.

"Captain Lacey, is it? A surprise to see you in Bath."

"Mrs. Westin." I took her hand, barely applying pressure to her fingers, and bowed. "A surprise indeed."

I released her immediately, and she took her hand back quickly but without snatching. "My daughter, Miss Westin," Lydia said, indicating the young woman at her side. Miss Westin curtsied prettily, and I gave her a polite bow. Chloe Westin had dark hair and blue eyes as Lydia did, though her face had a somewhat different shape from her mother's, the influence of her now-dead father. I hadn't met Chloe ere this, she having been sent to the country before I'd begun my investigation into her father's death. But I'd heard much about her from Lydia.

Lydia's assessing gaze took in my new suit and well-polished boots, and concluded, rightly so, that my circumstances had changed. She did not ask, however, because this would be both impolite and imply that our relations were still close. We'd shared an intimacy—we'd been lovers, not to mince words—but that had come to an abrupt end.

"My daughter is to be married," Lydia said. She

caught my eye, both of us knowing how things had ended with Chloe's previous fiancé. "To Mr. Grayson, a charming and very respectable young man. Are you acquainted with him?"

"No, I am afraid not." I bowed again to Chloe. "My felicitations, Miss Westin."

She smiled, her happiness genuine, I was pleased to see. "Thank you, sir."

The gentleman I remembered eyeing me so sharply in the Upper Rooms a few afternoons ago appeared at Lydia's side. I doubted he was Chloe's fiancé, he being closer to my age than hers, but then, one never knew with society marriages.

"Pardon my manners," Lydia said, though she'd been nothing but scrupulously polite. "May I introduce Mr. Harmon? This is Captain Lacey, who was helpful . . . in discovering what happened to Colonel Westin." She stumbled a little over the words, as though deciding exactly what to say as she spoke. Then she lifted her head, becoming once more the elegant and proud woman I'd first met on a half-constructed bridge in darkness and rain. "Mr. Harmon is my husband."

I could not stop my gaze flashing to the man again. He looked back at me in defiance, attempting but failing to mask his anger with neutral politeness.

He held out a rigid hand. "Well met, Captain." From the look in Mr. Harmon's eyes, he knew the full tale of how I'd helped Lydia, or at least most of it. I wondered how much Lydia had left out. But Mr. Harmon seemed to understand what my relations with her had been, because his eyes held both wariness and a warning.

"And you, sir," I said. Our handshake was as brief

as possible.

The only one oblivious to the tension was Chloe, who gave me another smile. "What brings you to Bath, Captain?"

"Honeymoon," I said, and wondered a second later why that had come out of my mouth. "I married very recently."

"Ah." This announcement pleased Mr. Harmon very much, though Lydia's eyes flickered. "Then you have my congratulations, sir."

"And mine," Lydia said, her words bumping into her husband's.

"Is your wife here?" Chloe craned to look around, trying to decide which of the ladies around us belonged to me.

"Indeed she is, but I've already —"

My quip that I'd already lost her in the crowd cut off as Donata stepped to my side, touching her fingers to my arm. She gave Lydia a cool look that held the smallest required politeness.

"Mrs. Westin," Donata said. "And Miss Westin. I'd supposed you'd left us for the Continent for good."

"As did I," Lydia said, her voice as controlled as Donata's. "My husband persuaded me to return to England."

"Best thing," Donata said. "Chloe will want her fellow countrymen." The warm look she turned on Chloe was genuine. "I heard of your engagement, my dear. My felicitations."

"Thank you," Chloe said. She did see the tension between the four of us now but was perplexed by it.

"And to you," Donata went on to Lydia. "It seems matrimony is in the air all around. Are you living in

Bath now?"

"For the Season," Lydia said. "And then we'll go to our home in Devon. I find I prefer life in the provinces."

"A very sensible arrangement." Donata moved her hand in her indifferent manner. "London is not for the faint of heart. I do hope you enjoy Bath. The orchestra at the Pump Rooms is quite fine this year."

How Donata would know this, I could not say, because she'd not visited the Pump Rooms yet.

"Thank you," Lydia said. "I imagine we will. Good evening."

We all said our good-byes, each of us as polite as could be. In the group, only Chloe was innocent. Lydia turned away stiffly, and the hand that stole to her husband's arm trembled.

"Married, has she?" Donata said as soon as the trio was out of earshot. "I am not terribly surprised. She was never one who could bear to be alone for long. Do you remember what I said about her when I first met you, Gabriel?"

"I do."

Donata had remarked, cigarillo smoke curling around her, that gentlemen had dashed themselves to pieces on the rocks of Lydia Westin before. Donata had been warning me, and I'd ignored her, to my peril.

"I see no reason to change my opinion." Donata gave a decided, feather-waving nod toward Lydia's back, squeezed my arm, and flowed back into the crowd.

*** *** ***

We learned nothing new that night. Grenville, Donata, and I encouraged gossip but the inhabitants of Bath had no information for us.

I had to conclude that Mrs. Collins had not come here as per usual. "So we move on to Brighton," I said to my assembled friends as we dined at home the next day.

Grenville had come to share our meal. He looked fresh and rested, though he'd stayed out with us until the wee hours then had gone to visit Marianne. If everyone could be as awake and lively as Grenville after a night of wine, gambling, and debauchery, doctors would prescribe it as a health cure.

"If we rush away, it will be remarked upon," Donata said. She'd had her usual lie-in, and she looked as bright as Grenville. I, who'd risen at my early hour to hire a horse and ride, wanted a nap.

"True," Grenville said. "Most people linger in Bath a month or more before turning to other pleasures."

"I will not cease looking for Mrs. Collins because the society in Bath will chatter if we leave before a month is out." The words were snappish, but I was frustrated.

"I did not expect you to," my wife said. "But we haven't even gone to the Pump Rooms."

"Yes, may we at least visit those, Father?" Gabriella asked. "Perhaps tomorrow morning, and we can leave for Brighton the next day."

Both Donata and Grenville looked amused at her eagerness. "We should stay at least a week," Donata said. "Remember, no one here is supposed to know you're searching for Mrs. Collins."

"And while we're placating the local populace, someone might do her harm," I growled. I took a drink of coffee, trying to still my temper. "I promised

Marianne I would look into the matter, and so far, I've done damn all."

"Not entirely." Grenville calmly went on cutting his sausages. "You've discovered Mr. Perry, who has a strange interest in Mrs. Collins. He married Mrs. Wolff, a great actress who is now blind. Why did he marry her? Because he admires great actresses? Or to make her do something for him? And what? We have established from David's Maddie that Mrs. Collins has a few hiding places—one here, where she has not been, though Mr. Perry arrived there and paid her rent. Why did he? Motive sinister, or motive benevolent? Did Mrs. Collins get wind of Mr. Perry coming to her rooms and took others, perhaps under an assumed name? She is an actress, as Marianne has pointed out. Marianne has been out on her own looking for her, talking to people at the theatres, though she's found nothing so far."

"Miss Simmons has even taken a part in a play here," Gabriella said.

Grenville ceased talking and stared at her. So did I and Donata. "How did you know that?" Grenville asked, keeping his voice even.

"She told me. She came to the door while you were out last evening to leave a message for you, Father. I thought it silly I shouldn't speak to her myself, so I did. We had a nice chat in the sitting room. Miss Simmons told me that she'd asked if the local theatres had any parts for her while she was in town, for verisimilitude, she said. One company did give her a part, and in fact, she's on tonight. I assumed she'd tell Mr. Grenville when he visited her. I do like Miss Simmons. I wish I did not have to pretend not to know her. It's ridiculous."

Finished, Gabriella picked up a piece of buttered bread and munched it.

We all regarded her in surprise a moment. "Miss Simmons did not bother to mention this," Grenville said in some irritation.

"May we go to the play, Father?" Gabriella asked. "A nice day out, I'd think—the Pump Rooms tomorrow morning, tea at the Upper Assembly Rooms, the theatre in the evening? If you and Mrs. Lacey haven't already made our plans, of course."

Polite, deferential, and still managed to tell me exactly what she wanted. She was certainly my daughter.

I ought to admonish Gabriella for not only allowing Marianne the house but speaking so frankly about Marianne's arrangement with Grenville, but I felt a flush of pride instead. Gabriella had a clear-eyed view of the world, judging individuals in it by their own merits. I could not scold her for that.

"The Pump Rooms, of course," Donata said before I could answer. "I had planned for the subscription ball at the Upper Assembly Rooms tomorrow, but a theatre jaunt would not be a bad idea. We can always wander into the ball later."

"I'll not be for the Pump Rooms," Grenville said with a grimace. "Never could understand putting on an odd-looking suit to walk into a bath full of other people. Not to mention the waters taste of rotten eggs. I will take my exercise walking the city."

"Hmm," I said. "Perhaps I will forego the Pump Rooms as well."

"Nonsense," Donata said. "The waters are quite healing. They will be good for your injured leg." She had a gleam in her eyes, a teasing one. She would herd me, half undressed in waistcoat and close-fitting drawers, into a pool full of water peopled with the denizens of the town, and she'd enjoy it.

"And I've never been to a spa," Gabriella said. "I long to see a mineral bath."

"But I have no wish to smell one," Grenville said. He gave us a salute with his claret. "Enjoy yourselves, my friends."

*** *** ***

The Pump Rooms caught my interest once we arrived, despite Grenville's aversion and my misgivings. The building of golden stone stood on the site of Roman ruins, some of which had been unearthed when the place had been renovated some twenty or so years before. Grenville had obtained a few curios from that excavation, which I admitted interested me more than the parade of ladies and gentlemen we found there the next morning.

We entered a grand room with a sort of counter I'd find in a public house, behind which ladies were dispensing drinks straight from what was known as the King's Pump. I'd been assured by Grenville that the pipes had been arranged so the water came directly from the fountain and did not pass through the pool in which bathers immersed themselves. Still, I understood his aversion when I lifted the glass of foul-looking water. It stank of a bog, and I had to hold my breath before I could drink it.

Gabriella made a face when she drank hers, but Donata emptied her glass without a qualm. "Excellent for the humors," she said. "Come along, Gabriella. We'll ready ourselves for a dip."

Bathing in public had never appealed to me. As a boy, I'd stripped off my clothes and played in the sea in the summer, or in the waters of the Broads. Dangerous, but I'd known no fear. In the army, modesty had often vanished in the face of necessity, but today I felt a bit uneasy as I donned a linen waistcoat and pantaloons and went out to what was known as the Hot Bath.

I had to admit that the water, pleasantly warm, did bite into my limbs and start to soothe them at once. My knee became looser, more relaxed, and the lingering pain in my ribs flowed away. The water, though it came up only to my chest, made me buoyant enough that leaving my stick on shore did not cause me disquiet.

Both men and women filled the bath this morning, from gouty gentlemen lowered in chairs, to ladies still wearing their bonnets. Heads turned when my wife entered with Gabriella—a lofty dowager viscountess was a sensation.

Donata retained her elegance in the thin dress that soaked through quickly. Gabriella splashed in after her, looking happy. Gabriella swam rather than walked, which earned her disapproving stares, but Donata did not admonish her.

When Donata reached me, I could not stop looking my wife over, she wet and draped with soaked material, her face flushed, her hair curling in the damp. She saw my look and gave me an arch one in return.

The company was mixed, old and young, healthy and infirm, wealthy and middle class. Donata greeted her acquaintances as Gabriella paddled or walked about the bath, enjoying herself.

The odor of the waters curled in my nose, and I did not much like being in the same pool as a man with open sores. But I had to admit my body felt warm, loose, and rested.

Our visit to the Pump Rooms earned us little more than a hot bath and a bad-tasting drink, and no new information on Mrs. Collins. Donata insisted we stay for tea, which we took while the small orchestra, above us in an iron-railed gallery, played tunes.

Later in the evening, after a light supper, we went to the theatre to see Marianne. The theatre was not the one in Orchard Street, where the famous Mrs. Siddons had begun. This one was on a side street, a bit smaller, but filled with spectators nonetheless.

I had not seen Marianne do much onstage before this, even when she was still in the company at Drury Lane. In those plays she'd been so thoroughly in the background I hadn't much noticed her behind the might of principal players such as Mr. Kean and Mrs. Collins.

We did not sit in the stalls—that would never do—but in a box high above the stage, rented by Grenville. Grenville sat at the front of the box, not disguising the fact that he'd come to watch his mistress on the stage. He gave Marianne a nod when she came out in her costume, and she acknowledged it with a nod in return. The entire house saw the exchange, and whispers began.

Marianne had been given a role in the melodrama as sister to the heroine, with more lines than I'd ever heard her speak. To my surprise, she was quite good. She so often referred to herself disparagingly as a "second-rate actress" that I'd assumed her talent to be indifferent. But while she did not have the rolling voice and grand delivery of a Hannah Wolff or Abigail Collins, she quietly became the role she played.

I believed wholeheartedly that she was young Miss Wight, worried about her future but plucky enough to do something about it. I laughed at her quips, became sad for her when she saw her plans crash, and applauded heartily when she came to take her bow. Grenville called, *Brava!* and had Matthias ready at the foot of the stage to hand her a bouquet of hothouse flowers.

"Is she not splendid?" Gabriella said, clapping. "Please tell her from me, Mr. Grenville, that I thought she was wonderful."

Grenville was pleased with her approbation and left us to visit Marianne backstage. The virtuous Lacey family, on the other hand, departed with the crowd via the front entrance.

"Captain Lacey," a man said.

I turned and found myself facing Spendlove's man, his face now bruised under his expensive hat. Behind him stood two men I did not recognize, but they had the bearing of parish constables. Behind those stood Spendlove himself, mist beading on his thick red hair. Even more astonishing, Pomeroy stood with him.

Pomeroy, a large man with a shock of thick blond hair, removed his hat and made me an apologetic bow. "Captain. Sir. Will you come with us, please?"

"No," I answered. "If you wish to speak to me, you may call on me at my house."

"Afraid not," Spendlove said. While Pomeroy strove to be respectful, Spendlove did not bother. "You may send your lady wife home, of course."

"His lady wife is going nowhere," Donata said frostily. "What is this, Mr. . . . . Spendlove, is it? And

Mr. Pomeroy? Please explain why you are accosting us in the street."

"Count your blessings, Madame, that Pomeroy here talked me into waiting until you emerged from the theatre at all," Spendlove said. "Now, I will speak with Captain Lacey."

"Indeed?" Donata fixed him with her chill gaze. "Please step aside, sir. Give your address to my footman, and my solicitor will call upon you tomorrow."

"I am afraid not." Spendlove repeated, rocking back on his heels. Pomeroy looked annoyed, but he had no intention of quieting Spendlove or leaving. Spendlove was commanding this expedition, Pomeroy's stance said, even if Pomeroy did not like it.

"Father?" Gabriella turned to me, her eyes wide, her slender body huddled into her coat. The wind was brisk, our breaths heavy in the icy air. If my daughter caught a chill because of Spendlove, I would happily strangle him.

"Let him speak," I said to Donata. "Be quick about it," I snapped at Spendlove. "And then go."

Spendlove looked positively cheerful, in no way intimidated by either my abruptness or Donata's haughtiness. "Captain Gabriel Lacey, I arrest you for the murder of one Mr. John Perry, of the parish of St. Giles in London. Found dead yesterday evening, starting to decay too, in your rooms above the bakeshop at Number 5 Grimpen Lane."

Chapter Thirteen

They at least let me take my family home, though it was only Pomeroy's insistence that allowed it. Spendlove had wanted to haul me into a coach with guards then and there and carry me straight back to London. He at last agreed I could return home and pack a valise, but this concession came because he was confident of my guilt, not for any thought of courtesy or regard for my comfort.

Pomeroy preceded me into the dining room of our splendid house, where we would wait while Bartholomew gathered my things. Spendlove came close behind me. The parish constables waited in the hall, and Spendlove's man stationed himself at the front door in case I made a mad dash for freedom.

Spendlove tried to keep Donata out after she sent Gabriella upstairs. "Not a place for you, I think, Madame," he said, his hand on the door handle.

"Nonsense," Donata said, pushing past him.

"Gabriel is my husband, and I demand to know why the devil you are arresting him."

Spendlove's light blue eyes glinted. "For murder, as I said."

"Supposed murder," Donata snapped. "We departed London on Tuesday last and have not returned since. How is Captain Lacey to have murdered a man in London from the Crescent? I believe I would have noticed his absence for enough time to journey up to Town, kill a man, and return. The entire society of Bath would have noted it."

"Madame . . ."

"I am Lady Donata Pembroke, *Mr.* Spendlove, and you will address me as such."

Spendlove turned to me. "Can you curb your wife, please, Captain?"

"No," I said. I leaned against the edge of the table to watch.

"Perhaps I will arrest her with you," Spendlove said. "She can join you in the cells until the magistrate sorts things out. A happy honeymoon for you, eh?"

Pomeroy broke in with a growl. "Have some respect, man."

"I have given Captain and Mrs. Lacey plenty of respect. I allowed them to return to this comfortable house, haven't I? A bit posh for my taste." Spendlove glanced around at the inlaid Hepplewhite sideboard, chairs, and table as though they offended him.

"You don't outrank me, Spendlove," Pomeroy said. "Let the captain defend himself."

Pomeroy's attitude made a change from his instant assumption of my guilt, as was his wont. He did not like Spendlove pushing in on his territory, it was apparent.

"We left London, as my wife told you, on the sixth of this month," I said. "Tuesday last, more than a week ago. Since then, I have been making my rounds at the assembly rooms, bathing for my health, and immersing myself in insipid gossip, as one does at watering places."

Spendlove, instead of looking disappointed, smiled anew. "Interesting you should say so, Captain. The coroner believes Mr. Perry has been dead a bit longer than a week, killed on the evening of the fifth of January. The night before you set off on your journey, in fact. Leaving London to come to Bath, which I'm told is not a fashionable thing this time of year."

"I'm on honeymoon, as you pointed out," I said. "Our journey was not as sudden as you make it. We prepared our leaving several days beforehand. I did not visit Grimpen Lane that evening. How did the man get into my rooms at all?"

"That is a mystery," Spendlove said. "Perhaps someone was there to let him in. He wasn't found for days, and the door was locked and all, or so your landlady says. She went up there last evening because she noticed a peculiar odor coming from above her shop. It's been cold, so I'm sure it took some time for Perry to start to stink. She thought maybe a cat had gotten caught up there. She takes her keys, goes upstairs, unlocks the door to your front room, and there he is. Sprawled in the middle of the floor, his head beaten in. Gave the poor woman a turn. She comes running out for the Watch, I got wind of it, and I came 'round. This gentleman, Mr. Perry, I understand, threatened you and had you beaten, didn't he, Captain? I imagine that made you angry."

"Of course it did," I said. "But I did not retaliate."

"One more thing," Spendlove said. He opened a little notebook and leafed through pages until he found what he wanted. "Lying next to the dead man was a walking stick with a gold head. On that head was engraved the words *Captain G. Lacey, 1817.*"

I heard Donata's intake of breath, and I clutched the walking stick I'd bought at the shop in the Strand. "It was the murder weapon?"

Pomeroy answered before Spendlove could. "Don't know for certain. Could have been, but there was no blood on it."

"Blood can be wiped off," Spendlove said.

"For God's sake," I said. "Why would I wipe the blood from a walking stick that obviously belongs to me and then leave the stick next to the body? I believe I would be wise enough to take it away with me."

"Not if you were interrupted," Spendlove said. "I see you have a new stick to replace the old. Perhaps you left it behind in your agitation to get away, perhaps you left it to throw us off the scent. After all, what man would leave a weapon with his name on it at the scene of a crime?"

"That walking stick has a sword inside it," I said. "A much quicker weapon, especially for a man with a weak leg, than trying to beat a strong, healthy man to death."

Spendlove shrugged. "You can, of course, tell all that to the magistrate. It is my job, and Pomeroy's, to run you to ground and bring you in. And gather evidence. We don't get paid until there's a conviction." His tone implied he did not worry that he'd miss out on his reward.

"I did not go to Grimpen Lane that day," I repeated. "I have not seen Mr. Perry since he interrogated me after he had me beaten and tied to a cot. I admit no love for the man, and I am convinced he either killed Mrs. Collins the actress, or has hidden her away somewhere, or has terrified her into hiding. But I did not kill him. You can ask up and down Grimpen Lane whether I came there, and you can ask Lady Breckenridge's household about my comings and goings that day. And why on earth would I leave the man in my own rooms to be found?"

"From what I've heard tell, you're not the cleverest of gentlemen," Spendlove said. "I mean no offense. You are thorough and come to conclusions, but usually through dogged stubbornness rather than keenness of mind. You stumble over what others miss, but by chance. Oh, yes, I enjoyed reading about your investigations in those little journals of yours. But you *would* be the sort of man to kill another in a foul temper then storm away and leave town, forgetting the little details of cleaning up after yourself. You might not be the only suspect in this murder, but you are a very good one, and we are taking you to London to the magistrate."

"Very well," I said, coldly angry. Spendlove had already decided my guilt, but the Bow Street magistrate might see reason. I'd dealt with him before, and he was no fool.

Donata put herself in front of me. "No, Gabriel. They cannot come and snatch you in the middle of the night, like police do on the Continent. I have solicitors; I have means. They must leave you be until they can gather enough evidence for an arrest."

Pomeroy cleared his throat. "I'm afraid that finding the man dead after the captain had an altercation with him was enough evidence for the coroner and the magistrates. Sir Nathaniel told us to bring you, sir. With reluctance, but it points to you."

"You still had the keys to your rooms," Spendlove put in. "Mrs. Beltan told me you'd decided, at the last minute, not to give up the rooms but continue to let them. Now why did you want to do that, eh? When you were moving into a posh Mayfair home?"

"My own business," I said in a hard voice.

"A very convenient business." Spendlove gave me another smile, his side-whiskers moving with it. "Never worry, Captain. If the magistrate binds you over for trial, you can now afford a very nice room in Newgate."

*** *** ***

Donata continued to argue, but I cut the altercation short by walking out of the house to the hired coach that would carry us back to London. My wife tried to stop me, pointing out I could at least leave at a sensible hour of the morning if I wished.

But I wanted to see the magistrate as soon as I could and clear this up. I told Donata I'd let her decide whether to stay in Bath, move on to Brighton, or return to London. Grenville was here and would look after her.

She was not happy with me. Donata maintained her chill, aristocratic façade even as she kissed my cheek and bade me farewell. Pomeroy helped me into the coach, Bartholomew came running down with my bag, and Spendlove climbed in close behind me, as though still assuming I'd bolt. The inside was a tight fit once Pomeroy was inside with us, three large men in a small conveyance.

The coach rolled through the dark streets of the elegant little town, around the famous Crescent and Circus and then through narrow, straight lanes back toward the road that led to London.

We took the route the mail coaches used rather than back through Chippenham. Snow began around Devizes. The canal company had overcome the problem of the steep hill that led to the town with several series of locks that stair-stepped up the rise. I couldn't see the canal now in the darkness and swirling snow, and I didn't much look out the window.

Pomeroy sat across from me, quiet and embarrassed. Spendlove, on the other hand, bade us a cheerful good night, folded his arms, leaned against the side of the coach and went to sleep. Or seemed to. Pomeroy started to speak once or twice, but I shook my head to silence him.

It occurred to me to wonder, as we traveled, whether Denis had asked one of his men, such as Brewster, to rid the world of the troublesome Mr. Perry for me. I dismissed the idea almost immediately. If Brewster or another of Denis's toughs had murdered Perry, they would not have left him to rot in my rooms. They'd have taken Perry's body away and thrown it into the river, with no one the wiser. They'd also have made sure they caught Perry alone, in his own house perhaps, or in a deserted street, not waiting until he'd fixed himself in my rooms.

I wondered what Perry had been doing there—

waiting for me? Why, when everyone had known I'd moved out?

I had another thought, one more chilling. I remembered Felicity leaving Donata's house to stay with her "pal" a few days before we left for Bath. Had she and Perry met, for whatever reason, in my rooms, and had Felicity struck him down? I did not like the idea, but it was one I could not shake.

We returned to London much faster than I'd left it. The coach changed drivers and horses in Marlborough, then Hungerford, Newbury, Reading, and Maidenhead, and then on into London. The sun had long since risen by the time we reached the metropolis, and we'd left the snow behind in Berkshire. Though clouds and cold hugged the city, some of the icy bite had gone from the air.

They took me straight to the Bow Street magistrate's house, clopping to it around from Long Acre instead of trying to make their way through Covent Garden market, thronged with its usual customers.

The magistrate's court occupied two narrow houses in Bow Street. Inside, the arrests of the previous night awaited a hearing with the magistrate, who'd decide whether to dismiss the case, fine the offender, or whether enough evidence existed to send him or her to Newgate to await trial. Because of the nature of my supposed offense — murder — I was taken to a private room to stand in front of Sir Nathaniel Conant, the current chief magistrate of Bow Street.

I'd come in front of him before, last spring, to support Colonel Brandon, when he'd been accused of stabbing a fashionable dandy at a Mayfair ball.

Conant was a thin, spare man with a dry voice, quiet despite the many years of watching the dregs of London parade before his bench. His only acknowledgment of our previous meeting was a slight nod of his head when Pomeroy brought me inside.

I was haggard, tired, and still cold. Pomeroy didn't look much better, but Spendlove seemed refreshed by his sleep on the road.

Sir Nathaniel took a seat at his large desk and signaled for me to stand in front of him. He began without greeting us. "Captain Lacey, the coroner has concluded that one Mr. John Perry died of heavy wounds to his head, inflicted there by another person. Because he was found in rooms you let, behind a locked door, for which only you and your landlady have the keys, and because an article of yours was left there that might have been the murder weapon, you have been named as a possible culprit. I want to point out that this is a preliminary interview, not a trial. From here I will decide whether you are to be taken to Newgate to await a trial for either murder or manslaughter, as I decide. Do you understand?"

"Yes, sir." I understood perfectly well.

"Very well, then, I—"

We were interrupted by the door opening again without anyone knocking. The floor creaked as a large man stumped across it, limping a little and supporting himself with a stick. The newcomer had a broad face, a mouth quirked into a perpetual half smile, and eyes that could look kind but had a hard, shrewd twinkle. Not much got past this man.

Conant rose and cleared his throat. "Sir Montague, I beg your pardon. I would have waited had I known you were coming."

"My fault entirely." Sir Montague Harris, magistrate for the Whitechapel house, hobbled to a chair and let out an "Ahh" as he sat. He stretched out his leg with another groan, planted his walking stick on the floor, and leaned his hands on it. "I ought to have sent word. I did not learn of Captain Lacey's arrest until a few hours ago, and I move slowly in the cold." He spent a moment wriggling in the chair then he pointed at Spendlove with his stick. "You, my boy, fetch me a footstool. The weather makes this gouty leg ache something fierce."

Spendlove's expression went wooden, but he said nothing as he picked up a crate the right height for a footstool and brought it to Sir Montague's chair. Sir Montague lifted his leg onto it with his hands and let out another noise of relief.

"Coroner's court concluded Captain Lacey was a person of interest?" Sir Montague asked once he was settled.

"Indeed," Mr. Conant said. "I was about to begin my questions."

Sir Montague waved to him. "Carry on, sir. I am only here for interest."

Mr. Conant, unmoved by the obvious tension between Spendlove and Sir Montague, cleared his throat, took up his pen, dipped it into his ink pot, and prepared to write. "Captain Lacey, you were acquainted with the deceased?"

"I would say *acquainted* is hardly the term. The man set ruffians on me and took me prisoner."

Mr. Conant looked up, raising his brows. "I did not hear of this reported to my patrollers. Or the Watch."

"Because I did not report it," I said.

"Why not?" Spendlove interrupted. "I'd have run out looking for a Watchman first thing upon escaping."

"I was more concerned with my immediate safety from Mr. Perry's ruffians," I said. I carefully did not mention Felicity. She might have nothing to do with Perry's death, but a dark-skinned prostitute might be more to a jury's taste as a culprit than a captain who'd fought with valor during the war. "And I needed to hurry to my own wedding before I missed it," I finished.

"Tell Sir Nathaniel where you *did* take refuge," Spendlove said, his eyes glittering.

I heartily wished Sir Nathaniel would send him away. "I went to Curzon Street. To the home of James Denis."

Another lifted head and raised brows from Conant before he wrote. He took his time, scratching out every word before speaking again. "Mr. Denis is quite notorious among the magistrates, Captain."

"Captain Lacey is his particular friend," Spendlove said.

Sir Montague broke in. "I would not put it quite like that. An uneasy truce, I would say, wouldn't you, Lacey?"

"Exactly," I said. I could not be certain Conant or Spendlove would believe me, but Sir Montague was perceptive. "I knew Mr. Perry would hesitate to bother me if he knew I was under Mr. Denis's roof. I needed to rest and recover in safety before I traveled to Oxfordshire."

"For your wedding, yes," Conant said. "When you returned to London, did you seek out Mr. Perry?

Or did he seek you?"

"No," I said. "I did not see him."

"But upon your return, you would have had ample opportunity to report what he had done to you," Conant said. "You could have had him arrested and prosecuted."

"I kept an eye out for him, of course," I said. "But I saw no reason to bother reporting what had happened. It would have been my word against his." I would have needed Felicity or Perry's ruffians as witnesses to prosecute him, and the likelihood of finding any of them was small, let alone convince them to come to court. I'd meant to deal with Perry myself, but of course, I could not say so to Bow Street's chief magistrate.

". . . *saw no reason to bother reporting what had happened,*" Conant murmured as he wrote. "Now let us come to the night of January fifth. What did you do that afternoon and evening?"

I tried to cast my mind back to the days before we'd headed to Bath, but it was a bit of a blur. "We were packing the household to remove from London for a holiday. I was integrating my household with my wife's at the same time, so I had much to do."

"You moved into the house of the Dowager Viscountess Breckenridge in South Audley Street," Conant said. "And not two days later decided to leave for Bath?"

"Yes."

Conant said nothing for a few moments as he continued to write. "You started to vacate your rooms in Grimpen Lane," he said after a time. "According to your landlady, Mrs. Beltan, you decided that instead of leaving the rooms entirely, you'd continue to rent them from her. Why did you suddenly change your mind?"

I shrugged. "I thought the rooms would be a good place for meeting people, without bothering my wife and her household."

Conant's brows lifted even higher. "Meeting people? What sort of people? Will you explain, please?"

Pomeroy answered before I could. "The captain styles himself an amateur thief-taker. Unhappy folk come to him to ask him to find their missing daughters or diamond necklaces and such. Even Mr. Thompson of the River Police asked the captain to help him look for game girls who'd gone missing."

"Yes, so I heard." Conant regarded me in faint disapproval. "Very well, you decided to keep your rooms, whatever your reasons. You retained the keys?"

"I did. To the outer door as well as to my flat."

"Did anyone else have keys?"

"Mrs. Beltan does, of course," I said. "If she gave them to someone, I would have no idea. But consider, Mr. Conant, the locks are quite old. I'm certain the doors and locks would yield easily to someone determined to get in." I gave Spendlove a pointed look, and his slight smile was his only answer.

"You are saying that either Mr. Perry or his killer broke into your flat?" Conant asked.

"I am suggesting the possibility," I said, trying to remain patient. "I did not go near Grimpen Lane that day. Too busy."

"Preparing for your journey," Conant said. "So you have told me. Can you speculate how a walking stick belonging to you came to be in the flat as well?"

"Maybe *it* broke in," Pomeroy said, sotto voce.

Sir Montague made a noise of amusement, but both Spendlove and Conant looked annoyed.

"Mr. Perry must have brought it with him," I said. "He'd stolen it from me, or had it taken from me, when he'd abducted me." Felicity had told me my walking stick had been left in the street, but one of Perry's men could have taken it to him.

I went on, "I cannot believe Mr. Perry had come to return it, so perhaps he was using it himself. Or it was left next to him on purpose to incriminate me."

"Perhaps," Conant said. "In any case, the coroner judges that, from the state of decay of the body, the man died somewhere on the afternoon or evening of the fifth. I must ask you to relate your exact movements."

"And I tell you, I don't remember. I was at the shops with my man until late, buying sundries for the journey, and then at home with my wife."

"You did not leave the house after you entered it that evening?"

"No."

"And her household staff will corroborate this? They saw you every moment?"

Not every moment. Barnstable had brought a light repast to Donata's boudoir, and then he and the rest of the servants had left us well alone.

"I give you my word I was in the house from five in the evening until six o'clock the next morning, when we departed for Bath."

"Mrs. Lacey can confirm this?"

"She could. But I do not want her brought here and questioned."

Conant's dry voice grew stern. "Captain, this is a case of murder. It is my duty to decide who should be brought to trial for it. I will question whom I must. I need you to explain to me exactly where you were, and I need to ask whoever was with you for the truth. A witness puts you in Grimpen Lane during the hours Mr. Perry must have met his death. I will tell you, it looks very bad for you, Captain."

I blinked. "What witness?"

Conant looked stubborn. "I will say only that it was a lady of very good character. She swears up and down she saw you return to Grimpen Lane and enter the door that led to your rooms at eight o'clock in the evening."

"She could not have seen *me*," I said. "Is she certain? It is very dark at eight in the evening."

"True, but she maintains that she saw you in the light from the bakeshop," Conant said. "She knew it was you. So you need to tell me, Captain Lacey, exactly where you were and what you were doing at eight o'clock on the evening of January fifth."

Chapter Fourteen

In bed with my wife, were not the words I wanted to say. I was not prudish, nor my appetites less than healthy, but Donata was a lady, and I did not want to embarrass her.

No, even if she had been the most ragged of street girls, I would not have wanted to give her name. It was none of these gentlemen's business what I had been doing in the privacy of my chamber.

"The witness was mistaken," I said. "There must be a number of tall men in London who resemble me, who walk with a limp, even. I have been mistaken for others before—in fact, I have been told more times than I care to that I resemble the late Lord Breckenridge."

"The witness was quite positive," Conant said. "You were known to her."

I could not imagine who they were talking about. "Not Mrs. Beltan, was it? Her shop gets very busy of an evening when she's selling off the last of her bread, and she might have mistaken someone for me, or been wrong about the hour or day when she'd seen me."

"Not Mrs. Beltan," Spendlove answered before Conant could speak. "Mrs. Beltan never saw you. As you say, her shop keeps busy."

"What we have," Conant broke in firmly, "is a witness putting you entering your rooms on the night in question, and you claiming you were nowhere near."

"I *was* nowhere near." I started to feel desperate.

"Then we will have to ask your household and your wife to confirm your whereabouts."

I got to my feet, too agitated to sit. "Damn and blast, gentlemen. I am recently married. Where do you think I was?"

Pomeroy guffawed, and Sir Montague let out a dry little chuckle, while Conant did not change expression at all. Pomeroy said, "Don't want Mrs. Lacey on the witness stand saying that to the court, do you?"

"I have no wish to make my wife a laughingstock," I said. "It is unfair to her. You have already made things awkward for her by dragging me off in the middle of the night. I hardly want to tell her that she can save me from the noose only by confessing she let me give in to my ardor."

Conant cleared his throat. "Then what we have is the witness' words against yours and your wife's."

"I'm afraid so." I sat down again, letting out a breath. "But if I had left the South Audley Street house that evening, someone there would have seen me. There is always a footman in livery at the front door, kitchen staff always in the kitchen, some servant or gardener in the back. My man tends to keep an eye on me wherever I am, Mr. Spendlove here has had a man following me about, and I have had yet another man watching me in case someone tries to abduct me again. Ask any of those people whether they saw me that night."

"I intend to." Mr. Conant let out a long breath, wiped his pen, and laid it down. "I will do you a favor, Captain. I do not feel I have enough evidence yet to keep you for trial, but I must request that you remain in London and return to me if I summon you. Will you give me your word that you will do that?"

"I give you my word." I could barely say the response in my anger, but I knew he was being lenient when he did not have to be.

"Sir," Spendlove broke in, his face reddening. "Are you certain? The witness . . ."

"Will remain anonymous, and I will be ascertaining whether Captain Lacey was at his house as he claims. This hearing will remain open until I am satisfied one way or the other. Is that clear?"

Spendlove did not look happy. Pomeroy got to his feet with his usual energy. "I'll go round to South Audley Street and question the staff, shall I?"

"No, I will," Spendlove said.

"Pomeroy will do it," Conant said with a frown. "You, Mr. Spendlove, are too adamant to obtain the conviction. I want someone less eager to prove the captain guilty."

"Pomeroy used to be his sergeant," Spendlove said. "He's hardly a neutral party."

Pomeroy answered, still sounding cheerful. "I resent you thinking I'd let sentiment stand in the way of me job. But if you think I'll let the captain off because he used to scream at me in the mud of the battlefield, then we'll send another Runner."

"I will decide," Conant said. He stood up. "Please leave me, gentlemen. I have many more cases to hear today."

Beneath my anger and exhaustion, I let out a breath of relief. I'd not see the inside of Newgate today.

"Wait for me downstairs, Captain," Sir Montague said. "I might be a few minutes getting out of this chair, and I want to speak to Sir Nathaniel."

I agreed, and departed, passing a grinning Pomeroy and glowering Spendlove.

Downstairs, I stepped out of the fetid air of the house to cold, brisk winter wind along Bow Street. It was mid-afternoon, sunshine trying to break through scurrying clouds. A coach—I assumed Sir Montague's—waited in front of the house, so I waited with it.

Spendlove exited behind me, putting on his tall hat. He paused when he saw me, and came close. "Mr. Denis won't protect you forever," he said, not bothering to lower his voice. "He might wriggle you out of this, but I vow to see the pair of you where you ought to be—dangling from nooses side by side." Without giving me time to respond, he turned his back and walked away.

"Have a care of him." Sir Montague limped out of the magistrate's house, his face twisting as he came down on his bad leg. "A word in your ear, my boy."

I waited. One of the foot patrollers came out to help Sir Montague into the carriage, but Sir Montague waved him off.

"Spendlove has a bone to pick," Sir Montague said. "He usually does. But he is dogged in his pursuit of Mr. Denis, even more so than you are. You have compassion. Spendlove has none. Do not stand in his way."

I hadn't intended to, but Spendlove seemed bent upon standing in *my* way. "You sound as though you speak from experience."

Sir Montague's usually good-natured countenance became serious. "A few years ago the Queen's Square magistrate lent Spendlove to me to assist on a case. Spendlove arrested the culprit I had in mind, who was suspected of a few murders. Before I could question the man—I believed he had not acted alone—Spendlove had beaten him almost to death. Spendlove said he believed the man worked for Mr. Denis, and he'd been trying to get information about Denis out of him. The suspect died of his injuries before he could be brought before me. To this day, that case remains unsolved."

"Good Lord. Was the man connected with Denis?"

"Who knows?" Sir Montague gestured with his large hand. "Spendlove has embarked upon a crusade against Mr. Denis, and he's ruthless in his pursuit. All others must fall before his obsession. I've suggested Spendlove be dismissed, but unfortunately, the other magistrates say he's a very good thief-taker, which is true. He lives well on his rewards for convictions. However, I would not put it past Spendlove to kill Perry himself and leave him in your rooms for you to be blamed." He shrugged and let out a sigh. "But perhaps I go too far. If Spendlove had killed him, I believe he'd have made certain

Perry was found sooner and you arrested right away. And so, I repeat, have a care."

"I will. Thank you, sir."

"Besides," Sir Montague said, his cheerful twinkle returning as he signaled the patroller to come help him, "*I* want to have the joy of catching Mr. Denis. It must be carefully done. Spendlove will blunder, and any charges against Denis will not stick. Nice to have seen you, Captain."

Sir Montague let a patroller push him up into the carriage, and then he touched his hat to me and settled back into the seat. The carriage jerked forward into the traffic of Bow Street, Sir Montague raising his hand in farewell.

*** *** ***

I decided to walk to Grimpen Lane myself and see what I could see. Before I did, I went back into the Bow Street house to find Pomeroy and ask what had become of my walking stick.

"Sir Nathaniel has it locked up tight," Pomeroy said when I finally ran him to ground. "If it turns out not to be the murder weapon, I'll bring it back to you." He strode off again, and I had to be content with his answer.

I walked the short way around the corner to Russel Street and into Grimpen Lane. I tapped my way along, the wind tugging at my coat and hat. It occurred to me that, bundled in my coat with my hat pulled down, I was as anonymous as the next man who passed me. I was tall, but I was not the only tall man in London, and many gentlemen used walking sticks. Whoever had professed to see me might have spied any man in a greatcoat bundled up against the cold. Unless the witness had stood directly in front of me and spoken to me, she could not possibly have known whether I was the gentleman she'd seen.

I stepped into the bakeshop, breathing a sigh of relief to be out of the wind, and removed my hat. Behind her counter, Mrs. Beltan slid formed loaves into the bread oven of her fireplace, wiped her hands, and came out to see me.

"Bad business, Captain," she said. "What nonsense, accusing you of murder. I told that Runner, Mr. Spendlove, you wouldn't have done such a thing, and that you were gone to Bath, but he had a bee in his bonnet. *I* never saw you near that night, and I usually notice your comings and goings."

I leaned on the counter, soaking up the warmth of the place. "Do you know who told them I entered my rooms? One of your customers, perhaps?"

Mrs. Beltan shook her head. "I doubt very much it was one of *my* customers. The ladies come in, they know what bread they want, they tuck it into their baskets, and out they go. They usually are in far too much a hurry to be watching who's going up to the rooms above. Someone's telling lies, I'm certain. Now then, Captain, before you go—your new wife wouldn't turn up her nose at fresh-baked bread or a cruller or two, even if she is an aristocrat. A gift from me?"

"*I* certainly wouldn't say no, Mrs. Beltan, but my wife is still in Bath."

"Never you mind. I'll give you something to take with you, and you come back when she's here for more."

So saying, Mrs. Beltan went behind the counter to her kitchen and filled a cloth-lined basket filled with good-smelling baked breads. I would feast tonight.

As I left the shop, my gaze went across the street to the house opposite and its upstairs window, with the curtains open the exact width they were every day.

I stopped. A woman who claimed she knew me by sight, who swore it was me going into my rooms. Sir Nathaniel never could have meant Mrs. Carfax, could he?

Despite living across from the woman for years, I barely knew Mrs. Carfax. We nodded at each other in passing, occasionally exchanging greetings and remarks about the weather, but that was all.

Mrs. Carfax was widowed and had lived in this cul-de-sac for ten years, so Mrs. Beltan had told me. She and her companion were thin and spare, with narrow faces and graying hair under large bonnets. Mrs. Carfax and Miss Winston dressed similarly, bowing to fashion only in the most cursory way, forgoing the braid, lace, netting, ribbons, or feathers so loved by Donata that made her gowns works of art.

I thought I saw a movement behind the curtain upstairs. On impulse, I crossed the narrow street and knocked on the door of the house.

And knocked. I backed a step and looked up again. There went the curtain, with the face of Mrs. Carfax peering around it. I waved at her and pointed at the door.

The curtains snapped all the way closed. For the first time since I'd lived in Grimpen Lane, Mrs. Carfax had muffled her window during the hours of daylight.

I knocked on the door again, annoyed. And again.

At long last, the bolt was drawn back, the door opened a crack, and Mrs. Carfax's companion peered out.

Though the two women were similar in looks and build, I saw the differences between them as I studied Miss Winston a foot away from me. Miss Winston had large brown eyes and the regular features of a once-pretty woman. She'd suppressed the prettiness by scraping her hair into a severe bun and wearing a frock of drab brown that washed any color from her face.

"Good afternoon, Captain," Miss Winston said. "Mrs. Carfax does not want to see you."

She shut the door. Or tried to. I put my foot inside it and forced the door open. Miss Winston looked at me in pure terror as I grabbed the door handle and held on.

"Miss Winston, I assure you I did not harm that man," I said. "Mrs. Carfax was mistaken."

"She made no mistake." Miss Winston tried to shut the door again.

I clung to it. "Let me speak to her."

"She don't want to."

"Please, Miss Winston." I heard the desperation in my voice. "The magistrate is ready to charge me for a crime I did not commit. Let me convince her I was nowhere near Grimpen Lane that night."

Miss Winston debated, her eyes narrowing, intelligence trying to overcome her fear. Something in me must have been persuasive, because she at last gave a nod. "Wait here."

I was reluctant to move my foot and let her shut the door, but I conceded, released the door handle, and backed a step. The door closed, but Miss

Winston did not shoot the bolt. I heard her ascend the stairs inside, and after a time, voices raised above.

The door was too thick for me to discern what was said, but after about a quarter of an hour, footsteps sounded again. Miss Winston opened the door then reached behind her and dragged an unhappy Mrs. Carfax outside with her.

Mrs. Carfax was the plainer of the two women, her eyes like faded blue sky. She kept her head ducked, her shawl pulled tight, as though appalled Miss Winston had made her come out without a bonnet and concealing coat.

"We should speak inside," I said. "The day is too cold."

Miss Winston shook her head. "No, you must say your piece. She'll not let you in."

I doubted anything male had entered their rooms in a decade. "Mrs. Carfax," I said as gently as I could. "You could not have seen me here the night of Mr. Perry's death. It was the fifth of January; do you remember? I was at home with Mrs. Lacey, packing to remove to Bath. I was in sight of my wife or her servants, or my daughter and my daughter's aunt and uncle the entire evening. So you see, it could not have been me you saw."

Mrs. Carfax shot me a quick glance, blue eyes the only color in her face. "It was you, Captain. I know it."

"I take it you saw me from your window?" I asked, looking up at it.

Mrs. Carfax pulled her shawl closer. "That is correct. From the window."

"Mrs. Carfax, in the years I've known you, you

have always closed your curtains as soon as the daylight fades. You keep them closed until dawn, never varying. In winter, the darkness comes early, not much past four. How then, were your curtains open for you to look out at eight in the evening?"

"I on occasion crack them open to look out into the street. Such as when I hear a noise."

She was lying. Her face was flushed, her gaze everywhere but on mine.

"Have we not been neighbors and acquaintances for years?" I asked her. "You know that man wasn't me, Mrs. Carfax. If you saw any man at all."

"It was you." Mrs. Carfax's voice grew more firm as the words came out. "I have told the magistrate."

I tried to speak patiently, but my words had an edge to them. "Has someone put you up to this? Told you to say these things? Mr. Spendlove, perhaps?"

Her eyes flickered, but I could not tell if she feared the name of Spendlove or her fright came from me towering over her, demanding she answer.

"If he has threatened you, I will stop him," I said. "Forgive me for upsetting you, but I might be fighting for my life. I've only just gotten married."

I realized at that moment exactly how much I wanted a long, happy life with Donata. Wanted it, longed for it with everything in me. The preparations for the wedding, the ceremony, and the shortened wedding journey had all rather obscured the realization that I had done the deed.

At this moment, in the street, cold wind cutting through me, my thoughts coalesced to one incandescent point—I had married my lover, a woman who'd challenged me from the moment I'd met her. I wanted to embrace every moment I had with her.

Mrs. Carfax remained rigid, not looking at me, but Miss Winston softened a little. "The Runner, Mr. Spendlove, did question us. He had poor Henny in quite a state."

This was the first time I'd heard Mrs. Carfax's Christian name, or at least her pet name. "Did he instruct you to tell the magistrates you'd seen me?"

Mrs. Carfax broke away from Miss Winston. "I *saw* you, Captain. That is all." She gathered her shawl about her and ran back inside the house, slamming the door behind her.

Miss Winston remained with me, her look troubled.

"I am correct, am I not?" I asked her. "Mr. Spendlove made her say these things."

"I believe so. Mr. Spendlove spoke to her in Mrs. Beltan's parlor. He sent me out, quite forcibly, and shut the door. When he'd finished and emerged, Henny was pale and sick, and she had to be taken home and put to bed. She never would tell me what he'd said."

Spendlove had threatened her with something, that was certain. Whatever he'd said he'd do to her, I would stop him.

"I know you did not kill that man, Captain," Miss Winston said. "I will be prepared to say so if I must."

"You are kind," I said. "If you can persuade Mrs. Carfax to change her mind . . ."

"I will endeavor. Good night." Miss Winston nodded to me then went back inside the house and closed the door.

I was left alone with my basket of baked goods and the winter cold.

I turned and walked across the lane again to the bakeshop, borrowed keys from Mrs. Beltan, because I'd left all mine behind in Bath, and opened the door to the stairwell that led to my rooms.

The smell met me. The cold cut it a little, and the wind coming in behind me helped, but the stench of death lingered.

I went slowly up the stairs and unlocked my front room. I stood in the doorway, the chill of the stairwell embracing me, and studied what was before me. John Perry's body had been removed, but no one had bothered to clean the blood from the wooden floor. The blood had dried, the large brown stain a reminder of the violence that had occurred here.

I held my breath against the smell as I crossed the room, avoiding the stains, and opened the front windows. Cleansing winter air poured in, bitterly cold.

I searched my rooms, hoping to find something the Runners had missed. I was not optimistic—Pomeroy was thorough. I found no blood in the bedchamber; all in that room was as I'd left it. The struggle hadn't come this far.

I locked the door to my flat again when I departed, but I let the windows stand open. I wanted the stink gone, and I had nothing to steal.

A large man waited for me at the street door. He had a deep scar on each cheek, his nose had been broken, and his eyes were watchful. He stood in front of me so I could not move around him, but he said nothing at all as I stopped on my doorstep.

"Where is Mr. Brewster?" I asked. "I thought he was my minder."

This man was apparently not as talkative as Brewster. He stared at me, popped open his mouth, said, "Watching South Audley Street," and popped his mouth closed again.

"Was he here the night Mr. Perry was killed?"

Again the stare then the little noise as he opened his mouth. "No one were here. Mr. Denis said to watch you and your family, not your rooms."

"Hmm." I contemplated the darkening street. "And now you are watching me?"

A nod. Very well. The man could watch me find a hackney to take me home. I was tempted to hand him the basket to carry for me, but I did not think he had a sense of humor.

He still did not move. "His nibs wants to see that old biddy across from you."

I was not surprised to hear Denis had learned that Mrs. Carfax was Spendlove's witness, because Denis had eyes everywhere. But I did not like Denis's interest. "If you mean Mrs. Carfax, tell his nibs to leave her alone."

The man only stared at me. I finally stepped around him, laid the keys back on Mrs. Beltan's counter, and made my way out of Grimpen Lane. Denis's man followed close on my heels.

As I made to climb into the hackney coach at the stand in Russel Street, I had a bad thought. If Denis wanted Mrs. Carfax so adamantly, this man might take it upon himself to go to her the moment I rode away and drag her to Denis any way he could.

"Get in," I said to him. "Take *me* to see Mr. Denis."

The large man did not like this idea. I saw him think about it, his mean-looking eyes never leaving me. At last, he gave an abrupt nod, turned from me, and climbed onto the back of the coach.

I pulled myself inside the best I could, and the carriage sprang forward. I hadn't managed to close the door, and it swung on its hinges, banging against the latch but not catching. I reached for it, but a helpful citizen outside grabbed the door and slammed it shut as we rolled on into Covent Garden.

Chapter Fifteen

It was dark by the time I descended in Curzon Street. Denis's man climbed down and disappeared inside the house, and the emotionless butler came out to help me from the hackney and inside. Again I had no appointment, but this time the butler put me into the elegant but unfriendly downstairs reception room while he went to tell Denis I'd arrived. I paced without sitting down.

I waited about half an hour before the butler returned and ushered me to Denis's private study. His desk this evening held a few large sheets of paper, which he perused without animation. One page I saw before he carefully turned it facedown contained the detailed drawing of a sculpture, a very old and rare sculpture I recognized from books. At present, the sculpture was in Rome. I wondered where it would end up. Because Denis would have had plenty of time to clear his desk before I entered, I knew he'd wanted me to see the page.

Denis motioned me to a chair, which his butler had arranged in front of the desk. When I sat, the butler set a goblet of brandy on the small table next to the chair, the brandy positioned in the exact center of the table. The butler had done this before when I'd visited—I wondered how often he practiced the move.

I did not wait for Denis to initiate the conversation or ask why I'd come. "Leave Mrs. Carfax alone," I said.

The flicker in Denis's eyes might have been humor. "I have no wish to beat upon small elderly widows. I seek merely to ask her why Mr. Spendlove convinced her to tell a lie to the magistrate. If we know more about her, we can intervene and remove Spendlove's influence."

"You mean you will render her more afraid of you than of him," I said. "You seem confident you can thwart Mr. Spendlove. He made it clear his life's work is to see you hanged."

Another glint of almost-humor. "I am familiar with crusades against me. You have commenced one for a few years now."

"I have not necessarily given it up. You murder people, or cause to have them murdered. I am surprised you haven't murdered me."

"I believe I have explained." Denis folded his hands on the desk. "Though you are a thorn in my side, I find you a very useful thorn. I have no wish to see Mr. Spendlove drag you in for this crime, which I know you did not do. I would not be surprised to learn that Spendlove himself killed Mr. Perry to throw suspicion on you in order to get you into court. There he can put you under oath and ask all sorts of questions about me, or perhaps bargain with you—details about me and my life for your freedom. Such a course would take him nowhere, but he would try."

The thought that Spendlove had pursued Perry and killed him in order to pin the blame on me had occurred to me. I was not certain Spendlove would go that far, but I did not know the man well enough to judge. A person obsessed with what he believed could go to any lengths to prove his point. He might even murder to show his disapproval of murder.

"What do you propose to do?" I asked.

"About Spendlove? We shall see. About you being accused of murder, I have already taken steps. Consider letting me speak to Mrs. Carfax. It would help."

I did not want poor, wretched Mrs. Carfax brought here to him. "She is a timid woman with a weak heart, who has difficulty speaking to anyone but her companion, and certainly not to a man like you. However annoyed I am with her, I will not let you make her ill. Her companion, on the other hand, is a bit more forthcoming. I will persuade Miss Winston to discover what Spendlove threatened Mrs. Carfax with and to tell me. But no hurting either of them."

Denis gave me a cold look, this one without any amusement at all. "It is not in my nature to bully the weak for no reason. If I am hard on a man, it is because he deserves it."

Admittedly, the murders I had known Denis to commit were of men who'd done terrible things. One had tried robustly to kill Denis and me, and another had helped procure innocent young women for a man of perverse appetites. I'd looked the other way on both. But I'd also seen Denis's hold over otherwise respectable gentlemen, including me. Denis had located my estranged wife and daughter when I'd been unable to, and then seen to it that my first marriage ended cleanly. I might have found the means, via Grenville and other friends, for the divorce, but I was forever in Denis's debt for bringing Gabriella back to me, and he knew it. For that service, I now cooperated with him, however reluctantly.

"You will let *me* speak to Miss Winston," I said sternly.

Denis made a faint gesture with his fingers. "Very well, but I advise you to do it soon. Mr. Spendlove will not wait long to try another way to convince the magistrate to send you to Newgate."

I knew he wouldn't. I was certain Spendlove had someone following me even now.

I took a sip of the brandy I knew would be very good and stood up. "Stay away from Mrs. Carfax and Miss Winston. I will tell you what I discover."

He did not look impressed. "Tell me exactly what you discover, and it will not be necessary."

"What about the incendiary device?" I asked. "Have you found out anything in that direction?"

Denis's coolness increased, as though I'd committed a social gaffe by asking. "My inquiries proceed. I will send you a message when the person is found. Good evening, Captain."

I made him a curt bow. I did not bother to thank him for his time, he made a dismissing motion, and I left him.

I walked up South Audley Street to my new home, moving slowly now. Because her ladyship was still away, no doorknocker hung on the black-painted panels and no footman waited expectantly in his place outside. My key was still in Bath, and I had to rap with my knuckles on the door of the house in which I now lived to gain admission.

*** *** ***

Barnstable had remained in residence while we'd journeyed to Bath. When he found me cold and damp on the doorstep, he had me inside and upstairs in a trice, a hot bath prepared before I was out of my clothes.

Barnstable had learned of my arrest and was aghast. "Taking a gentleman in the street with no provocation," he said as he shook out and folded my coat and shirt. "What is the world coming to? If a man gets himself murdered in your rooms while you are far away, why is that your fault? I am certain her ladyship will give the magistrates an earful."

I was certain as well. "I was not far away when the murder occurred, unfortunately." I lowered myself into the hot water and let out a sigh. Barnstable knew how to draw a bath. "I was here, in this house, in her ladyship's chamber. You might have to swear to that in court, Barnstable. It will not be pleasant. I apologize."

"Of course I would swear, sir. We all will."

"No lying. That will not help."

Barnstable looked offended. "Of course not, sir."

He left me to soak. I was happy to let the dust of the road, the stink of Bow Street, and the sweat from my worries float away. Barnstable had learned I was not a man who liked being ministered to in the bath — I preferred to scrub myself — and let me alone.

Today I did no scrubbing. I lay back in the hot water and let its warmth and that from the fire settle over me. I knew Sir Montague's presence at my hearing had been the only thing that had kept me from residing in Newgate this night instead of in this comfortable dressing room. I felt a wash of gratitude for the man. I also knew that if I thanked him he'd look surprised, modest, and then wise, telling me he'd only done his duty.

Melancholia hovered again, but I'd learned in the last few years that activity helped me stave it off. When I was walking about being frustrated by people, my leg hurting, the darkness stayed away. I had no time for it.

When the water began to cool, I hauled myself out of the bath, wrapped myself in the dressing gown Barnstable had left, and let him shave my face.

After that, Barnstable wanted me to eat. I humored him by devouring some of the bread Mrs. Beltan had given me, which Donata's cook toasted and buttered for me, then I left again, clean and warm, out into the cold.

I took a hackney back toward Covent Garden. Now that Perry's demise had made her old lodgings safe, Felicity might have returned to them. I could easily see her killing Perry, battering him to death in fear as she fought him. If she had killed him, accidentally or not, I'd send her away, out of Spendlove's reach. I had no wish to see Felicity hang for someone like Perry.

I had the hackney drop me where Great Wild Street, Drury Lane, and Great Queen Street more or less came together in a triangle. From there I picked my way north to the passage I remembered had emerged onto Drury Lane. Or thought I remembered — I had been hurt and insensible when Felicity had dragged me out of it, my vision a bit blurred.

After trial and error, I found the right lane, with the house that had lodged Felicity at its end. A landlady was home in her rooms in the bottom floor and opened the door to me. She was half drunk and said she hadn't seen Felicity for days.

I asked to be let up to Felicity's rooms regardless. I thought the landlady would refuse me, but she must have liked my bearing, not to mention the few shillings I dropped into her palm. She wanted only to return to her gin bottle, so she handed me a large key and waved me away.

Felicity lived in two rooms, a sitting room in front of the house, and a bedroom in the rear. I had to light a stump of candle that I'd brought with me in order to see anything, but I recognized the low bed as the one I'd been tethered to. I'd been tied with scraps of linen, which still lay on the floor. The rooms were cold and smelled of damp. Felicity had not been back here.

I went through them anyway, looking for some clue as to where she'd gone. A few frocks hung on pegs behind a curtain in the bedroom, and a cupboard in the corner held her linens and stockings. One slipper, the beading torn off, the satin soiled, rested forlornly in the bottom of the cupboard.

The top of the night table next to the bed was empty, but the single drawer revealed a small book bound in leather. I opened it to find a New Testament, printed in small text.

The book was not new—few but Grenville and those of like wealth could afford new books. Most people bought them secondhand and kept them carefully. This testament was well-worn and much read. Pages had been marked with old ribbons, a few passages underlined with drawing pencil. *Suffer the little children, and forbid them not to come unto me,* was one. Another was *It is easier for a camel to go through the eye of a needle, than for a rich man to enter into the kingdom of God.*

I closed the book, wondering. Felicity had not written her name in the testament, so it could have belonged to a former lodger, or could already have been in the table when the landlady had purchased it. Or Felicity could be lonely and frightened, drawing comfort from scripture.

I returned the book where I'd found it, went back downstairs, gave the landlady another coin—which she stared at a moment before quickly dropping it inside her bodice—and departed. I walked Drury Lane to Russel Street and so to Covent Garden, and began asking the game girls there about Felicity.

"Whatcha want *her* for, Captain?" one of the regulars said, "When you can have *me*?"

They enjoyed teasing me. I dispensed shillings to them, and they gathered around me like birds to a man scattering breadcrumbs.

"I heard you was rich now," another said. "Married to a gentry mort, an' all. Lucky Captain. Now he has money for his girls."

"Who are going to tell me where Felicity is," I said, trying to sound stern. I handed out more coins. I knew much of it would go to their men, or to parents who sent them out to whore to feed the family. But if I gave them enough, they'd manage to keep a little for themselves.

"I saw her," one of the quieter girls volunteered. The waif could not have been more than fourteen, and here she was, in worn finery, waiting for a gentleman to take her up for money. "I was walking behind them tonight. She had a bloke. They turned off to Maiden Lane. That was 'bout half an hour ago."

"Thank you." I handed around more coinage. "If you see her again before I do, tell her to come and talk to me. She can send a message to South Audley Street or to Mrs. Beltan's bakeshop. Tell her I mean her no harm."

"She won't believe ya," the first girl said. "But we'll tell her."

Hands reached out to me, this time to stroke my back or pat my arms, accompanied by a chorus of thanks and ribald suggestions. I backed away carefully, trying to make certain none of their fingers dipped into my pockets for more of the money I was freely handing them.

They laughed at me, and I made them a bow, turning away as soon as I deemed it safe. As it was, I discovered as I walked away, one of them had lifted my new handkerchief.

I made my way out of Covent Garden down Southampton Street to Maiden Lane. I walked along slowly, peering into dark openings or passages. The street was busy, filled with carts and wagons, people passing as they hurried through the cold to whatever errand they had to complete this night.

I did not see Felicity, with or without a gentleman. I paused to ask a young lady who eyed me hopefully whether she'd spied my quarry. The girl was interested in nothing but my money, but as soon as I gave it to her, impressing upon her that I wanted only information, she told me she'd seen Felicity and a gentleman walk into the tavern opposite.

I thanked her graciously, receiving a surprised stare, and left her.

The tavern was not the Rearing Pony, which was my local haunt on this street. This tavern, the Hen and Hound, was further along Maiden Lane, nearer Bedford Street. The regulars peered at me when I entered, but they did not seem unduly hostile to a new face in their midst. I ordered an ale in the taproom and flashed still more coins to ask the landlord whether he'd seen Felicity.

The landlord snatched up my offering but refused to answer. The barmaid, on the other hand, stepped close to me as she filled her tray with more tankards. "I know that one," she said. "She ain't nothing but trouble. She's upstairs. Are you her gent? Because she don't deserve you if you are. She's with another, love, I'm sorry to tell you."

"I'm a friend," I said. "I'll wait."

The barmaid gave me a shrug, as if to say, *Just as you like.* Her look held sympathy for me and disgust at Felicity.

I waited, sipping ale and keeping my eye on the door the barmaid had indicated led to the stairs. I was halfway through the ale when I heard a thump on the floor above. The landlord, barmaid, and everyone around me either did not hear it or ignored it, but I did not like it.

The sound hadn't been the rhythmic pounding of a man and woman taking their pleasure in a rickety bed. The sound had been that of a body falling.

I set aside my ale, walked to the door to the stairs, opened it, and slipped inside the stairwell. No one paid me any attention. I ascended the enclosed staircase, bracing my gloved hand on the wall close beside me.

Two doors led off a small landing at the top; the sounds came from the door on the left. That door was locked, but the latch easily broke under the shove of my shoulder.

The room was small and cold, dimly lit with tallow candles. Felicity huddled in the middle of a threadbare rug, facedown and naked, her skin gleaming with sweat, her back striped with a crisscross of red welts. The man standing over her, his fine lawn shirt open to expose a rather pasty chest and twist of brown hair, was busily beating Felicity with a long strap of leather. She tried to protect her head with her hands, flinching as the strap came down.

I slammed the door, and the man swung around.

I recognized the weedy gentleman as a member of one of Grenville's clubs. I could not remember his name or in which club I'd met him, and at the moment, I did not care. Before he could draw a breath to shout at me, I had snatched the whip from his hands, hauled him across the room, and slapped the whip across his chest.

Chapter Sixteen

The man's eyes bulged, but with indignation, not fear. "Damn you! What the devil do you think you're doing?"

"Preparing to beat you senseless," I answered.

"Bloody hell, man, what is the matter with you? It's only a game."

Felicity had sat up, arms around her legs, knees drawn to her chest. She rocked a little, her face wet with tears.

I grabbed the man by the back of his neck and jerked him around to face her. "Does she look as though she's enjoying your game?"

"She likes it. They want a bit of the lash, don't they?"

I'd heard of gentlemen going to certain brothels for more exotic pleasures than simple coupling, but I could not believe that Felicity, who was bravely trying not to cry, had agreed to this. She'd been hired for the night, and this gentleman had decided what he wanted to do to her.

I shoved him against the wall and punched him full in the face. The man's head rocked back into the whitewashed plaster, and blood streamed from his nose.

He finally started to show fear as I pulled back my fist again. "I'll have the law on you," he bleated. "Captain Lacey, isn't it? Grenville's toady? I'll have you in court."

Was I to be cowed and apologize? Tell him I did not mean to interrupt him whipping a young woman for his enjoyment?

I punched him again, and again. It felt good to my fists. When I released him, he slid down the wall, blood and tears on his cheeks.

I shoved the gentleman down on his face and cracked the lash once across his back. The whip split his thin shirt, drawing a narrow strip of blood. He cried out.

"Can't you take a flogging?" I asked him through my rage. "You wouldn't last a day in the King's army." I'd been flogged, and I'd ordered floggings. Never pretty, and they were damned painful, but they got their point across.

"I'm not . . . in . . . the army," he wheezed.

"Neither is she. Now get dressed, and get the hell out."

I raised the whip again. The man scrambled out of my way, snatched up his coat and waistcoat from where he'd folded them over the back of a chair, and fled the room.

I dropped the whip in disgust and turned back to Felicity. She'd remained curled in on herself, but her head was up, and she tried to smile, though her eyes and cheeks were wet with tears. "Well, now, that was something to see."

"Are you all right? Are you badly hurt?" I crouched down but kept myself at arm's length from her.

"I'll weather it." Felicity raised her slim shoulders. "He was right, you know. He promised to pay to do what he wanted. I just didn't know what he'd want until too late."

"Do not justify that bastard to me." I was shaking a little, my fists still clenched. "He is filth."

"He's a posh gent, Captain. He'll prosecute you."

"And then I'll reveal his shame to the world, and possibly pummel him again. I care nothing for him, Felicity. He has no business hurting you."

She shrugged again. "It's the way of the world."

"It is a bad way. Get dressed, and we'll leave this place."

Felicity rose from the floor without bothering to cover herself. I spun around and faced the wall, and she laughed at me. She took her time while she dressed, slowly sliding on each piece of clothing, then finally she asked me to do up the buttons of her frock.

I turned around to find her fully dressed, her back to me. I pulled the placket together over her slender spine, hiding the angry welts on her dark skin, and competently did up the buttons.

She grinned at me when she turned around. "You're skilled at that, aren't you? I knew you were one for the ladies."

I did not answer as I escorted her out and down the stairs. The landlord met us at the bottom, his lips pushed out in a surly expression.

"Ye owe me for the room."

Felicity took a firmer hold of my arm. "I already paid you, you greedy pig."

His lips pushed out further. "That gent was a lord. If he brings the law down on me place, I'll be finding you, girl. And you." He switched his glare to me.

I dug into my pocket, fished out the last of my coins, and dropped them into his hand. "For your trouble," I said. "If the lordship bothers you, tell him to call upon Captain Lacey. I'll make certain he does you no harm."

The landlord eyed the gleaming silver on his palm, and then he closed his hand around it and spun away, as though fearing I'd take it from him again. He returned to his taps and completely ignored us.

I led Felicity out into the night. The street was freezing, her wrap was thin, and she clung to me.

"If you're in the business of handing out coin, Captain, you can pass some my way. He never paid me."

"Sorry, that was the end of my money. Let us get you home."

Felicity halted, her hand dropping from my arm. "Not to your posh lady's in Mayfair again. I've had enough of toffs to last me a lifetime. And I ain't going anywhere near Mr. Denis."

"Your own rooms," I said. "They should be safe enough now."

That she agreed to. We did not talk as she led me up the streets and through Drury Lane to the narrow passage to her lodgings. It was far too cold to speak, the wind carrying away any breath.

Felicity had recovered her spirits by the time she took me upstairs to her cold rooms and shut the door. "You can stay all night if you like. You need someplace warm to lay your head, since your lady's not in London. And I can properly thank you for rescuing me."

Felicity was lovely, but she did not entice me. Even before I'd proposed to Donata, she'd offered, and I'd declined. Felicity had a vulnerability about her, despite her obvious courage and resourcefulness, that I could not bring myself to take advantage of.

"No, thank you," I said. "An evening of uninterrupted sleep is what I need."

Her smile vanished. "It's not just for gratitude, or for pay. We'd be a man and a woman, not a game girl and her flat."

I knew she would not understand all my reasons, so I said, "I've only just married."

She looked slightly mollified. "And your wife, she's a formidable lady. I wager she'd have you sleeping in the scullery if she found out you were with the likes of me, wouldn't she?"

"I rather think she'd bar me from the house altogether."

"Is she not one to look the other way on a man's weakness?" Felicity asked, her cocky smile returning.

"No, indeed."

I went to Felicity's fireplace and built a fire with what little wood was left in the box, using the flint and steel I carried in my pocket to strike sparks to tinder. Felicity plopped herself down on the room's only chair and let me work.

That left me nowhere to sit but the floor. I made

myself as comfortable as possible on the hearth rug, carefully stretching out my bad leg, the slowly growing fire starting to warm me.

"I want you to tell me the entire story of Mr. Perry," I said. "Beginning to end. Leave nothing out."

"Ain't much more to tell than I already told you. He wanted to talk to you about something. Either you or Miss Simmons."

"Miss Simmons?" I remembered walking with Marianne through the dark, and being relieved that she'd gone home safely to the house on Clarges Street. "Why?"

"Devil if I know, do I? Perry comes to me, says he knows I know you, and do I want to make a whole guinea for the night? I couldn't say no to that. I am supposed to distract you, that's all. Then his toughs come out of nowhere to beat on you, and then he says I have to keep you or he'll have the law on me, or he'll sell me off to Jamaica. He could do it, 'cause I know a girl he did it to. All the questions he asked you about the theatre I didn't understand." Felicity laughed. "He thought a lame man like yourself, unguarded, would be easy to take. The fool."

"Well, he succeeded, didn't he? With your help."

Her smile died. "Not my fault. I told you, he forced me."

"I know he did. Now, what did he want me to tell him?" I asked this half to myself. I knew now of his connection to Hannah Wolfe—what had he feared I'd learned at Drury Lane? What had he to do with Mrs. Collins, if anything? I could not ask him now, because he was conveniently dead. For the convenience of whom?

"I don't know, I'm sure," Felicity said. "Mr. Perry didn't get down on his knees and confess his sins to me. I'm just glad he's gone."

"Did you kill him? I wouldn't much blame you if you had."

"No." Felicity sounded downcast. "Didn't get the chance, did I? I was hiding from him, not following him to see if he'd notice me. Besides, he died in *your* rooms, didn't he? Sure you didn't whack him with your walking stick? You did a fine job of it on my gent tonight."

"No, I did not kill him, though Bow Street would like to think I did." I shifted my body as the heat from the fire grew stronger. "The trouble with this problem is I don't know its players. Marianne is my connection, and I confess I know very little about her theatre life. This entire conundrum has been very like a play itself."

I'd been seeing Perry as a grand villain—not surprising after he'd had me beaten and hauled off the street. Mrs. Collins, the tragic heroine, spirited away or murdered. Mrs. Wolff, Mr. Coleman, and Marianne—the heroine's faithful retainers, loyal until the final curtain. I was not certain who played the romantic hero—perhaps I hadn't met him yet, or perhaps he didn't exist. Or perhaps he was me, the fool who ran about the stage wailing in despair without doing a bit of good.

"I am walking in circles," I said. "I dragged my family and friends to Bath, when the solution is likely in London. I was about to drag them off to Brighton to scour that town as well."

"Cheer up," Felicity said. "I bet your little girl liked Bath. It's pretty, I'm told."

"She did." The thought of Gabriella pulled me to my feet. I had to help myself up using the warming brick wall for balance, but I managed. "I am finished, Felicity. I believe I will turn the entire problem over to Pomeroy and let him run up and down the country looking for the missing actress. Perry, a threatening man, is dead. I will spend all the time I can with my wife and daughter and leave Mrs. Collins in peace."

Felicity rose with easy grace and reached out to steady me. "You know you'll never do that. You're like a dog after a bone."

"Thank you," I said. "But perhaps Mrs. Collins might be safer if I leave her alone. Someone tried to send her an incendiary device—if I find her and expose her, they might try again."

"Unless Mr. Perry did that," Felicity said.

"Perhaps he did, and then someone killed him. No, Mrs. Collins is still in danger, depend upon it."

"You see? You'll never give it up, and you know it."

I let out a breath. "At the moment, I only want my bed."

Felicity's grip on my arm softened. "Sure you don't want to stay? My bed's a bit narrow, but it would be warmer for all that. Your bed will be empty and cold tonight."

I gently pried myself from her. "Then I will make sure the footman tucks in plenty of hot bricks."

"Ah, well. Can't say I didn't offer."

She showed no regret, but I did see a flash of loneliness in her eyes. Very brief, then gone. She might not necessarily want *me* to fill that lonely place inside her, but she wanted someone.

"Thank you," I said. "For everything."

"Thank *you* for pulling that lunatic off me," Felicity said. "Couldn't see your way to thanking me with something a little more solid than kind words, could you? Like a crown to see me through the next weeks?"

"I gave everything I had left to the landlord," I said truthfully. I did not have enough even for hackney fare back to Mayfair. "I will return with a coin tomorrow."

"I don't believe you. But you're kind to say it. Good night, Captain." Felicity stepped close to me again, wound her arms around my neck, and kissed me full on the mouth. She danced back, laughing, as I pulled away.

"Good night," I said, giving her a dignified bow. I was pleased to hear her laughter, even at my expense. It meant the cruel man who'd beaten her hadn't left a darkness in her.

*** *** ***

I departed the house, found a messenger boy, and directed him to South Audley Street with a message for Barnstable to send a carriage for me. I told the lad the butler would give him a shilling for the message, as I had no more money. The lad gave me a wary eye, but he went.

While I waited, I walked about, lost in thought. Part of me truly did wish to give up the wearisome investigation. Another part of me admonished me, telling me I could not abandon Mrs. Collins and also Marianne, who was very worried. Marianne must know more than she was telling me, and so might Mrs. Wolff and Coleman. They might not know what they knew, but even so, I should speak with them again.

The curiosity that was my besetting sin rose again. Drury Lane theatre was not far. I knew there would be a performance tonight, but perhaps I could speak to Mrs. Wolff while the play was going on.

Nothing for it. I tramped down the cold but crowded streets and made for the back door of Drury Lane theatre.

Unfortunately, I was unable to get in. Mr. Kean was performing tonight, and a large man, not Coleman, was stationed at the door to keep those without tickets from slipping inside. He was a surly man and not inclined to listen to me. When I asked him to find Coleman or Mrs. Wolff, he did step inside to inquire, but returned a few minutes later to tell me they were too busy to see the likes of me. I'd have to return after the performance.

I decided tomorrow would do. I made my way back to Covent Garden, where I'd told the boy to send the carriage, and found Lady Breckenridge's coachman waiting for me.

I at least had a warm ride home, with coal boxes inside the comfortable landau to cut the cold. When I arrived at the South Audley Street house, Bartholomew was there, and also the party from Bath. Mrs. Lacey, Gabriella, and Peter, Bartholomew informed me, were upstairs and had already gone to bed.

"Mrs. Lacey made the journey in one go?" I asked in surprise. "I would have thought it too tiring for her."

"She was adamant, sir." Bartholomew gave me a warning look. "Her ladyship's not in the best of tempers at the moment. Just thought I'd give you a hint, sir."

Meaning he advised me to quietly go to my own chamber and leave Donata until morning. Donata's maid passed by above, her face grim. The entire house seemed tense, not the haven of peace I'd sought.

I thanked Bartholomew for looking after everyone and climbed the stairs, my leg aching from the cold and all the walking I'd done. I decided I would leave Donata alone, not because I feared her mood, but because she would need to sleep. She'd be exhausted from the long journey.

When I entered my bedchamber, Donata rose from my armchair. She was clad in a blue silk dressing gown, her hair in a single plait under a white lawn cap. We stared at each other a moment, then Donata rushed to me.

"Gabriel." She flung her arms around me, and I swept her into an embrace, burying my face in her neck.

This was why I'd married, to come home to the soft warmth of a woman, to lose myself in her and forget my sins. I held her and felt the pain inside me ease.

Donata pulled back to look up at me, her dark blue eyes holding fury. "Gabriel, what in heaven's name possessed you to let yourself be *arrested*? Running off to Bow Street in the middle of the night? What the devil were you thinking?"

Chapter Seventeen

I took a step back, releasing her with reluctance. "I went because Spendlove was about to insist we make a family party of it. All of us in Bow Street together."

Donata turned away from me, her nightdress swirling about her slipper-clad heels. "Good Lord, Gabriel. The entire town was agog with it."

"I am pleased I could supply the diversion. I came to London to clear things up so you could return home to quietness. I haven't quite finished yet, but you can see I managed to keep myself out of Newgate."

"Bloody hell." She swung to face me. "I have three solicitors employed to handle various situations for my family, and *they* keep solicitors for more complicated events. If you had waited, I would have had all those solicitors on our doorstep, ready to do battle for you. You wouldn't have had to leave ignominiously, dragged from our house like a common criminal."

"I was accused of murder, Donata. That is common enough."

"*Accused*, yes. There is no reason for you to be tried for it until they have the evidence. This man, Spendlove, has an obsession about you. You know that, and yet you let him sweep you up without regard to what might happen to you. Do you think your daughter wanted to watch you be bundled away by Runners, leaving her alone with strangers? She was quite upset."

My anger fled before the wave of worry for Gabriella. "Is she all right?"

"Gabriella is resilient," Donata said. "But she is angry at you. When I explained that you ignored all offers of help to let yourself be hauled to Bow Street, she was most indignant."

"As you are."

"Indeed, Gabriel. I would go so far as to say I am furious. How could you?"

"Because, damn it, it occurred to me that you might not want a battle between Spendlove, Pomeroy, the patrollers, and myself in your dining room. I thought I'd take myself and my sordid life out of your house."

"*Our* house."

"*Your* house, Donata." My sleeplessness, temper, exhaustion, and worry got the better of me. "Your house, your leases, your life tenancy, your money. Everything protected so I cannot touch it. I prefer it that way. You married *me*, a man who is in scrape after scrape and to whom finances are wavy lines on a piece of paper. When I'm about to touch you with one of my scrapes, I will do my damnedest to leave you out of it."

Donata planted herself in front of me again, her anger matching my own. "Is that what you believe? That I married you to have you hang on me like an illicit lover, while I dole out an allowance? No thank you. I had such a wretched time of my first marriage, I thought I'd try marrying a man who could be a partner and friend. Foolish of me for supposing you might feel the same."

"I *do* feel the same, devil take you. What I do not want is to drag you into disgrace, which I have done only days after our wedding. I wanted to sort it out and spare you the humiliation."

"Oh, it is far too late for that. The newspapers are making a meal of us. That is another reason I'd prefer you to have the solicitors handle things instead of bursting about like a lit firework."

"A lit firework is what I am. I have no idea how to stay home and be quiet. That is why my first wife fled me for a stolid Frenchman. The poor woman was terrified of me."

"You might take note, Gabriel, that I am *not* that poor woman. I met her—she must have been quite pretty when she was young, because that is the only explanation for your madness in marrying her."

I stopped, startled. "When did you meet Carlotta?" I'd done my best to keep the two ladies apart.

"I made it my business to, when she was in London for the divorce. Do not worry; she had no idea at the time who I was other than a friend of Grenville's. I did not take her to task for being a limp ninny, though I longed to."

I was torn between laughing and shaking her. I

settled for scrubbing my hand through my hair. "You do not have a good opinion of women, do you?"

"My opinion is my opinion, regardless of whether the person is male or female. Lady Aline is a fine specimen, not a mean bone in her, nor does she find it necessary to pretend to be frail and weak. Louisa Brandon is a kind woman with a core of steel, though she ought to have bashed both her husband and you over your heads years ago."

"I quite agree. And *you* are the most exasperating woman of my acquaintance."

"I believe I am. That is what you look for in a bride, is it? The first Mrs. Lacey must have been very exasperating."

"She was."

"Then I am pleased to carry on the tradition."

Her eyes sparkled, and her color was high. She was outraged, and I'd embarrassed her. Donata had been subjected to endless gossip about her first husband; I doubted she wanted to go through it again with me.

"Spendlove would not have waited for your London solicitors," I said, trying to speak evenly. "If I had not gone alone without fuss, he would have found a way to punish *you* for it, or perhaps demand that the parish constable lock us both up for the night. Your neighbors would have had much more to talk about then."

"My family never would have stood for that, do you not understand? My father wields much power and has influence in high places. Mr. Spendlove is only a commoner who works for the magistrates. His position is tenuous, while mine is unshakable. The newspapers might twit me about my choice of husbands, but I will weather such things. Spendlove, on the other hand, had better have a care."

I balled my hands. "Perhaps I dislike using my wife's position to pry myself out of trouble. I see that often enough—I saw it tonight—gentlemen who think nothing of running roughshod over others and hiding behind the security of their family's position. Do you wish me to be such a man?"

"Of course not. But when you are in trouble, I only ask that you trust me to remove you from it. I can. Allow me to."

I drew a breath to continue, but I let it out again. Donata was right that I had enough pride in me to float one of the Montgolfier brothers' balloons, but I knew I'd never make her understand. I did not want her to have to clear up after me. She'd married all of me, the rough underside as well as whatever polish I'd acquired—not that there was much of the polish left.

Donata's dark blue eyes narrowed. "I have not convinced you, have I?"

"We shall see."

"Hmm." She folded her arms over the dressing gown, the blue embroidered with oriental patterns. "I suppose we have had our first quarrel. Who has won, do you think?"

"No, this is by no means our first quarrel. I believe we have had plenty in the past, beginning with the billiards game in Kent. You did your best to ruin my shots every time."

She shrugged. "I dislike to lose. I was a bit generous in tallying up my points, I will admit. I waited to see whether you'd say a word, but you never did. You paid up like a gentleman."

"I'd never accuse a lady of cheating."

"Not out loud anyway." The corners of her mouth turned up the slightest bit. "If you are not happy with my tally, we shall have a rematch."

"I would not mind. I will trounce you thoroughly."

Her brows rose. "Threatening a lady? And this hard on the heels of me being so very angry with you. I still am. Your overblown sense of honor is most aggravating."

"I'd rather have too much honor than not enough."

We regarded each other warily. Outside, winter wind swept against the walls, rattling shutters and howling through the eaves. Inside, I was truly warm and comfortable for the first time in years, and I was grateful. I had enraged this woman I had only just married, and humiliated her. And yet, she had not shown me the door.

Donata unfolded her arms. "Regarding me in that way will not help you, Gabriel."

"Hmm? Regarding you in what way?"

"As though you wish to devour me."

I felt something else stir through my frustration. "I beg your pardon. I will endeavor to school my expression."

She came to me, took my large and weather-beaten hands, and set them on her waist. "I do not mind. Please proceed."

I did. We spent the rest of that night infusing the room with still more memories, continuing to lay to rest Lord Breckenridge's ghost.

*** *** ***

I breakfasted the next morning with the Auberges

and my daughter, all of whom expressed thankfulness that I was not rotting in Newgate. Though Donata had told me Gabriella had been angry with me, this morning her relief had washed that away. I wished she felt comfortable enough with me to hug me in joy when she saw me walk into the breakfast room, but her smile and happy words would have to be enough.

Gabriella informed me as I ate that Grenville had returned with them, but Marianne had chosen to stay in Bath, to finish her run in the play and also to look out for Mrs. Collins. I did not like the thought of Marianne in Bath alone, but I was still convinced that the greater danger was here in London.

I partook of sausages, toast slathered with plenty of fresh butter, and a large pile of eggs, and best of all, strong, rich coffee, which Bartholomew kept pouring into my cup. I'd told Bartholomew to send Felicity the coin I'd promised her—for her assistance in the problem of Mrs. Collins, I'd be careful to let everyone, including Felicity, know.

I was almost finished with my meal when Barnstable brought in a letter and laid it beside my plate. "Hand delivered, sir," he said.

I'd come to recognize the spare, slanting hand of James Denis, and broke the seal a bit hesitantly.

I have found the man who created the incendiary device. Be at my house at ten o'clock this morning. Denis.

A command, as always, but never mind. I wanted to see who he'd cornered, and Denis had known I would.

I told Bartholomew to send word to Grenville to join me. I was not certain if Grenville would be awake after his journey from Bath, but I wanted his insight when we faced the culprit.

Grenville arrived in his landau at half past nine. Though the time was far earlier than his usual rising hour, he was washed, shaved, and immaculately dressed. He showed no surprise that I wasn't in Newgate awaiting trial—Bartholomew must have told him the entire tale of my adventures, which the lad had pried from me this morning.

"I must ask you what on earth you did to Stubby," Grenville said as soon as we rolled away together in the carriage. "He interrupted my supper at Watier's last night and demanded to know why I'd befriended a ruffian like you. He would not go into detail, but he also would not let me enjoy my meal until I gave him the rough side of my tongue. When he realized I was about to cut him, he apologized and then blamed you for his bad behavior."

I listened to all this, perplexed. "Who the devil is Stubby?"

"Lord Andrew Kenton Stubbins, only son of the Marquis of Chester. Known to his friends since Eton as Stubby. Ostensibly because his surname is Stubbins, though other chaps unkindly claimed the nickname meant something else. What the devil did you do to enrage him so?"

"Is he a weedy gentleman, pale hair, pale eyes, sharp nose?"

"Looks as though he doesn't see the out of doors much?" Grenville asked. "Or lifts a finger to do anything for himself? Yes, that's the chap."

"I thrashed him," I said.

Grenville started to laugh then he stopped. "Dear God, you are not joking. How did that come about?"

I shrugged, not much wanting to talk about it. "I

found him beating Felicity. With a whip. I took the whip away from him and gave him a taste of it."

"Good Lord." Grenville let the laugh come then. "I had no idea he was a follower of the Marquis de Sade. No wonder he did not want to speak in too much detail in the middle of Watier's."

"I hope I dissuaded him from the practice," I said.

"I doubt it. He is ready to punish you, Lacey. I would not be surprised if he either brings you up before a magistrate or claims a suit against you."

What a nuisance. If this Stubby did try to prosecute me, I'd have to go to Donata, climb down from my high horse, and ask for her offer of solicitors.

"He would risk me revealing his proclivities in front of a public court?" I asked.

"He might; and he'd deny them. I wonder what made him take it up?" Grenville snorted a laugh. "Perhaps the chaps at school were not the only ones to call him *Stubby*."

"Perhaps."

My amusement was small, though. I hadn't much wondered whom I'd beaten last night in the public house, but I knew I would have done the same even if I'd been aware I was manhandling a marquis' son. When I'd been at Harrow, a duke's offspring and the son of the lowest gentleman had been the same to me. I'd been up before the headmaster often enough for engaging in pugilism with any and all of them. Not much had changed, it seemed.

We'd arrived at Denis's door. Instead of being made to wait in a reception room while we were announced, the butler took us straight to Denis's study.

On one occasion, when I'd arrived with Grenville, the men who worked for Denis hadn't let him upstairs. This time we were both shown in as though Grenville had been expected.

I noted that Denis had more bodyguards standing in his study today than usual, with two more placed outside the door. Brewster was one of the two guarding the door, and he gave me a curt nod as I passed him.

A man, flanked by two of Denis's bodyguards, stood in the center of the study. There was nothing remarkable about him—he was perhaps half a foot shorter than me, his build strong but not overly athletic. His clothing was that of an ordinary man: frock coat, trousers, and boots that could have been bought at any secondhand shop. His hair was light brown and thinning on top.

He did not seem in any way unusual; that is, until he turned his head and looked at me. Then I saw a face that had been hardened into something with no humanity in it. His eyes, hazel, were cold, colder even than Denis's. He regarded me without interest. I was nothing, and neither was Grenville.

I did not wonder now that Denis had positioned extra guards throughout the house. The man also had a peculiar odor about him, which I recognized from my army days as saltpeter. The scent of a man who constantly mixed dangerous concoctions.

"Captain," Denis said. He did not rise or offer either of us a chair. "This is Thomas Ridgley. He is the man who made the device sent to Abigail Collins at Drury Lane in August of this past year."

"Why?" I asked Ridgley before I could stop myself. "Why would you do such a thing?"

Chapter Eighteen

Ridgley didn't shrug, didn't twitch. He looked straight at me when he answered, his face expressionless. "Hired, wasn't I?"

"Hired by whom?"

Ridgley closed his mouth and fixed his gaze on a point between me and Grenville.

"He has not told me," Denis said. "Not yet."

Ridgley betrayed no fear at this veiled threat. Either he was a fool or so hardened nothing frightened him at all.

Denis continued, "He is Cornish by birth but has lived in London and elsewhere for most of his life. He made incendiary devices for the emperor Napoleon as well as for the Prussian army, also for rulers of the Italian states and Russian generals. His loyalties are fluid. This he told me for nothing."

"My services are in demand," Ridgley said.

"Quite." Denis moved a paper on his desk and

turned his focus to Ridgley. "In August an unnamed person came to you and asked you to put together a box that would explode upon its opening. Why did you agree?"

"Money."

"How much money?"

The question must have touched upon what Ridgley considered confidential, because he closed his mouth again.

"How did you do it?" Denis asked, as though he hadn't noticed Ridgley ignoring the question.

The words came out flat and uninflected. "Gunpowder and primed cord, flint poised to scratch across rough paper to create a spark when the box was opened. If it had gone off, it would have done extensive damage to the woman's face and hands. Might even have killed her."

I took a step forward. Standing here listening to him so cold-bloodedly explain how he'd set a trap to maim Mrs. Collins made me angry. Who knew how many other such devices he'd made, how many others he'd hurt or killed with them?

Grenville shot me a cautioning look, but I could not stop myself. "Coward," I snapped at Ridgley. "Only a coward finds a way to kill another person while he hides in safety. You don't even have the courage to face your victims."

Ridgley did not blink. "Not *my* victims. I am hired for my services."

"Even worse," I said.

Denis usually tried to quash me when I lectured in my hot-tempered way, but this time he said nothing, only let me run down.

Denis was another man who dispensed justice

from afar, but my assessment of Denis when I'd first met him, that he had no feelings, had proved to be wrong. Denis was a man of deep feeling, but he'd long ago learned to mask those sentiments for his own survival. I wondered if Ridgley was the same or whether he'd ever had a conscience at all. Looking into Ridgley's unmoving eyes I saw nothing, only a frightening emptiness.

Denis went on, "You made the device to order. Did you take it yourself to the delivery company?"

"No. Was picked up, and I was out of it."

"Was the person who came for it the same as the one who hired you?" Denis asked.

Ridgley was silent a moment, as though debating whether to answer. The debate didn't trouble him— he was simply weighing what he told freely versus what he kept tightly inside.

"Not the same person. Man who took it from me was a nervous fool. Surprised he didn't blow himself up with it."

"Tell me the name of this person," Denis said.

"Don't know. Thin chap, not very tall, large teeth, like a horse."

The same description had been given by the clerk at the delivery company, and that description did not fit Perry, Coleman, or even Spendlove. Whoever had taken the package from Ridgley, none of us had seen him yet.

"Now we come to it," Denis said. "I need the name of the person who asked you to make the device in the first place. Or his description if you never learned his name."

Ridgley did not debate this time. He instantly closed his mouth and stood in silence.

Denis regarded him without heat. "The captain does not like my methods, but I have found them effective. Captain, you and your guest may wait in the sitting room if you like. My butler will bring you refreshment. Or you may go about your business, and I will send for you again when I have further information."

I wondered why he'd sent for us at all if he hadn't yet managed to pry names from Ridgley. Perhaps Denis had thought Ridgley might be more forthcoming under my brand of temper. Or perhaps he'd wanted me to get a good look at Ridgley in case the man escaped him. Denis knew I'd search for him, send Bow Street after him, do whatever I could to bring him down.

I debated whether to concede to Denis's wish that I leave. Grenville, I could tell, was sickened by the proceedings. Not a year ago, he'd been stabbed in the chest by a villain, only because the villain had thought him in the way. Grenville had narrowly escaped death. His wound still ached when he was distressed, I knew. From the pain in his eyes, it was aching now. I ought to send him away to spare him this gruesomeness.

There were too many people in the room. I wasn't certain why I suddenly felt that, but I was reminded of times in battle, when men clustered together for safety, or so they thought. But in truth they proved to be in more danger when artillery rained down. One blast could take out many.

I looked again at Ridgley's stony face and expressionless eyes. I saw something in there, resignation, perhaps. He knew Denis would never let him go.

My gaze moved to his clenched fists. Denis would not have let so dangerous a man into his study without his lackeys searching him thoroughly. But the odor of saltpeter and his unworried stance woke instincts I'd tried to push aside since leaving the Peninsula.

I was moving forward at the same time Ridgley brought up his fist. "His hands!" I bellowed. "Get down!"

Grenville, who'd traveled in wild and dangerous parts of the world, dashed for Denis, who was slowly rising from his chair. Grenville grabbed him, and they went down together behind the desk. Denis's pugilists seized Ridgley, but I shouted at them.

"No! Let him go!"

The lackeys understood after a half second, and they boiled away from Ridgley, seeking cover. I grabbed Ridgley's arm, clamping down with heavy fingers to pry open his hand. With a strength that belied his size, Ridgley threw me off and flicked his thumb across whatever small device he'd hidden in his fist.

It would have killed him. At the last minute, I seized a strange, compact stick from his hand, sparks from the powder burning through my glove. Too late to snuff out the fuse—the sparks would ignite the explosive in the next second. I threw the thing as hard as I could to the other side of the room and dove for the floor.

The ensuing explosion roared like cannon fire. A sheet of fire raced up one of the walls, and bricks and pieces of plaster burst outward to rain down over us. The lackeys began climbing to their feet, shaking their heads from the noise, coughing in the smoke.

One grabbed a rug and started beating at the fire.

The door had burst open, Brewster and the second guard dashing inside in alarm. Through the smoke and confusion, I saw Ridgley get competently to his feet and slip out of the room.

I tried to yell, but only succeeded in drawing in a lungful of foul smoke. I scrambled to my feet, using Brewster as a lever, and ran after Ridgley.

I never felt my bad knee as I sprinted into the hall, taking a breath of relatively cleaner air. Ridgley was on the stairs, moving quickly but quietly, not panicking, not drawing attention to himself. The butler was coming out of the backstairs below, looking up in concern. I saw Ridgley remove another small object from inside his waistband.

"Get back!" I shouted at the butler, then I leapt over the landing's railing and onto the stairs, tackling Ridgley.

I felt a sharp pain in my shoulder, and then I was unclear what happened after that. I remembered myself snarling in rage, my large fists balling, and me punching Ridgley over and over again. The animal in me, fearing for its life and enraged at that fear, was beating the life out of its hunter.

"Lacey!" Grenville's voice from above me cut through the fog. "He's down. Don't kill him, for God's sake."

No, if I killed him, we'd never discover who hired him to make the device. I stilled my blows, the pain in my shoulder proving to be a slice from a small knife. The pain in my knee, which I'd ignored in my berserker fury, came back to me in a flare of agony.

Brewster reached down and helped me to my feet, as I was too shaky to stand on my own. Grenville watched from the landing above, his gloved hands gripping the railing, his eyes dark in his sharp, pale face.

Ridgley lay on the stairs, his face a bloody mess. He was still awake — barely — but the look he gave me was neutral, uncaring. No defeat, shame, or defiance.

Denis emerged to stand at the top of the stairs near Grenville. His coat was askew and a small bruise darkened his cheek, but otherwise he looked unscathed. Grenville was breathing hard, but Denis's chest barely rose and fell.

Unlike Ridgley, who still showed no emotion, Denis's eyes were filled with fury. "Search him again," he snapped. "And then bring him back upstairs."

"Damn it," Brewster said under his breath as he parted Ridgley's coat. "We searched him. Thoroughly. I swear to you, Captain."

"Strip him," Denis said from above. "Make damn sure he has nothing in his hands, in his mouth, or up his ass. Then bring him to me. In the dining room — my study is too full of smoke."

So saying, Denis turned his back and strode around the landing and into the dining room. He didn't slam the door, but he didn't need to. His rage had put cold fear into his men, and they bent to take it out on Ridgley.

Grenville came down to me and helped me descend the rest of the stairs. I collapsed to a chair in the lower hall, pain flooding me. I'd left my walking stick above, but I didn't care at the moment.

"Thank you, Lacey," Grenville said. He crouched on one knee in front of me, his usually perfect hair mussed, his face stained with sweat and soot. "No one but you noticed. He might have been the death of us all."

"Reminded me of war days," I said, my voice ragged in my dry throat. "An enemy could roll in an incendiary device to a cluster of men, or send in a man to destroy himself and a handful of us. A cowardly way to fight, but it fulfilled its purpose. Men died or were terrified."

"Terrified is a good way of putting it." Grenville gave me a shaky grin. "Your Mr. Denis even thanked me for shoving him to safety, and said he owed me a favor."

"You have my sympathy," I said.

"I noticed you not diving for safety," Grenville said, losing his smile. "But charging headlong. You could have killed yourself, old chap. What would I have told your wife?"

Cold washed through me. A moment ago, I'd felt a small amount of pity for Ridgley with Denis's men so happily going at him, but the pity dissolved. A man like Ridgley had no concern for hurting others, and anyone, including Donata and my daughter, could have gotten in the way of one of his devices. Let Denis have him and do his worst.

"I need to get home," I said. I started to my feet and fell back as more pain streaked though my knee and my shoulder. "I am growing too old for this."

Grenville rose from his crouch, looking as haggard as I felt. "No need to worry, my friend. I'll fetch your stick, and Jackson will take us home. Won't be a trice."

He left me and sprinted up the stairs with an ease I envied. Grenville and I were of an age—why did he have the energy that deserted me?

Grenville had to wait when he was nearly at the top, while Brewster and the other lackeys dragged Ridgley, now divested of his clothes, his head lolling, around the landing and into the dining room. The closing door had a chill sound of finality.

*** *** ***

Grenville took me to his house on Grosvenor Street, bypassing Donata's. He did this without asking leave, and I was grateful for his decision. I did not want Donata or Gabriella to see the horror of myself. I could clean myself up at his home before returning to my own.

Grenville's footman Matthias was horrified enough. The valet, Gautier, on the other hand, sat me down to patch up the scrapes on my face and the cut on my shoulder, and most painful of all, my burned hand.

Later, bandages applied, I met Grenville in his private sitting room, brandy already in my good hand. The sitting room contained shelves upon shelves of trinkets from Grenville's travels, from gold statuettes from Egypt, to ivory pieces from the Japans, to woven carpets from the Ottoman Empire. Every time I came into this room, I saw something I hadn't seen before, this time a Chinese porcelain bowl, so delicate and perfect, the porcelain translucent, that I stared at it from a few paces back before I left it alone to sit down.

"Ming dynasty," Grenville said, seeing my interest. "Fifteenth century."

I carefully eased myself into a chair, thankful that Grenville liked his comfort. "Never let someone like Ridgley in here," I said, trying to make my voice light. "Disaster."

Grenville poured brandy for himself and sank onto a gilded chair covered with leopard's fur, the feet carved into animal claws. "You may joke, but that was a terrifying experience. I've met hard men before, Mr. Denis included, but Ridgley is merciless."

"Abigail Collins is right to be afraid. I had considered the possibility that she used the threats to pretend fear, to take herself away for other reasons, but I have changed my mind. Ridgley's device would no doubt have killed her, had not Coleman been canny enough to soak it in water. I myself would have fled as soon as I was able."

"I hope to heaven whoever was vile enough to hire Ridgley has not found her." Grenville took a deep drink of brandy. "Marianne is still in Bath asking questions—after meeting Ridgley, I wish I hadn't left her there."

"I have no doubt Denis is busy taking care that Ridgley will build no more devices." I moved my mind from speculating upon what Denis might do to the man. "Ridgley knew Denis would never let him go, hence his preparation with the device. He likely kept several at hand in case he needed them. But he isn't a fanatic—he was prepared to die to keep from being questioned, but when he saw the opportunity to escape in the confusion, he took it."

"And you went after him, knowing he could have had more devices about his person." Grenville shook his head and raised his goblet to me. "I commend you, my friend. But never do that again. I believed I aged ten years this afternoon."

"I had to stop him," I said. "No matter what."

"Yes, well." Grenville blew out his breath and took another drink. "We will have to report this to a magistrate. Ridgley's lodgings will have to be searched for more devices, for the safety of his neighbors. How a person can be that uncaring, I do not understand."

"I met a man like him before," I said, remembering. "Only one, thank God. I had a soldier under my command who killed without emotion. Enemy soldiers and our soldiers alike, with no remorse. When a man kills in war, he feels *something* — terror, victory, compassion for the fallen, admiration for a man who fought well to his death. This soldier had none of that. For him, the person he killed had simply gotten in his way. He obeyed orders to the letter, so I made certain I and my sergeants were careful how we phrased our commands to keep him from doing more harm than good. He finally fell in battle at Albuera, and none of his fellow soldiers were much grieved. I disliked ever looking at the man. There was nothing in his eyes."

"Well, God save me from meeting another like Ridgley," Grenville said.

We both went silent a moment, soothing ourselves with drink and the quiet comfort of the room. I finished my goblet of brandy and rose to pour another.

"Do you know whether Marianne has found out anything?" I asked, resuming my seat. "Has she sent any word?"

"A letter arrived from her this morning," Grenville said. "Marianne reported that she's found only one interesting thing. An actress she befriended in Bath swore she saw Mrs. Collins earlier in the autumn, but not anywhere near a theatre. She saw her at a church one Sunday morning, staying well to herself. Mrs. Collins wasn't praying fervently or anything, only taking in the service. But that was months ago, and the actress hasn't seen her since. And the actress did not speak to Mrs. Collins or draw close to her, so she might have been mistaken."

"That is more than we've learned so far," I said, feeling my interest return. "The question is, why did Perry pay the lease on her flat? To have an excuse for discovering whether Mrs. Collins was there? Or because Mrs. Collins asked him to? Was Perry her friend or her foe?"

"If he was a friend, then why did he abduct you and have you beaten? Not the actions of a friendly man."

I took another sip of brandy while I thought. "He questioned me about Drury Lane and why I'd gone there. I assumed he thought I knew where Mrs. Collins had gone. But perhaps he thought *I* was a danger to her and wanted me to stay away from her. But who knows what Perry had in his head? We'll never know, because someone beat him to death."

I took leaned back in my chair and tried not to grow discouraged. The balm Gautier had smeared on my hand was cool, the burn starting to feel a little better.

"We should turn our thoughts to his murder," Grenville said. "Who would want to kill Mr. Perry? Ridgley, perhaps, if Perry hired him and Ridgley feared exposure. But who else *could* have? You, because you were still in town and had a bit of a grudge against the man." Grenville held up his hand, touching his forefinger. "Ridgley, although he would likely have found a way to blow up Perry without being near him." He touched his next finger. "Mr.

Spendlove, to throw blame on you." He moved to his next finger. "Who else?"

"Brewster, on orders from Denis," I said. "Though I am certain Brewster would have disposed of Perry's body and cleaned up my rooms. Denis would have insisted."

Grenville lowered his hand. "Unless Denis thought having you take the blame for Perry's death a way to rid himself of you."

I shook my head. "If Denis wants rid of me, he will not go about it so clumsily as having me accused of murder. A charge might not stick. No, he'll do it irrevocably."

"Please do not speak like that." Grenville looked pained. "Again, I'd have to explain your demise to Donata, and I wish to be spared that. Have pity on me, Lacey."

"Denis had the opportunity to kill me in the Norfolk marshes, and he did not. I believe he is keeping me alive and well for reasons of his own."

"You do not make me feel better. But let us return to the question of who else could have killed Mr. Perry. Felicity? She was very afraid of him."

"I considered her from the first," I said. "Apparently the blows were heavy, but Felicity is strong, and a woman afraid could make them. I'm not sure, however, that she would have remained in London after she'd beaten him to death, continuing her trade as though nothing had happened. Surely she'd have removed herself."

"Felicity does have an arrogance about her, despite her fears. She might think herself safe." Grenville shrugged. "What about this Coleman fellow? He'd be strong enough."

"True," I said. "He is very protective of Mrs. Wolff, who was married to Perry, for heaven's sake. Coleman might have seen Perry as a threat to both Hannah and Abigail, and decided to keep both ladies safe for once and for all. Why in my rooms, I do not know, but perhaps Perry went there to look about, and Coleman found him there."

"Worth pondering. And asking him. You might take your friend Pomeroy for that."

"I do not want to if he's innocent," I said. "Pomeroy enjoys arresting people. And then there's the problem of Mrs. Carfax and her evidence."

I told Grenville the tale of Mrs. Carfax and my certainty that Spendlove had made her tell the tale she did.

"Hmm," Grenville said. "I agree with Denis that you should make her see that lying for Mr. Spendlove is not a good thing. I have a proposal — let me talk with Miss Winston and Mrs. Carfax for you. Or Miss Winston alone if Mrs. Carfax proves too reluctant. I have been told I have a certain charm."

"By all means," I said without smiling. "Charm them. They are apt to look upon me as though I'm a beast readying myself to spring upon them. I suppose in spite of my politeness, I have not learned the correct demeanor."

Grenville's lips twitched. "You were born to be a soldier and shout at people. You are excellent at it. I was born to coerce, which is how I survive. Also, you are tall, which unnerves others, especially sheltered spinsters. My more modest height is less intimidating."

"You have an uncanny knack for mocking others and yourself at the same time," I said, "and yet making the mocking sound like a compliment."

"I told you, I learned young how to coerce. You speak to the robust and protective Coleman, and I will take the gentler Miss Winston. Better action than waiting for Denis to send word what he's learned from Ridgley, if he learns anything at all. It is too bad about Denis's study burning, though. I found it quite a tasteful room."

*** *** ***

Grenville and I shared his carriage to Covent Garden, he departing for Grimpen Lane and Miss Winston, I turning off to Drury Lane theatre.

A performance had been scheduled for later today as well as several tonight, so the theatre was alive with people scurrying about to ready the place. I did not bother to knock at the stage door, which opened and closed often as I watched. People strode purposefully in and out, including men carrying planks of wood and tools for repairs. I simply blended into the chaos and found myself inside.

Gone was the dusty silence of backstage when I'd visited before New Year's. The theatre had emerged from its dormancy and was now filled with actors and workmen, the quiet replaced with sounds of hammering, shouts, rapid conversations, laughter.

I made my way down the hall, ignored by others intent on whatever task they needed to complete. No one stopped me; no one questioned me. Coleman was nowhere in sight.

The room where I'd spoken to Hannah Wolff while she sewed costumes lay at the end of the hall. Making my way to it was much slower today as I navigated around hurrying people and other obstacles. I was nearly knocked into by a man swiftly emerging from a room that looked like a comfortable parlor.

"Coleman, I asked for hock about a hundred years ago . . . ah." The man stopped and peered up at me, and I recognized the actor, Edmond Kean. "You are that army captain, are you not? Have you found Mrs. Collins yet?"

I had to shake my head. "I am afraid I have not."

"What the devil does the woman mean leaving me in the lurch at the season's start? We've had to give her parts away—didn't want to, but there it is. Not to mention she promised us all that money. Well, I suppose that's gone now. Do tell Coleman to bring me the hock. I am devilish thirsty."

Chapter Nineteen

Kean turned abruptly and walked back into his room, but I pushed in before he could close the door. "Money?" I asked. "What money?"

Kean shrugged, not bothered that I'd accompanied him. He wandered away from me to a dressing table containing a mirrored stand with a drawer. "For the theatre. She was going to invest in it. The committee was very happy, and had made plans for new and enormous sets. I suppose that's a wash now. A pity; she was very interested, and she has the blunt."

My thoughts spun rapidly. "Would her investing in Drury Lane unnerve someone enough that they'd frighten her off or even try to kill her?"

Kean looked blank. "My good fellow, I have no idea. I can think of no reason why anyone would *stop* her. If they wanted to see her ruined, they'd let her go ahead and invest. Running a theatre is not for the faint of heart. You lose money faster than pouring it down a well. The committee would never discourage someone from giving us funds, and neither would I." He looked me up and down, as though seeing me for the first time. "Did I not hear you've recently married a wealthy widow? And are friends to Mr. Grenville?"

I made a bow. "I married at New Year's. And, yes, I have the honor of being Mr. Grenville's acquaintance."

"Any chance either would be interested in funding plays? Lady Breckenridge is a patron of the arts, and so is Mr. Grenville. I wish to give my King Lear, even if audiences insist on the version with the happy ending. Philistines."

The disgust in his voice was unmistakable, but I happened to like the happy ending. Life was sad enough; no need to rush to the theatre to witness more tragedy. "People want to feel uplifted when they leave a play," I suggested. "To know that all ended well."

Kean gave me a deprecating look. "You are teasing me, Captain. If you want happy endings, watch comedies. But do not be deceived by them. As I always say, dying is easy; comedy is difficult."

Kean turned away from me then and made for the sofa at the end of the room. As he'd done when I'd talked to him on the stage, he seemed to lose all interest in our conversation, or even remember I was there. He sank down and took up a newspaper from the stack strewn on the couch. "Now, where the devil is that hock?"

*** *** ***

I left Kean's room and again made my way down the hall toward the room at the end. This time I reached it, tapped, and heard a woman's voice bidding me to come in.

I opened the door and stepped inside, and immediately averted my eyes. A young woman with red-blond hair stood in front of Hannah in nothing but a thin muslin skirt and a strip of cloth wrapped around her breasts. Hannah was pinning the skirt, her blind eyes closed while her hands moved competently.

"Who is it?" Hannah asked.

The young woman sent me a cocky smile over her shoulder. "A handsome man come to beguile us."

"If you mean Mr. Kean, tell him to go. I am not ready for him yet."

"It isn't Mr. Kean," the young woman said. "*He* ain't handsome. Who are you, sir?"

"Captain Lacey," I said. "The friend to Miss Simmons."

"Ah," the young lady said. "I hear our Marianne landed on her feet. Catch her speaking to the likes of us anymore. Too high and mighty now. I wager she'll get that Mr. Grenville to marry her."

I thought it best not to answer this. "May I speak to you, Mrs. Wolff?"

Hannah let her hands fall from the actress. "Of course, Captain. Do run along, girl. I'll finish with you later."

"Right you are." The actress winked at me. "Tired of being a pincushion anyway."

The actress snatched up a jacket and brought it to me, indicating I should help her with it. I set aside my walking stick and settled the thin and rather threadbare coat over her shoulders. I avoided touching her as much as I could, but she nestled back into me, giving me a cheeky smile, before she turned away.

"Thank you, sir. You are a gentleman. Tell Miss Simmons I wish her luck."

I gave her a polite bow. "Mr. Kean is looking for Mr. Coleman. I believe he wants wine."

"When doesn't he?" the actress asked. "That and a bit of the other." She laughed and spun out of the room, but at least she remembered to close the door.

Hannah put aside her pins, making sure all were safely on the table beside her before she rested her hands in her lap. "I have a knack for fitting costumes," she said before I could comment. "My hands know where everything should go. Please, sit down, if you can find a chair in the mess. Have you come with any news?"

I picked up an empty chair from the other side of the room and carried it closer. I feared to move anything in the other chairs, in case she would have to find something on them after I'd gone. "I have not been able to lay hands on Mrs. Collins, I am sorry to say. We have found the man who made the incendiary device sent to her."

"Well, that's a mercy. Has he been arrested?"

"Not quite." I wasn't certain how to explain his interrogation by Denis, so I merely said, "He is being detained. He is reluctant to name who hired him, however."

"Oh." Her brows drew down in worry. "I heard you had a bit of bother over the death of Mr. Perry."

"I did. But luckily, a magistrate believed me when I said I had nothing to do with it." I leaned forward, resting my hands on my stick. "Why did you marry him, Mrs. Wolff? He was a dangerous man."

Hannah shook her head and smiled a little. "Because I owed him money, dear. Much money. My late husband and I both did. We tried to pay, but we never had enough. When Mr. Wolff passed, Mr. Perry thought it would be a fine thing to take a famous actress as his wife. He'd forgive the debt, he said, if I did so. I knew I faced debtor's prison and complete ruin, so I married him. He was never violent to me, though never respectful to me either. When I had my accident and lost my sight, he was no longer interested in me. Lately he'd begun to threaten me again, wanting his money. I am too old and feeble to be a good wife, which was what he'd paid for, wasn't it?" Hannah shook her head, but she kept her wry smile. "So I left him. I took up lodgings with my sister and her husband, and Mr. Coleman collected me from their house and brought me here every day. Perry never went to the magistrates—he dared not. I could tell the magistrates an earful about *him*." She sighed, her bravado deflating. "But I cannot lie to you. Mr. Perry's death is a release, and nothing more."

"Mr. Coleman is devoted to you. Do you think he is devoted enough to rid you of Mr. Perry?"

"Coleman?" Her tone turned incredulous. "Dear heavens. Coleman is not the violent sort. Very strong, yes, but gentle as a lamb. Besides, he was in here with me all the day they say Mr. Perry died. We were very busy, and he spent the day assisting me. He took me home in the evening and then stayed and supped with us. My sister will confirm that. I will vow Coleman went nowhere near Mr. Perry that day."

"I dislike to be rude, Mrs. Wolff, but you are

blind. Would you know if Coleman slipped out of the theatre that afternoon, made the short walk to Grimpen Lane, and came back again? He would not have been gone long."

Hannah's look turned pitying. "Well, of course I would have known. I can't see him, dear, but I can hear him. Coleman is not a silent mouse, you must know. And people have a *presence*, Captain. As you do sitting there now." She pointed straight at me. "A room is different with another person in it—people make noise when they breathe or fidget, and everyone has their own odor, you might have noticed. Coleman never left my side that day. I had a mountain of work making last-minute repairs, and he had to help me or I'd never have gotten it done. I will swear this to the magistrates if necessary. And others will swear it too. There were many people in and out, Coleman next to me all the time."

She spoke calmly, confidently, with no fear. She either believed in Coleman absolutely, or she was lying herself blue for him. I had learned from experience that in the case of crime a person could speak quite convincingly and not say a word of truth.

But in this case, she was right that Coleman would have other witnesses—the actors and actresses going in and out of this room, her sister who'd served Coleman dinner.

"Where is Coleman today?" I asked. "He is not minding the door, and Mr. Kean was most put out he could not find him."

"Mr. Kean is put out about many things." Again Hannah gave me her smile. "Coleman is helping repair the sets. Horses are fine beasts, but when someone has the grand idea of bringing them on the stage, they forget what havoc they can wreak. More than one of the sets must be rebuilt, and quickly."

Her calm and sparkle of humor told me this was not the only or the largest disaster she'd witnessed in the theatre. I wished I could while away the winter's day sitting here with the glass of hock Kean had asked for, and listen to her tell stories of the stage. She had been an amazing actress, charming the young Gabriel Lacey and most of the audience with me. I would have liked to remain here and hang on every word delivered in her low, melodious voice.

As it was, I had errands to run, and she had her own work. Her fingers twitched, anxious to return to it.

"Thank you, Mrs. Wolff." I rose and restored the chair to its position. "I will let you know as soon as I have word of Mrs. Collins."

Hannah gave me a grateful look. "Do. If my husband had been threatening poor Abby, she will be safe now."

"I hope so," I said, and took my leave.

*** *** ***

I looked for Coleman and saw him where Hannah said he'd be, standing on a ladder, pounding what looked like a giant trellis with a hammer. He was surrounded by other men who were also pounding things, the area behind the stage resembling a village after a severe windstorm or some other disaster.

I saw that I'd never get near Coleman today, and so I went out.

I met Grenville at the Rearing Pony, the tavern on Maiden Lane I frequented. Grenville was there before me, and the landlord's wife, Mrs. Tolliver, who always had a warm, rather seductive smile for me, brought me a tankard of ale.

Grenville wanted to hear of my interviews at Drury Lane first. I recounted everything, from meeting Mr. Kean and his information that Mrs. Collins wanted to invest in the theatre, to Hannah's revelation about her marriage.

"Interesting," Grenville said when I'd finished. "She is adamant about Mr. Coleman. But he looks after her, and she is fond of him, and naturally she would wish to protect him."

"If Mrs. Carfax *did* see a tall man going into my rooms that night, she might have mistaken Coleman for me." I took a sip of ale, enjoying its thick flavor.

"I wager Mrs. Carfax saw nothing at all," Grenville said. "I will tell you what I learned from Miss Winston, whom I managed to charm into speaking with me inside Mrs. Beltan's bakeshop. She is most unhappy with Mrs. Carfax, but she says Spendlove has Mrs. Carfax very frightened, and Mrs. Carfax will obey him without question. Something to do with *Mr.* Carfax, but Miss Winston does not know what. Dear Henny, she says, refuses to tell her."

"Mr. Carfax is dead and gone," I said. "Ten years now, I think."

"Perhaps, but who knows what scandals he got up to before he went? Perhaps he owed his tailor, and Mrs. Carfax is terrified of that getting out." His lips twitched as he lifted his ale.

Most aristocrats owed large debts to tailors, bakers, and candlestick makers, and many never paid them. Grenville might find this worry amusing, but to Mrs. Carfax, a respectable widow of the middle class, such a thing might be anathema. Spendlove might have threatened her with debtor's prison, the same thing Hannah Wolff had faced, or simply have threatened to shame Mrs. Carfax to her respectable friends. Being shunned was a lonely thing.

Grenville went on. "Miss Winston is inclined to agree with us that Mrs. Carfax's claim to have seen you was not well-done. Miss Winston refuses to cow to Mr. Spendlove and promises to do her best to talk Mrs. Carfax out of it."

"Well, that is something," I said.

We finished our ale, continuing our speculations. I noticed we carefully avoided the topic of Ridgley and what Mr. Denis might discover.

Grenville drained the last from his tankard and dabbed his mouth with his handkerchief. "I believe grub is in order. Anton told me at breakfast that my abrupt comings and goings have thrown him into disarray. He cannot possibly create any dishes for me until next week—and only then on condition that I cease running about the country. I don't much fancy sawing through the beefsteak here, so shall we adjourn to one of my clubs to dine?"

Anton was Grenville's prized chef. If Grenville indulged the man a bit too much, I could not blame him. Anton was an artist with food.

However, the idea of a good meal cheered me, and I agreed we should go. Grenville chose Watier's, and we enjoyed a dinner prepared by a chef of nearly Anton's calibre.

Our meal, unfortunately, was ruined by the arrival of Lord Andrew Kenton Stubbins, otherwise known as Stubby.

When Stubbins spied me upon entering in the dining room, he turned a fine shade of red. His suit was immaculate this evening, though the tight style of it and his leg-hugging pantaloons only enhanced his spindly build.

Stubbins glared at me for a time before he drew himself up and marched over. He was flanked by three men in suits of the first stare of fashion, the shoulders of their jackets padded out ridiculously wide, their collars so high I wondered that they could turn their heads. Their nearly identical costumes might have been comical if Stubbins' rage had not been so vicious.

Grenville gave the foursome one of his cool, disdainful looks as they stopped before our table. The three gentlemen behind Stubby looked uncomfortable—if Grenville cut them or was seen rebuking them, they stood to lose all respect in their circles.

Stubbins was enraged beyond fear. "Damn you, sir," he said to me, letting his voice grow loud. Heads lifted, conversations ceased. "How dare you sit here and eat among us? Did you think I would forget?" He had the full attention of the room now. He squared his already artificially squared shoulders and said, "Sir, name your seconds."

So, Stubby Stubbins' answer to me humiliating him was not to take me to court or to have me arrested. It was to challenge me to a duel.

Chapter Twenty

Instead of answering, I swallowed my food and took a sip of smooth claret. Grenville calmly laid down his fork and cleared his throat. "His second would be me," he said, bathing Stubbins in a chill look. "Yours?"

"Chetterly and Danielson." Stubbins jerked his thumb at two of the gentlemen behind him.

Grenville made a show of extracting a card and carefully handing it to one of the seconds, who stretched out a stiff hand for it. "Call on me tomorrow at three o'clock, Mr. Danielson. We will arrange matters."

The gentleman who took the card nodded once. Grenville lifted his fork and knife again, cutting into his roast, giving it his full attention. I kept my gaze levelly on Stubbins until he gave me a final hostile stare and turned away with his friends.

"Let us find a better place," Stubbins said in a

loud voice as they exited the dining room. "This one is too *odorous*."

"Interesting," Grenville said once Stubbins had gone and conversations began again. "He has come up with a way to punish you without his deeds coming to light in public. I will do my best for you, my friend."

The role of the second was not only to stand by a duelist and make sure the other party attended and obeyed the rules. Seconds met with each other to set up the place and time and to try to convince the two duelists to reconcile their differences in a less dangerous way.

"Thank you." I gave him a nod. "But do not worry about me. I have fought duels before and have emerged unscathed."

Grenville gave me a wry look. "I know. That is what concerns me."

*** *** ***

I swore Grenville to silence on the coming duel, preferring not to tell Donata until everything was set. If Stubbins fled to avoid the appointment, I might not have to tell her at all.

Keeping secrets from my wife was not the way in which I'd planned to begin the marriage, but some things I would have to be careful about revealing. I was not very worried about the duel, as I was a dead shot, though Stubbins might find a way to cheat. But me planning to stand in the way of a bullet might upset Donata.

Donata, however, was busy with her own concerns for the next few days, the chief of which was readying Gabriella for her come-out. Donata took Gabriella to a modiste to fit her out with an entirely new wardrobe. Considering some of the fantastic ensembles Donata could appear in, I was not easy about this, but Donata laughed at me and assured me she knew how to dress a modest debutante.

Gabriella's clothes were only a small worry. Far greater was the thought that I'd have to watch young men dance with her, flirt with her, and even propose to her. It bothered me greatly. I'd only just found Gabriella — was I to lose her so soon?

I kept my thoughts from these troubling directions by turning over the problems at hand. I decided to pay a visit to Hannah Wolff's residence, having pried the direction from Pomeroy. I wanted to speak to her sister, and perhaps gain an impression of Perry and who might have killed him.

Hannah's sister and brother-in-law, Mr. and Mrs. Holt, lived in what once had been a grand old house near the Strand, now cut in half and let to the middle classes. The remodeling had created a staid, if more practical, dwelling. The door was plain and unadorned, and so was the maid who answered my knock.

Hannah's sister and brother-in-law went with the house and the maid. They were a plain, quiet couple, both of them small in stature and tending toward stoutness. I had a thought that perhaps Mr. Holt had murdered Perry in order to protect Hannah, but upon meeting him, I was not so certain. He'd never be mistaken for me, if Mrs. Carfax had seen anyone at all. Additionally, I could not imagine this gentleman with the stooped shoulders and soft belly easily beating Perry to death. Perry had been on the short side but strong. I remembered him kicking my ribs with great force. The ribs had healed, but the stiffness remained.

Hannah's sister had hair turning from gold to gray, which she wore bundled under an old-fashioned mobcap, a few wisps of hair floating loose. Mrs. Holt offered me tea, which was served by another maid, this one half bent with rheumatism. The maid, the sister, and the brother-in-law looked surprised when I helped the maid with the heavy tray.

The two were devoted to Hannah, her sister said when the maid had gone. Such a tragedy about her sight. She'd been the best actress in the world — even Sarah Siddons was a rough-voiced upstart compared to Hannah. Of course Mrs. Holt and her husband took care of Hannah now, and at least Hannah could continue her work in the theatre, which she loved. John Perry had been a horrible, sneering man, and she was well rid of him.

They did confirm that on the night Perry met his death, Coleman had brought Hannah home at half past seven, and they'd all taken supper. Coleman hadn't departed until almost eleven, after which Hannah had gone to bed.

Mr. and Mrs. Holt were kind people, if somewhat dull and fixed on their favorite topic, Hannah Wolff. I politely drank the tea, though I preferred coffee, and ate some overly sweet cakes. They remembered courtesy and asked me about myself and my life in the army, though it was clear they had little interest.

I took my leave fuller of tea and cake and with few ideas about Perry and his role in all this.

Grenville invited me to his house that evening, having had his meeting with Stubbins' seconds about the duel. Stubbins had requested that we postpone our appointment until Lady Day, saying he had business to take care of at his estate. Grenville's tone when he relayed the information to me told me what he thought of Stubbins' courage.

"He stated that not meeting until March would give you time to put your affairs in order." We were ensconced in Grenville's sitting room, supplied by Gautier with brandy and cheroots. "And he is aware that you are newly married and is generously allowing you to say good-bye to your wife." Grenville took a pull of the cheroot he was smoking then drank a mouthful of brandy. He exhaled the smoke. "He is rather confident of his chances of potting you."

I raised my own lit cheroot and sucked smoke into my mouth. The cheroot, blended with the trickle of fine brandy, produced a heady, smoky, rich taste. "He might be. But I will shoot him in the shoulder, and honor will be satisfied."

"I rather think he's asking for the extra month or so to practice. Have a care, Lacey."

"I will simply have to get my shot off first."

Grenville laughed, but I saw the worry in his eyes. Truth to tell, I did *not* want Stubbins to shoot me, not now when my life was starting to be good for me. If I killed him, I'd be arrested for murder, and I did not want that either. But the upcoming battle did not frighten me—I would deal with it when I saw the ground, the weapons, and how shaky Stubbins was or was not.

Matthias entered at that moment and handed me a piece of paper. It was a note, not sealed and had no direction. Hand delivered, Matthias said, and the messenger was waiting.

The letter bore one line on the entire sheet of expensive paper—typical of Denis. *I have news. Bring Grenville.*

I passed the note to Grenville and nodded at Matthias. "Tell the messenger we're on our way."

"Not so much a messenger as an entire carriage," Matthias said. "Do I tell the coachman to wait?"

"Yes." I tamped out the cheroot with regret. I'd been enjoying the indulgence. "We will be down directly."

*** *** ***

Denis had sent his luxurious coach, empty, no doubt to ensure we came to him at once. One of his pugilist footmen helped me in, then Grenville, and we pulled off through a rather sharp rain south toward Curzon Street.

As we halted in front of number 45, the rain increased, bringing with it a chill mist. This was a good afternoon to be inside with a fire and more brandy, not rolling about London, no matter how comfortable the conveyance.

The interior of Denis's house was warm, even in the halls and stairwell. Denis had told me not long ago how he'd grown up on the streets of London, sleeping in dung carts for warmth. Now that he could, he chose to live in extreme comfort.

We were ushered into his study. Most of the room was still intact, though the wall near the fireplace had burned completely. Dust cloths covered the floor, and new paneling leaned against the blackened bricks, waiting for workmen to install it.

There was no sign of any workmen now, nor of Ridgley. Denis met us alone with only Brewster as a bodyguard.

Denis, as composed and well-groomed as ever, was sitting at his desk when we entered. The only souvenirs from the disaster with Ridgley were a fading bruise on his cheekbone and more coldness in his eyes.

"It is a tricky business," he said after we'd seated ourselves, "prying information from a man who neither fears death nor has anyone in the world he cares about. One's threats have little teeth if the man has no hidden terrors."

"Are you saying he told you nothing?" I asked.

"I am saying one has to search more diligently for the threat that will pull out the necessary information. I did find that leverage, and he did finally speak." He paused. Denis wasn't one for dramatics, but I daresay he enjoyed making Grenville and I wait for his next words. "The person who hired Mr. Ridgley was not a man, but a woman."

"Ah." I said.

"A woman?" Grenville sat forward. "Good Lord, that's monstrous. Lacey, why do you not seem more surprised?"

"Because nothing about this case surprises me anymore," I said. "And Mr. Kean told me I should be looking for a rival, another actress, either in her company or at another theatre. Mrs. Collins is very successful after all."

Denis waited until we'd quieted again. "The reason I bade Mr. Grenville join you is that while Mr. Ridgley would not give up a name—I suspect he never knew it and never asked it—he did describe her." Denis fixed Grenville with a look. "She had blond hair, large blue eyes, a pointed face, and could make herself look younger than she truly was. He described the gown she wore as something he'd never seen before — a red dress fairly plain but with large panels of painted cotton about the bottom, depicting people in a desert land."

My lips parted. I'd seen Marianne in that very frock last summer — Grenville took Marianne to the most exclusive modiste in London, and he had provided the cloth, which he'd purchased a few years ago during his last trip to the Ottoman Empire. The cloth had been hand-woven for him — there could not be two gowns the same.

Grenville was out of his chair before Denis finished speaking. Brewster took a step toward him, but Denis signaled Brewster to still.

"He lied to you," Grenville said, his face red. "He must have."

"I do not think so," Denis said. "I am skilled at interrogation, Mr. Grenville. He described Miss Simmons to the letter, and I doubt he could have invented the details of her garment."

"Let me speak to him," Grenville said. "If he's not lying, he's at least mistaken."

Denis shook his head. "I am afraid it is no longer possible to speak to him."

Meaning Ridgley was dead. Though I could not be sorry for the world to lose such a man, Denis's finality sent a chill through me.

"I agree with Grenville; it is absurd," I said. "Marianne Simmons would not hire a murderer to deliver a dangerous device to Mrs. Collins. Marianne had given up the theatre; she had no reason. The theatre never meant as much to her as it does to Mrs.

Collins or Mr. Kean."

Or perhaps Marianne had simply been skilled at hiding her emotions. When Marianne and Abigail Collins had come to London to try their luck, Abigail had risen quickly while Marianne had been shoved into far lesser roles, for far less money and very little fame. Such a course of events might make any woman bitter and jealous.

Still, I could not believe it of her. I said, "Why then would Marianne come to me and beg me to help her find Mrs. Collins?"

Even as I said the words, I knew what Denis's answer would be. "To try again? Ridgley did not supply me with her motives, gentlemen. He neither knew them nor cared. He only described his client."

"What of the man?" I asked. "The nervous gentleman who took the device to the delivery firm?"

"Ridgley had no idea who he was either. The man picked up the device from Ridgley and paid him the second half of his fee. Ridgley never saw him or the woman again."

"Did he tell you how much the fee was?"

"One hundred guineas," Denis said. "Half when Ridgley was hired, half on delivery. The woman counted out the coins readily enough, he said."

Grenville looked ill. His face had gone gray, his eyes pinched with white. He supplied Marianne with plenty of money these days, pouring cash into her hand almost as quickly as she could spend it.

"He had to have been mistaken," Grenville said, his voice rasping. "There must be another such woman. Marianne cannot have done this."

But I saw the worry in his eyes. The description could fit more women than Marianne, true, and another actress could have played the part to throw suspicion on her. If not for the detail of the gown, a unique dress that had been created for her and had debuted to much praise, I would not hesitate. Marianne was quite pleased with that dress, I happened to know, and would not have taken it to a secondhand shop; she was proud she'd sold none of the clothes Grenville had given her yet. But then, a cloth manufacturer might have decided to make a fabric similar to that which the mistress of so popular a man wore; and another modiste could have copied the dress, eager to imitate to please her clients.

"There must be another explanation," I said.

"Where is Miss Simmons now?" Denis asked.

"In Bath," Grenville answered. "Oh, dear God, she persuaded me to leave her there." He sat down, his hands going to his face.

"Then we will return to Bath and find her," I said. "We will let her defend herself before we condemn her."

Grenville lifted his head. He drew out a handkerchief and wiped his mouth. "You are right, of course, Lacey. By all means, let us speak to her."

He surged to his feet again. Then the very fashionable, always correctly courteous Grenville staggered past Brewster and out of the room without a farewell.

I rose. "What of Ridgley?" I asked Denis, who hadn't moved. "I take it he is dead?"

"He is no longer a threat," Denis answered. "You would not like anything more I could tell you."

"He was a cold bastard."

Denis inclined his head. "He was." He unlaced his fingers. "I rarely come across a man that evil, but

Ridgley certainly was. Most people have some capacity for caring, no matter how otherwise terrible that person might be. Even me." He gave me a small smile. "But Ridgley had nothing. He was an empty shell. I regret that what he told me is something you do not wish to hear, but I cannot help that. I can only report what I discovered."

"Yes," I said. "Thank you for your help."

He lifted a brow. "That thanks clogged your throat, but I will accept it. Remember — Ridgley spoke no names, only descriptions."

With that, Denis closed his mouth, waiting for me to go. I gave him a nod and departed the room. I thought about his parting words as I tramped heavily down the stairs, to find that Grenville had gone out into the rain alone without bothering to wait for me or a conveyance.

Chapter Twenty-one

I caught up to Grenville, who was striding hatless through the cold rain—at least he'd let a lackey bundle him into his greatcoat. Denis's carriage crept along behind me, and I stepped in front of Grenville, herding him back toward it.

"You are the most famous man in Mayfair," I said. "If anyone sees you charging about like a madman, it will be all over London by this evening. Get in."

Grenville gazed back at me, unseeing, for a moment. Then he nodded and allowed Denis's footman to help him into the coach. I climbed in behind him, the warm interior a relief.

"There will be another explanation," I said as I took the seat opposite him.

Grenville scrubbed his hand through his hair, further mussing what the rain had wet. "Yes, yes, I know that, but it came as a bit of a shock."

"I assure you, Grenville, if I'd thought Marianne

capable of seeking out someone like Ridgley, I would have warned you off her long ago."

"You did try to warn me off. Remember? You told me to take up with her at my peril."

"Peril to your heart, I meant. Not to your person, or anyone's person. But let us think. An actress can make herself resemble whom she pleases, including another actress. Marianne was in the Drury Lane company a long time, and with the strolling players with Mrs. Collins before that. There are plenty of women who would know Marianne well enough to be able to mimic her."

Grenville's face had regained some color, but he still breathed hard. The light from the lanterns inside the coach glittered on the rain droplets in his hair. "Yes, I see all that. I beg your pardon; I did not mean to embarrass you. But what about the clothes Ridgley mentioned? That gown was unique."

"Actresses know about costumes. This woman might have found a fabric that looked similar, or faked it somehow. Ridgley had never met Marianne—the woman would only have to resemble her for a short time. Say this lady wore the distinctive gown, dressed her hair in Marianne's style, and possibly made sure others saw her going to her meeting with Ridgley. Easy enough to throw away or burn the dress when she finished, redo her hair or get rid of the wig, and no one would be the wiser."

Grenville drew another breath. "Yes, that makes sense." He went silent a moment, staring at the rain streaking the windows. "Who would do such a monstrous thing, Lacey?"

"Any number of people, unfortunately. I'd rather ask Marianne herself, though, who she believes capable of pretending to be her."

I was not certain Donata would be pleased that I wanted to hie quickly back to Bath, but I did—at once. I could reach there far faster than I could send a letter and Marianne could return. If Spendlove or Pomeroy got wind of what Ridgley had told Denis, Marianne was in danger of being arrested. I needed to hear her story and keep her safe.

"We should leave for Bath at once," I said.

"Indeed." Grenville turned his head and looked out the window. He looked pale and not happy, as though his motion sickness had come upon him again.

I gave him a warning look. "Do nothing impetuous concerning Marianne until you have spoken to me first. We need to go carefully, and not alert Spendlove."

He gave me a shaky nod, then a short laugh. "Do you know, Lacey, finally you are learning what it is like for me to deal with *you*."

"Amusing," I said. I knocked on the coach's roof. Though we'd passed Donata's door three houses ago, I had the coachman stop to let me down where we were. "I will prepare for the journey. You have Gautier give you a hot bath and plenty of brandy."

"Do I look that awful?"

He didn't. Even with the rain and his agitation, Grenville managed to appear flawless. "No, but if you have a bath and brandy, you might go to sleep and return to your rational self when you awake."

Denis's footman pulled open the door and eyed me impatiently. I took up my walking stick and climbed down, giving Grenville a brief good-bye.

"You make the devil of a nursemaid, Lacey,"

Grenville growled.

I gave him a salute, thanked the footman, and walked through the rain back to Donata's home.

*** *** ***

Bartholomew wanted to relieve me of my rain-spotted clothes, Barnstable to plop my wet body into the bath, but I did not have the patience. I did, however, stop for my daughter, who emerged from a chamber above as I ran up the stairs.

"Mrs. Lacey is attempting to drown me in garments," Gabriella said as she met me on the landing. "It is unbelievable how many gowns I must wear in the space of one day."

I stopped, the mad whirl of the morning slowing to a breath of sweetness. "Mrs. Lacey is an expert on these things," I said.

"She is indeed. I am not ungrateful; I'm merely uncertain I will be able to concentrate on conversation and manners when I'm worried about rushing off to change clothing for the next event. And if I spend all my time at my toilette, I'll never have a moment for anything else."

I gave her a fond smile, my heart warming away from the horror of Ridgley, the shock of his confession, the fear for Marianne. "I quite agree with your dilemma. I too am now required to throw off and put on a new suit as soon as an hour changes."

Gabriella reached out and patted my arm. "Then we will grow used to it together."

A wonderful sentiment. Gabriella was relaxing around me. I suddenly wished all my troubles at the bottom of the Thames, with nothing to do but bask in the presence of her. I had so much wasted time to erase.

"Father, I could wish to see Miss Simmons again." Gabriella cut through my thoughts. "I rather like her. Could we not invite her to dine with us when she returns? Surely it would not be so terrible a thing to have an actress sit at our table. Mrs. Lacey invites actors and actresses to dine, and Lady Aline Carrington invites them to her soirees. She says other ladies of the *ton* do as well."

"Very famous actresses," I said. "And yes, those ladies are quite proudly displayed, sometimes asked to perform. Mrs. Lacey is correct that there would be talk if Marianne came to dinner with us while you are here, but I can convince Lady Aline to invite her to a supper and have us come as well. Lady Aline gets away with much."

Gabriella listened, intelligence in her brown eyes. "I find it all so very silly."

"As do I." I dared rest my hand over hers. "It is a moot question at the moment, in any case, as Marianne is still in Bath."

"No, she is not," my daughter astounded me by saying. "No one knows where she it. Mr. Pomeroy came while you were out. Mr. Spendlove arrived with him, but Mrs. Lacey would not allow him the house." Gabriella's smile told me Donata had been at her acerbic best. "They were looking for Miss Simmons. Mr. Pomeroy said that the patrollers in Bath sent word that Miss Simmons had disappeared, and they have no idea where she's gone."

*** *** ***

I had some idea. At least, I hoped I did. The trouble was, how to reach her hiding place without Spendlove or Pomeroy following?

"Cleverly," my wife said when I told her of my

plans. "Tomorrow night is my first at-home. There will be a crush. You will make certain all the men following you about see you here, then you will leave surreptitiously. Lady Aline would be happy to help, I know. From there you depart London."

"Grenville will want to come." If I slipped away and left him behind, he'd be furious.

"Leave Grenville to me. You will travel much more covertly without him. Barnstable will enjoy keeping up the pretense that you are still in the house after you've gone, and he will make certain the rest of the staff do as well."

Donata looked quite eager, and I realized she was enjoying herself.

I touched her cheek. "You are impossibly good to me. Why could I not have married you years ago?"

"Because you were away from England, and I was married to an ogre," she answered without sentiment. "By the bye, Mr. Pomeroy delighted in hinting you'd tried to hide the fact that you were sharing my bed at the time Mr. Perry met his death, even though it would save you from being tried for his murder. You are a fool sometimes, Gabriel."

"I am a fool much of the time," I said. "But I refuse to have Bow Street sniggering, and speaking about you without respect."

Donata gave me her sharp stare. "Very noble of you. But I will allow them to snigger all they please if it keeps you from the noose."

*** *** ***

The scheme went as Donata planned. The next evening, the house began to fill, carriages lining up outside the front door to deposit guests dressed in the latest new fashion for the Season, the ladies glittering with jewels every hue of the rainbow.

Grenville arrived, his sangfroid in place. His manners were impeccable, and he engaged his acquaintances in conversation with his usual wit. I saw the tightness about his eyes, however, and the lines around his mouth when he looked at me.

For verisimilitude, Grenville talked as freely to me as ever, letting the crowd know I was still one of his favorites. In private, this afternoon, he'd lost his temper with me.

I'd thought it only fair to tell him of my plan to search for Marianne. As predicted, Grenville wanted to accompany me, and I had to argue a long while to convince him to remain in London. He at last conceded that staying behind and helping Donata with the pretense that I was still in Town would be better for the purpose. But he was very angry that I would not let him go to Marianne in my place. I tried to explain that the great Grenville could not move about the country with the anonymity I could, and he agreed, but he was still angry.

I made certain to circulate among the guests, which was difficult, as they occupied every inch of the stairs and the foyer, spilling well into the public rooms and even into the garden behind the house, as cold as it was. When parties began to leave, I walked several of them out, waving them off as their carriages pulled away.

At the time arranged with Lady Aline, I slipped away through the dark garden and through a small gate to the mews. Lady Aline's coachman waited with her landau only a few feet from the gate. I climbed inside on my own and crouched on the floor.

The coachman drove around to South Audley

Street, and Bartholomew assisted Lady Aline into the landau. Bartholomew tipped me a wink before he shut the door, and then Lady Aline pulled all the curtains closed.

"This is terribly exciting, Lacey, my boy," the stout lady said as I eased myself onto the seat and brushed off my trousers. "I haven't done anything so underhanded since I slipped away from my governess to meet the stable boy and let him kiss me silly. Oh, do not look so surprised. I was a lovely gel when I was seventeen, and I was forward. Quite, quite forward. I pursued gentlemen with ardor until I realized what silly creatures most of them were. I am unmarried by choice, Lacey. Turned down any number of proposals."

I would have married her in a trice. "It is good of you to help."

"Only too glad. Never forgive Donata for not allowing me to the wedding, though. Was it splendid? Was she very beautiful?"

"It was," I said. "And she is."

"And you are good for her. I see the change in her. She was so very angry at Breckenridge, rot his black heart. She needs someone who likes her and will let her shine. I have faith that you will do it."

Her expression said that if I did not, Lady Aline would come after me any way she could.

"I am doing my best to make her happy," I said. "And I like her very much."

"Took you a bit, didn't it?" She gave me a grin, which animated her large face. "Donata is not your usual wilting female. She is robust, and not all gentlemen appreciate that in a lady."

"I do," I said.

"I know. That is why I did not kick up a fuss when you proposed to her, even in your straightened circumstances. Donata has plenty, but she needs a good companion to see her through the rest of life. Bless you, my boy."

Lady Aline's praise was hard-won, and I warmed under it.

We reached her townhouse not long later. I stayed in the coach until it rolled to the mews behind it, then I took the horse already prepared for me and rode west out of London. At Cranford I gave up the horse for the chaise Donata had caused to be hired for me. We had decided that if Spendlove did see me leaving London and followed, I'd turn back at this milepost and let him wonder.

I was confident I had not been followed. Spendlove and his patrollers would have been watching the area around South Audley Street, not looking for a lone horseman riding away from a lane near Oxford Street. In Cranford saw no one furtive, and none paid much attention to me as I gave up the horse, had a quick bite of bread with ale at the coaching inn, and left for Berkshire.

*** *** ***

I decided to go past Hungerford, all the way to Great Bedwyn, where I wasn't known, to break my journey and put up at an inn there. It was dawn when the chaise pulled into the town, with bells tolling in churches in Great Bedwyn and up and down the canal. I slept a few hours of the early morning, ate a small breakfast, and set off on a hired horse north toward Froxfield.

The house where Marianne kept David looked quiet. The door was closed, and though smoke rose from the chimney, no little boy played in the snow in front of or behind the house.

Marianne might not be here at all. I'd have wasted a journey and risked being followed to Marianne's secret refuge.

Banishing these cheerful thoughts, I dismounted the horse, left it to paw for grass beneath the snow, and rapped on the door. It opened a crack, and Maddie, David's caretaker peered out.

Her expression softened to relief, and she pulled the door wide. "It's all right," she called over her shoulder. "It's that captain."

David was playing on the floor in front of the settle. He looked up when I came in, his eyes narrowing in puzzlement as he struggled to remember who I was.

Marianne came down the stairs in the corner, heels clicking on the stone steps. "I meant to send word to you," she said without greeting. "But it was damn difficult to get away from Bath undetected. I finally managed it, thanks to the help of a few friends. We might stay here forever; we haven't decided."

I thought by "we" she meant herself and David, and perhaps Maddie, until another woman came down the stairs behind her. This woman was a few years older than Marianne, though her exhausted look and the stoop to her shoulders made her seem almost elderly. She wore a white mobcap and a dress not much different from Maddie's—likely borrowed from her.

I thought I did not know the woman, until I looked again. And then I stared in astonishment.

"Cease gawping, Lacey," Marianne said. Her eyes

held triumph behind her tiredness. "May I introduce you to Mrs. Collins? Abby, this is my neighbor, Captain Lacey, who has been tramping about England hunting for you. I found her," Marianne said to me. "No thanks to you."

Chapter Twenty-two

I could not cease my staring. I had to plant my stick and lean heavily on it. "Good God."

Mrs. Collins reached the foot of the stairs and stepped off, becoming the poised, graceful lady I'd watched take so many bows at Drury Lane.

Marianne almost smirked at me. "It seems I had no need to engage you after all, Lacey. Sorry for your trouble."

"*Marianne.*" I clutched my walking stick so that I would not stride across the room and shake her. "You must explain what has happened."

Marianne lapsed into a true smile. "I am sorry; it was too much to resist teasing you. To be fair, Abby found me. She heard I was performing at the theatre in Bath, and she managed to get covertly into my rooms and wait for me. Frightened the life out of me, she did, but then I was overjoyed. Abby disguised herself well—I would not have known her if I'd passed her in the street."

"Then we likely did, several times." I gave Mrs. Collins an admiring nod.

"I have had much practice," Mrs. Collins said. Her voice hinted of the musical quality she used on the stage, but I heard true tiredness in it. "Please do not give me away, Captain Lacey. Marianne has told me much about you, and she claims you are a man of honor."

"Indeed, I will tell no one where you are," I said. "Until you wish me to. But you are well? You were not hurt?"

Mrs. Collins drifted across the room to the settle. David gazed up at her without fear. A smile crossed Mrs. Collins' face, and the look in her eyes was . . . I was not certain. I saw pain there, and resignation, but also fondness.

David stared at her, distracted from playing with his ball. Mrs. Collins sat on the settle, took up the ball and bounced it to him. David laughed and tried to catch it, hurrying after it when he missed.

"I left London of my own accord," Mrs. Collins said to me. "After the incident with the package, I knew I had to leave. It was not worth my life to stay. I will retire gracefully until the danger is over, then make a return if I feel I can, if anyone will have me."

"And how can you be certain when the danger has passed?" I asked. "Mr. Perry is dead; is it not safe for you to return to London now?"

Mrs. Collins shook her head. "Mr. Perry was never the danger. At least, not to me. In this instance, he was trying to help me, though I did not like his motives for doing so."

"And someone killed him."

"Not I," Mrs. Collins said quickly. "I did not know of his death until Marianne told me as we traveled here."

I pulled a kitchen chair from the table and sat down on it near the settle. There was room next to Mrs. Collins, but I, still the admirer, could not bring myself to sit myself down beside her, as though we were friends.

"Please begin from the beginning," I said. David, watching me, lifted the ball he'd retrieved and put it to his mouth. "What led up to you receiving the device and deciding to go into hiding? You stating you will retire and try to return later are not the words of a woman devoted to the theatre."

Mrs. Collins gave me a weary smile. "It is difficult for me to stay away, but I was terrified. It began with small things meant to trip me up on stage or be late for my entrances. One of my costumes was found cut to ribbons the day of a performance. Mrs. Wolff had to hurriedly substitute another for me, which tried her sorely, but she finished it, bless her. Letters, unsigned, telling me I had gotten above myself, and needed to watch out. Small things that one can shrug away most of the time, but when they started to come thick and fast, night after night, it was unnerving. I would forget my lines or give a listless performance. The other actors were not happy with me, I can tell you. When the package came, and Coleman said it might have killed me, I knew I had to leave. Someone in that theatre hated me. It made me cold, that hatred."

Marianne sat herself next to Mrs. Collins. She showed nothing but sympathy, no guilt at all as Mrs. Collins listed the deeds against her.

"You've been at Drury Lane how long?" I asked Mrs. Collins. "Six years, is it?"

"About that, yes, when Marianne and I came in from the country. What rubes we were!" She laughed a little. "It was a struggle to find places, but we did."

"And fortune smiled upon you."

"Yes," Mrs. Collins said. "I have been very lucky, I know that."

Marianne gave a snort. "Much more than luck, Abby. You've always been a fine actress. I knew that the moment I met you. Why do you think I hung on you so?"

"We helped each other," Mrs. Collins said. "Marianne has always been good to me. That is why I revealed myself to her when I learned she was in Bath. I'd been growing worried about my safety, hearing Bow Street Runners had come to town. I wanted no one finding me. No one."

"In this case, the Runners were looking for me," I said. "They frequently are."

Mrs. Collins flashed a smile that made her somewhat plain and round face blossom into astonishing beauty. I was reminded of how Mr. Kean could look aged and stooped one moment, tall and robust the next.

"Are you so very dangerous?" Mrs. Collins asked me.

"They believe so, but I assure you, I mean you no harm."

"I know." Her eyes were brown . . . or perhaps hazel . . . or gray. I could not tell in this light, and the color seemed to change with her mood. "Marianne says you are to be trusted, and so you are."

"High praise from Marianne," I said dryly. "She

bestows it on so few. I asked how long you'd been at Drury Lane, because I wondered when the pranks to frighten you began. It was fairly recent, was it not?"

"There are always jealousies and tricks, but you are correct, Captain. These particular problems began last year—I'd say about April or May. We were well into the theatrical season. I did not pay them much mind at first, being far too busy worrying about performing, but as we wound down and started planning the next season they began to happen more often. I grew to dread going into my dressing room each night, wondering what new delight I would find waiting for me."

"When did you decide to invest money in the theatre?"

I waited, watching her reaction. Mrs. Collins looked puzzled, then her eyes widened in amazement. "About the same time. But good heavens, if anyone was upset by that, why did they not say so? Why would they want to frighten me enough to make me cease *acting*?" She shook her head. "No, you must be mistaken. Me giving money to the theatre would help it remain open, letting actors keep their roles. With my investment, we would be able to hire more help, including someone for the costuming so Mrs. Wolff can retire. She is wearying as much as she protests, and I would like to see her settled to enjoy the rest of her life. Drury Lane theatre is always teetering on the edge of bankruptcy. Everyone knew I planned to put in my money, and I heard nothing but praise because of it."

"But with you partly owning the theatre, perhaps you'd never become dislodged."

"Nonsense. I love the stage, but it is tiring. I had

been contemplating taking fewer roles to give myself a bit of rest, and I said so. But now I'm damned if I'll step aside because someone is trying to frighten me."

"Good for you, Abby," Marianne said. "Captain Lacey will find the person out, and you will be safe."

"You have much faith in me," I answered. "I am still a long way in the dark."

Maddie, who had listened to all this while forming a pie crust at her table, broke in. "Depend upon it, Captain, it is an angry rival. Sift through that theatre and you will find her."

"It is one thing I do not miss," Marianne said. "The petty anger, the false friendships, broken as soon as you are no longer useful or are seen as a threat. More drama backstage sometimes than on it."

"Indeed," Mrs. Collins said, laughing her light laugh. "But to go so far as to send me a box that would explode in my face." She shivered. "That is a person with no conscience."

She was right. I rose to my feet. David continued to stare at me over his ball.

"Thank you, Mrs. Collins. I will do my best to find this culprit, because I too am frightened by his audacity. Who knows what he might try next?" I looked at Marianne and made a little nod at the door. "I will not tire you with my presence. Thank you for answering my questions, and I am pleased to see you alive and well. Remain here until I give you word that all is safe."

Mrs. Collins extended a plump hand to me, which I took, finding it warm and soft. "Well met, Captain. I will heed your advice and remain here, until I hear from you that all is well."

Her faith in me both buoyed me and worried me.

Mrs. Collins looked straight into my eyes, her smile all for me, until I felt I would do anything for her. Such was her power.

Marianne took my unspoken request and followed me outside. "I'll be staying on with Abby," she said. "I want to look after her. Tell his nibs."

The horse had wandered a bit. I tramped after him, Marianne following, but this made certain we were out of earshot of the house. I caught the horse's reins, trying to decide how to proceed.

"What did you want, Lacey?" Marianne asked. "It is cold out here, so you had better tell me quickly."

I took my time folding the reins in my hand. Only a fool wrapped reins around his hand or wrist—if the horse bolted, it guaranteed a broken wrist at best, or for the fool to be dragged to death at worst. "We found the man who made the device delivered to Mrs. Collins," I said. "Denis found him, I should say. His name is Ridgley. He claimed a woman hired him to fashion the parcel." I at last looked up at her. "A woman who closely resembled you."

Marianne's eyes widened. "Resembled *me*? What on earth are you talking about?"

"He described you. Golden curls, blue eyes, pointed face that looked girlish, and he mentioned a gown, the one with the cloth Grenville brought from Constantinople."

Marianne's mouth had dropped open as I spoke, and now she drew a sharp breath. "Good Lord. But the woman he described is not me, despite the gown. I'd never dream of hurting Abby. Where is this Mr. Ridgley? Once he looks at me, he'll know his mistake."

He is no longer a threat, Denis had said. "I'm afraid

he's dead. I would not have wanted you near him, in any case. Ridgley was very odd, almost inhuman. He might not have admitted one way or another whether you were the person who hired him, even if he saw you."

"But you believed him. I see it in your face." Marianne pointed a stiff finger at me. "That is why you rushed out here to Berkshire to find me, is it not? You had no idea Abby was here."

I gave her a conceding nod. "I admit, I was worried when I first heard the explanation, but I was unwilling to take him at his word. Mr. Denis did not believe it either. He posited that another actress could have pretended to be you, and I am inclined to agree."

"Well, that is a relief. I would have liked a little more confidence from you, but I know you have a suspicious nature. Believe me, I would never hurt Abby. She was a friend to me when others would not be."

"I do believe you. I did not only come here to confront you with that news—I wanted to be sure you were safe. The Runners are still nosing about, and whoever is trying to hurt Mrs. Collins has not been found. Lying low here with her is best."

"The Runners." She made a derisive gesture. "The Runners never did a thing to find Abby or discover who wanted to hurt her. None cared but me."

"And me," I said. "Do not lump me in with Spendlove, I beg you."

"What about *him*? I notice you have not mentioned my protector in all this. Did *he* believe I'd hired a man to make an incendiary device? I see in your face that he did. You are terrible at lying."

Marianne balled her fists, her eyes filling with anger and hurt. "*Damn* him."

"He believed it only as long as I did. The news was a shock, Marianne. Especially when Ridgley described what you wore. The dress is distinctive and unique."

"And a description of it was printed in all the newspapers at the time. Everyone knows every gown Mr. Grenville's current courtesan wears. And fair hair and the childish look is all the fashion. Just see the artificial curls on your ladies of the *ton*."

"Even so, you cannot blame him," I said. "Even I hesitated at first, and I have known you a long time."

Marianne paced agitatedly, her boots leaving prints in the thin snow. "*He* should have had no hesitation at all. Devil take him." She swung to face me. "Please inform Mr. Grenville that I will not be returning to his house. I will leave all the jewelry and all the money, not to mention the lovely gowns, and I will find some way to repay him for what he has spent on my son. But I do not wish to see him again. I'll stay here with David as long as I can and then return to other lodgings in London. Did you also take my old rooms at Ma Beltan's? If so, I'll let them from you, Lacey."

"For God's sake—"

"No, do not try to reason with me. I am not in the least reasonable at this moment. You may tell him from me that I have tired of him never trusting me. He either takes me as I am or not at all. I care nothing for how rich he is."

I held up my hand as Marianne started pacing again. "I am not your go-between. If you wish to tell Grenville of your disappointment, you must tell him yourself. My interest is to clear up this problem and return Mrs. Collins safely to London."

"But that is all *I* ever wanted. And now I am accused of hiring strange men to make dangerous packages, and the man who is supposed to be my protector believes it. *I* am the fool. I ought to have looked for Abby on my own and never mentioned anything to you gentlemen."

"But you did ask me, and I am trying to help," I said. "Please push your indignation aside for the moment, and let us solve this."

"Do not bleat to me about pushing aside anger. That is rich, coming from you. Your temper has gotten you into more trouble than any of my piques ever did."

"I know that, but it is only because you have large blue eyes and can make yourself appealing when you want to. Now, please think. What other woman could have pretended to be you to hire Mr. Ridgley? Who in the company could have done this?"

Marianne's brows drew together. Wind began to stir the trees and the halo of curls around her face. "I do not know," she said after a time. Her voice had lost its edge, and she spoke wearily. "I told you, even if Abby quits the theatre altogether, no one could guess who in the company would take her roles. She had no understudy yet for this year. Mrs. Carter, the other principal, already has plenty to do. The committee might choose a lady from the chorus, but more than likely, they'd hire someone from the provinces or a principal from another company. We can never be certain what decision the committee will make."

"But anger and jealousy are not necessarily

rational. Perhaps whoever it is has grown tired of seeing Mrs. Collins succeed again and again. She decided to put an end to Mrs. Collins' career, whether that end benefited her or not."

"True. But I am no longer close to the theatre, am I? There might be a new actress I know nothing about who is doing these things. When I was there I didn't pay much attention to the rivalries, I must admit. I did my job, collected my pay, and tried to find a gent who would give me more. Acting can be a tedious chore, if you must know. Exhausting. Why so many wish to take it up is beyond my understanding."

"Then why did *you* take it up?" I asked, genuinely curious.

"I told you before, to make a bob or two. And people in strolling players don't ask nosy questions. Well . . . they do, but if you don't want to answer, they make something up about you and leave you be."

"Did you join them because of David?"

Marianne looked surprised. "No. David came along after that. If you must poke your nose into my affairs, I will tell you it is because of David that I say Abby was a friend to me when others wouldn't be. She stood by me when I had David, and she helped me take care of him—helped me set him up with Maddie, in fact. Others wanted me out of the players, wanted Abby to say I should be left by the side of the road, but she never did. *She* was why I survived, why David is alive and well today. I can never, never repay her for that."

Tears filled Marianne's eyes as she looked at the house in the clearing, smoke drifting from its neat chimney.

"Why did Mrs. Collins, in particular, stand by you?" I asked. "What is she to you?"

Marianne laughed a little as she turned back to me. "A friend. A dear, dear friend. You will probably never understand, Lacey, with your overblown sense of honor, so I will tell you that what she did for me was extraordinary. Her own husband fathered my child. Yes, you heard me aright. Mr. Collins came to me for comfort when Abby was too busy being an actress for him. David was the result. And Abby, instead of condemning me as she ought, remained my friend and helped me through it all, especially when David turned out . . . as he is. She loved me better than she loved her husband, you see, which enraged Mr. Collins to no end. Not in a hermaphroditic sort of way, I am sorry to disappoint you, but a love like that of sisters, or even a mother for a daughter. She's an astonishing woman, is Abby."

I listened in silence, my respect for both women rising as she spoke. Marianne regarded me with a defiant look, as though waiting for me to condemn her for the adultery, but I could not. She had done what she had done for reasons only she and Mrs. Collins understood. My own past was not blameless, so I had no business judging her. The affairs I'd conducted after my first wife had left me, as I sought solace for my torn-out heart, had not always been well-done.

Also, as she told me the tale, an idea began to stir through my morass of emotions. I touched the thought, waiting for it to wriggle away, but it did not.

"Rivals," I said. "Some never leave it behind, my wife tells me."

"Is that all you have to say?" Marianne wiped her eyes with her fingers. "And me spilling all to you."

I drew a long breath, the fog clearing from my brain. "I believe you, Marianne," I said. "You had nothing to do with the persecution of Mrs. Collins. Nothing at all."

"Thank you very much. I am pleased you have listened at last."

"Some women are obsessed with rivalry, Donata tells me," I said, remembering my wife's voice ringing with conviction. I repeated her words. "Ladies of the *ton* wake in the morning planning how they will best their enemies that day."

"I am sorry to hear it," Marianne said. "Perhaps they ought to take a brisk walk and feel better."

Rivals. Actresses, someone pretending to be Marianne, Coleman on hand to render the parcel harmless.

What result had come about with Abigail in hiding? The theatre company not only had to replace her with another actress, but her scheme of investing in the theatre went away. If Mrs. Collins bought into the theatre, she would have a stronger say on who came in, and also who went out.

I opened my eyes, realizing I'd closed them. Marianne was staring at me, her face pink from the cold. My hands were growing numb despite my gloves, the horse prodding me gently with his warm nose. "I must leave for London," I said abruptly. "Tell Mrs. Collins good-bye, and that I will do my best to restore her to London."

Marianne raised her brows. "If you say so. I see

the fire in your eyes, Lacey. What the devil are you about to do?"

I led the horse to the large stump in the clearing I used as a mounting block and hauled myself onto his back. I looked down at Marianne who was watching me in bewilderment, the vestiges of her tears lingering.

"I need to ask a gentleman about a box."

Marianne continued to look perplexed. I nudged the patient horse forward and rode for the track out of the clearing, leaving Marianne and the cozy cottage behind.

Chapter Twenty-three

When I reached Drury Lane theatre late that evening, the company was between performances. A lighter drama had just finished, and *Othello* would commence next.

As before, the theatre was bustling—actors, dressers, scene builders, stage hands, and others whose function I had no idea of rushed through the corridors. I moved through them all the best I could, back to the room where Hannah Wolff did her sewing.

This chamber was no less chaotic, with piles of clothing rising around Hannah like islands from the sea. Two women sifted through the costumes, dropping clothing here and there. A man in a close-fitting tunic and hose, his Shakespearean garb incongruous on the modern sofa, lounged near Hannah to talk—mostly complaints, I heard as I walked in and observed the clutter.

The actor spied me and broke off his tirade about an actress treading on his lines, and the chatter dropped away. Hannah turned her face to the door, though her hands never ceased moving the needle through fabric. "What is the matter? Who has come?"

"Mrs. Wolff," I said. "It is Captain Lacey. I must speak to Mr. Coleman."

"He's run off his feet, Captain. Poor man. Wait until after the performance. Enjoy it. Mr. Kean is brilliant."

"I'm afraid this cannot wait. Tell me where he is, and I will fetch him."

"I will," the actor said. "Dull as church, waiting for Ma Wolff to finish my rags."

He shot off the insult as he got lazily to his feet and brushed past without looking at me. In spite of his fine Elizabethan doublet, his face was pockmarked, his teeth crooked and broken. Fine feathers on insolent ugliness.

"He's a pig," one of the actresses said to Hannah, loud enough for the departing actor to hear. "Do not heed him." She lifted what looked like a long piece of embroidered silk from a pile and walked uncaringly out of the room, the second lady drifting behind her.

I closed the door on them and came closer to Hannah. Her hands stilled as she tried to hear where I moved. "Do not tell me Mr. Coleman has done something dreadful," she said.

"I am not certain yet. But I very much fear I have something unpleasant to say."

"You leave her be," Coleman said behind me.

He'd yanked open the door, and now the giant man walked in, his large fists held at his sides.

"Mr. Coleman . . ."

I got no further. He advanced on me, his face mottled with anger. "Leave her be. She told me you'd been coming around. She don't know no more about Mrs. Collins. She's tired and needs to be left alone."

"Never mind, Mr. Coleman," Hannah said quickly. "The captain said he needs to speak to you."

"Why? What does he want?"

Hannah looked more worried. "I do not know. Let him speak."

Coleman stood between me and the door. He was much larger than I was and whole where I was lame. Even with my stick, I doubted I'd best him in a fight. I doubted Perry would have, either. I ought to have waited to bring Pomeroy with me, but I hadn't been certain, and Pomeroy would have arrested them both before they could say a word.

I decided to plunge in. "Mr. Coleman, when the incendiary device arrived here for Mrs. Collins, you knew exactly what to do. You knew it was deadly dangerous."

"I told you," Coleman said, scowling. "I smelled the gunpowder. I knew it from the army."

"I think you knew exactly what the box was," I said. "And what it would do. You'd thought it over and decided it was too dangerous and might hurt others, Mrs. Wolff included. So when the parcel came, you took it away from Abigail, doused it in water, and tore it apart."

Coleman stared at me, his lips parted as his face grew red.

"Coleman, what is the matter?" Hannah asked. Her mending slipped to the floor as her hands moved restlessly. "What are you accusing him of, Captain?"

I let my voice gentle. I hated to say this, but it must be done. "I am accusing him of nothing. I believe that you, Mrs. Wolff, commissioned the device and had it delivered here, with the express purpose of hurting or even killing Mrs. Collins. Coleman knew, and knew it was wrong. But the device helped anyway—Mrs. Collins fled, taking her plans for investing in the theatre and her threat to you away."

"No," Coleman said wretchedly. "You leave her be."

"What are you saying?" Hannah cried, her worry increasing. "I am a blind woman, Captain. How would I go about procuring such services, when I cannot even find my own way in the street?"

"You could have asked any number of people to help you. The theatre is full of actresses who could stand to make an extra coin. Was having a woman got up to look like Marianne your idea? You could easily have made the costume—you have much skill, as long as someone gives you pieces that go together. You told me so."

Coleman advanced on me. "You *leave her be.*"

"Coleman, no!"

But Coleman had already begun. He came at me, his big hands reaching for me. I stumbled as I scrambled to get away from him, meeting a pile of clothing on one of the chairs, and I fell to one knee.

I was tired from my journey, my bad leg aching from the long ride in the chaise. I did not want to fight, not now, but Coleman didn't care. He came after me, swinging one colossal fist at my face. I managed to block the blow and countered with one of my own.

Coleman's fists were huge and heavy. His bad breath washed over me as I twisted away, bringing up my walking stick.

Coleman grabbed the stick in both hands. I fought to keep hold of it. Hannah was shouting at us, pleading for us to stop.

I wrenched the stick from Coleman's grasp and brought it around. The stick struck Coleman in the side, and he grunted. He swung away, coming at me with fists again.

I rolled out of his way, using the seconds before he could change direction to haul myself to my feet. Coleman had strength and the might of a charging bull, but I had more agility, despite my injured knee. As he ran at me, I sidestepped and brought the stick down on his back.

Luck helped me then, because Coleman slipped on clothing I'd strewn over the floor. He went down on his knees, and I fell with him, pressing the brass handle of the walking stick to his throat. I was breathing hard, sweat running down my back in this warm room.

"Tell me the truth," I said.

Coleman's growl of anger faded to a pleading moan. "Leave her be. She never meant it."

"Coleman?" Hannah's gasp was loud behind me. "What are you saying?"

I saw Mrs. Wolff from the corner of my eye, on her feet in front of the sofa, but afraid to move from that spot.

"She didn't know what she was doing," Coleman said, tears in his voice. "Please don't let the magistrates take her."

"You think *I* had that device sent to Abby?

Bleedin' 'ell. Why the devil should I?"

I answered. "Because you stood to lose if Mrs. Collins invested in the theatre. It only occurred to me this morning that there could be a reason besides an actress ridding herself of a rival for a person wanting Mrs. Collins to go away. Marianne pointed out that even if Mrs. Collins departed, it did not necessarily mean the rival would acquire her roles. Mrs. Collins wanted you to retire, didn't she? And you were afraid she'd drive you away from your beloved theatre. So she had to go."

Hannah firmed her mouth, her helpless look vanishing. "You can never understand, Captain. Since my accident I have had nothing. *Nothing.* Only this piecemeal work of sewing costumes, the only way I am allowed to stay in this place that is my home. The theater was the only thing in my life, acting in my blood. I made Abigail Collins what she is, made the world see her greatness. And she thinks it's a kindness to send me home, to *retire* me, as though I am a horse what needs to be sent out to pasture. My disgusting husband, Mr. Perry, was all for it. He'd make sure I had to go back to him once I was sent away from here. He wanted to go in with Abby to invest a large amount of money, so he could have a piece of the theatre, so he too could tell me where to go and what to do. I'd been able to elude him here, but he was going to take even this sanctuary from me."

"And so you killed him," I said.

"*I* did not. I am a blind old woman, as I said."

I looked down at Coleman who knelt on the floor with his fists clenched, tears running down his face. I had traveled to London thinking this man had it in him to kill at Mrs. Wolff's command, but now that the goliath was sobbing on the floor, I was not so certain.

"Why did you think Hannah was the culprit?" I asked him.

"I don't know," Coleman said. "I was afraid. Mrs. Wolff was so angry at Mrs. Collins, I thought she were doing all the bad things to her. Mrs. Wolff knows this theatre like a mum would know her babe. She could have done the tricks, easy."

"Oh, Coleman." Hannah moved slowly to him. I let her come, watching her, though she still held a pair of shears. "Have you that little faith in me?"

"You have a temper. I've seen you."

"I do. It is true." Hannah stopped and smiled, her gaze remote. "When you saw me play Lady Mac and Gertrude, Captain, I was a haughty creature indeed. I was the highest actress in this company, and I wielded my power like a little empress. I made all dance to my bidding. I raged if I did not have my own way. I was awful. But God punished me. He sent Mr. Perry to me, took away my husband, and took away my sight. I had my comeuppance. Mr. Perry conspiring with Abigail to chuck me out was the final blow."

I moved the walking stick's handle from Coleman's throat and took a step back. Coleman remained where he was, not moving to rise or do anything else. "I thought she'd gone too far," he said. "So I doused the box, to make sure."

"And Mr. Perry?" I asked.

"I never went nigh him."

"I told you," Hannah said. "He came home with me that night and stayed for supper. He never left."

No, he hadn't. Two witnesses had confirmed it.

I studied Coleman, then Hannah, then Coleman again. I'd been wrong. Or had I been? My explanation was correct; I knew it, but I did not have all the pieces.

"I did not want to believe what I feared," I said to Hannah, who stood unmoving in the middle of the room. "I did not want to send a woman I admired so much to the gallows."

"But you would do it," Hannah said. "I hear that in your voice. I did not spend a lifetime learning how to imitate other people to not understand what sort of man you are."

I gave her a bow, though I knew she could not see it. "I would have let it go if the prankster had stopped at trying to ruin Mrs. Collins' performances. But then I met Mr. Ridgley. I cannot hold blameless anyone who would employ such a monster."

Hannah looked mystified, and Coleman clearly did not know who I meant.

"Mr. Perry is dead," Hannah said. "I admit I am glad of that, but I will say again that I never meant Abby any harm. I am put out with her, but I can argue with her and make her see my way. Mr. Perry was another matter. I still hope you discover who has tried to hurt Abby and bring her back again. Even if she doesn't understand me."

Hannah was half turned to me, the shears held loosely in her hand. Her face was troubled, her brows drawn.

Coleman crawled to her. He reached Hannah and wrapped his arms around her legs, burying his face in her skirts. It was a bizarre sight, watching the huge man weep on the small woman, but I knew who had the power in this room. It was not Coleman, and it was not me.

"My apologies," I said, feeling awkward. "I did not mean to upset you."

"Find Abby," Hannah said, stroking Coleman's shaking back. "And then you'll understand."

I had found her. But I would not betray her whereabouts to Mrs. Wolff and Coleman until I was certain Mrs. Collins was no longer in danger.

Without taking leave, I left the room. I closed the door on the tableau of Coleman kneeling at Hannah Wolff's feet, she looking down on him like a sad Madonna.

I made my way out of the back of the theatre, bypassing the rushing actors, including Mr. Kean, who strode past me without ever noticing me. I walked through the back passage, cold and exhausted, to Russel Street.

"Sir?"

A familiar blond giant loomed out of the fog, his light hair beading with moisture. He'd been lounging next to a carriage and a coachman, which I recognized as belonging to Lady Breckenridge.

"You all right, sir?" Bartholomew asked me. "Didn't know you was back."

"I am," I said. "I think."

"Your lady wife is here," Bartholomew said. "She's up in her box. Shall you go in, sir?" He looked over my travel-rumpled clothes and mussed hair, raising one brow. "Or would you prefer to retire home?"

Bartholomew was becoming quite the snob, the perfect valet in the making. I was in a foul temper, so to dismay him, I said, "Yes, I'll go up," and walked to the theatre's front entrance before he could answer.

By the time I reached the Breckenridge box, the play was well underway. Donata's box in this theatre was not as large as the one at Covent Garden, but still plenty opulent. The box's small foyer contained two gilded chairs with soft seats and an ebony table holding a decanter of wine and glasses. Double doors with panels picked out in gold led to the box itself.

Donata was already in her seat, Lady Aline next to her, Grenville beyond. I breathed a sigh of relief. Friends only, no cold glances of ladies and gentlemen I barely knew.

Donata rose to meet me, the bandeau in her hair glittering with diamonds. She touched my unshaved chin. "Did you find her?"

No pleasantries, no asking how my journey was, or if I were well. Donata was a woman who went straight to the point.

"I did," I said.

The three looked at me expectantly as Donata sat me down and resumed her seat, but exhaustion overcame me. Mr. Kean stepped onstage to loud applause, covering any conversation I might make. By the time he launched into his first speech, I was drooping on Donata's shoulder, and then I snored through the better part of Kean's brilliant performance as Othello.

*** *** ***

I slept through my usual early rising time and did not wake until Donata herself was up. I had spent the night in my own chamber, not wanting to go to Donata in my road-stained state, and too tired to wait for Bartholomew to bring a bath.

Barnstable had ordered one drawn by the time I rolled, groaning, out of bed in the afternoon, and Bartholomew hovered near to shave and dress me. I was ashamed of my assessment of Bartholomew as a snob last night; he was a godsend, and I was lucky he'd agreed to work for me.

Both he and Barnstable looked over my bruises from my fight with Coleman, but I said nothing, and they seemed to sense they should not ask, not at the moment.

Washed, shaved, and dressed in clean clothing, I entered Donata's boudoir. She looked up at me from where she sat at a small table, a newspaper open in her hands. Silver trays bearing plenty of food waited for us.

"You will take breakfast with me, will you not?" Donata asked returning to her newspaper. "You have had a long journey, and it is already two. The others will not mind if you do not go down yet."

"And you wish me to tell you everything," I said, taking the seat Bartholomew drew out for me.

"Exactly," my wife said, the paper still in front of her. "You were insensible last night, and I was kind and let you sleep. Grenville was most worried, but I told him that if something had gone amiss, you'd have said at least that before you nodded off."

"I would have attempted it." I let Bartholomew pile my plate high with meat, eggs, and toast. The long journey had made me hungry, and I only now realized I'd eaten very little during it.

"Still, it was most maddening of you to sleep through the entire play." Donata lowered her paper long enough to give me a severe look over it. "And the entertainment after it, and the short play after that."

None of which I remembered. How I'd come to be in her carriage on the way home, I had no idea.

I could have gone on teasing her, taking my breakfast in silence until I'd eaten my fill, but I decided to take pity on her. I gave her the tale, beginning with my arrival at the cottage outside Froxfield, my astonishment to find Mrs. Collins there, then my realization that made me rush back to London to question Mrs. Wolff and Coleman.

"I thought I had the answer," I said, running a finger around the rim of a thin porcelain coffee cup. "But they seemed truly bewildered by my questions. Still, Mrs. Wolff is the only one I can see to benefit the most from Mrs. Collins' departure. If Mrs. Collins is gone for good, or is so rattled she decides not to invest in the theatre, Mrs. Wolff's position is safe for the moment. At least, she and Coleman believe so."

"What about Mr. Kean?" Donata asked and took a sip from her cup of chocolate. The chocolate left a dark smear on her upper lip. I wanted nothing more than to taste it, but she licked it away and continued. "He might have been angry that Mrs. Collins wanted to come into the running of the theatre, perhaps for the same reasons Mrs. Wolff feared. Mr. Kean has the reputation for liking his drink a little too much, and for being difficult."

I shook my head. "I cannot see the theatre's committee readily letting Mr. Kean leave. He fills seats, and they know it."

"Perhaps," Donata conceded. She laid aside her newspaper and took up the first letter of her pile of post, lifting her knife to slit the seal. "Then it must be another actress, as you suspected before, for reasons of her own."

I sighed and sat back. "I believe I know nothing anymore. All my ideas have gone wrong. Perhaps marriage has muddled me."

She did not look up from her letter. "Do not be daft. If you are muddled, it is because so much is unclear. You have found Mrs. Collins, and she is well, which is the best thing."

"But not safe until I run her detractor to ground," I said, unhappy. I took a sip of coffee, allowing myself to enjoy it.

I could sit in this room forever, I decided. Drinking fine coffee, bathing in Donata's light scent, and watching her sleek head bend as she read her letters. She was a lovely woman, with a loveliness that went all the way through her. I thought of my encounter with Lydia Westin in Bath. Lydia had dazzled me two summers ago, making me believe I'd lost my heart to her, thoroughly and forever. My dear friend Louisa Brandon had told me that, in time, my heart would heal. I had not believed her.

I believed her now. Donata had eased her way into my life, and now I could not imagine myself without her.

She had a pile of correspondence to go through, my wife ever popular, which Barnstable had piled on a little table behind her. Quite a stack of letters, and one box.

I froze, my coffee slopping as my cup jerked. "Donata," I said. "What is the package?"

"Hmm?" Donata glanced at it. "Tea cakes from Gunter's. I ordered them as a little treat for when you returned. Do not worry so, Gabriel."

Perfectly reasonable. I ought to laugh shakily in

relief and say that my fears were getting the better of me. But I remembered Ridgley and the evil of him.

"Would you like one now?" Donata asked. She took up her knife again and inserted it under the seal, ready to pull the paper free.

"*No!*" I was up and over the table before the shout left my mouth. I grabbed Donata by the shoulders and jerked her to the floor.

I heard a scratch, smelled the foul odor of burning and gunpowder, and then a loud *bam* ricocheted through the room. Heat touched me, sparks, and fire. I rolled with Donata, pinning her beneath me, coughing from the smoke.

"Gabriel!" Donata's voice was harsh with terror. I felt great pain, heard Bartholomew's cry of alarm, and then something very heavy hit my back.

As I fell, Donata's warm body there to surround and catch me, my thoughts sharpened into astonishing clarity. In one moment, like a shimmering drop of suspended water, I saw who had driven away Mrs. Collins, murdered Perry, and now had tried to kill me.

Chapter Twenty-four

At four o'clock that afternoon, I stood at the front door of Hannah Wolff's house, where she lived with her sister and brother-in-law. Pomeroy and Spendlove were with me.

I hadn't wanted Spendlove there, but he'd insisted on joining us when I'd gone to fetch Pomeroy. Sir Nathaniel, the magistrate, had agreed. Pomeroy had expressed his aggravation loudly, but Spendlove had won.

I rapped upon the door, wincing at the pain in my singed knuckles. I also ached from where Bartholomew had tackled me, shoving me down and hitting me with a carpet to put out the fire that had caught my coat. The clothes had been ruined, but fortunately, the man inside had been spared.

The plain maid who'd answered the door the last time opened it again, looking askance at me and the two Runners. She did not want to admit us, and I had to stand in front of Pomeroy and Spendlove to keep them from simply barreling their way in. This maid had done nothing, and I could at least be polite.

We went into the foyer and then the front hall. The walls were plain dark wood, with framed panels of wallpaper at neat intervals, each rectangle holding a painting. The paintings were not very good, at least, not compared to the artwork I'd seen at Grenville's or Denis's. They were competent and pretty, what a cit could afford.

The Holts were both at home, the maid said, and would be down directly. When they entered, I again wondered at my thoughts. Hannah's sister and her husband regarded us with timid puzzlement, and Mrs. Holt asked the maid to send in refreshments.

"We'll not stay," I said. "I came to tell you that Mrs. Collins has been found. She is well, and she is eager to return to Drury Lane for the remainder of the season."

"What did he say?" Hannah herself stood in a doorway that connected with the next room, holding herself steady on the doorframe. "Captain Lacey, you found Abby?"

"I did," I said. "She will be back in London soon. Are you alone here? Where is Coleman?"

"Hasn't come for me. I was tired today, and my head hurts. And I am not alone. My sister and Mr. Holt are here."

I turned to the rheumatic maid who'd come in with the tea tray, which again I took out of her crooked hands and set on a table. "Please send for Mr. Coleman," I told her. "Mrs. Wolff will need him."

The maid turned to Mrs. Holt for confirmation. Mrs. Holt nodded, then started for her sister. "Dear Hannah, you should not be out of bed. You'll take a chill."

I stepped between them. "Not yet, Mrs. Holt."

Spendlove, who had been standing by with his beefy arms folded, finally exploded into impatience. "May we get on with this? That is, if you aren't about to sit down for tea and cakes. Perhaps we should wait until a royal duchess comes to call."

Mrs. Holt ignored him, while her husband's mouth popped open. "Excuse me, Captain Lacey," Mrs. Holt said. "My sister needs me."

"She does not," I said. "She needs Coleman."

"I'm not waiting for him," Spendlove rumbled behind me.

"Neither am I," Pomeroy said. "Sorry, Captain. Mr. Benjamin Holt and Mrs. Holt, you are being arrested for the murder of Mr. John Perry, and for procuring a device meant to maim or kill from one Mr. Thomas Ridgley. I will be taking you to a magistrate where he will hear my evidence and decide whether there is enough to hold you for trial."

Mrs. Holt stopped. She looked, not at the Runners, but at me, her eyes widening in amazement. "I cannot leave this house, gentlemen. I must take care of Hannah."

"Mr. Coleman will," I said. "Luckily for her, he's been looking after her all this time. I shudder to think what might have happened to her had he not."

"I do not know what you mean," Mrs. Holt said in indignation. "Everything I have done has been for my sister. I gave up my life on the stage so I could make certain she always had a decent place to live.

She is one of the great ones. I have always known that."

Mr. Holt had remained in place and silent, but he'd straightened from his stoop, which made his stomach look immediately less puffy. His head came up, and now he appeared to be a foot taller, almost as tall as I was.

"What is happening?" Hannah asked into the silence. "Martha, tell me."

"It was all for you," Mrs. Holt said, her voice firm. "Abigail Collins would have ruined you, cast you out, and you the best in the world. You took that woman to your bosom, taught her everything she knew, made her everything she is. She came here, pathetic and poor from the little traveling players, keen to make a go on the London stage. And what did she do in the end? She turned on you, she did. Mrs. Collins made you into her dresser and her teacher, keeping you as a drudge when once you'd been great, far better than she ever was. And she was going to give you the push. She could not do that. I would not let her do that."

Hannah's eyes were wide, her lips trembling. Her hand slid from its propping position, and she started to fall.

I sprang forward and caught her. This woman, who had seemed such a pillar of strength on the stage, was nothing more than a collection of frail bones. She was so light I barely felt her weight as I held her upright.

Spendlove looked belligerent at my rescue, but Pomeroy merely moved so neither of the Holts could run for it out the front door.

"I don't understand," Hannah said, tears in her

eyes. "I never wanted this."

"I did not want this for you either," I said. "But they tried to kill Mrs. Collins, and this morning, they tried to kill me. My *wife* opened that package."

The incident had made the fury in me rise in red incandescence. If they'd tossed an incendiary device at me as I'd made my way through a deserted passage or some such, I could have understood. I'd have blamed myself for not taking more care.

But they'd endangered Donata, and everyone in my house, and that was beyond forgiveness. Barnstable, who'd brought in the post, might have been hurt or killed by that package if it had gone off too soon. And dear God, my daughter might have seen the box, thought it innocent iced cakes, and snatched it up in playful eagerness.

"Your wife?" Hannah turned her face up to mine. "Oh, Lord. Is she well?"

"She is. But it was a near thing."

It made me sick to think how near. A harmless parcel from Gunter's, Donata had assumed it. I was keeping myself from contemplating the full of it, or else I'd fall here with Hannah and degenerate into a gibbering fool.

"Handy little devices," Mr. Holt said, no longer the dithering middle-aged gentleman. His voice was clear, filled with pride. "We had several made. Mr. Ridgley was obliging."

Good God. "Make a search of the house," I said to Pomeroy. "Carefully. Mrs. Wolff, you will come with me."

"You leave my sister alone," Mrs. Holt said. "She's not to be touched by the likes of you."

I ignored her. Without a word, I led Hannah

swiftly back through the room from which she'd come, into the hall, and thence out of the house. As we went, I heard Pomeroy's voice rise cheerily, reminding the Holts that they were under arrest. Spendlove curtly called in the patrollers who'd waited without, and they flowed through the front door as I took Hannah out of it.

She looked up at me, the once great lady of the stage, now faded, tired, and grieving. "What have I done?"

"Not you," I said. "Not you, Mrs. Wolff. This is not your fault."

"Yes, it is." She rested against me, closing her eyes against the glare of winter sun she could not see. "I was always such a prideful creature. I took credit for shaping Abby, but she has the gift. She could have done it without me. But I suppose I poured all my troubles out to my sister, and she took it much too serious. Martha has always been protective of me, proud she sacrificed her career to look after me, the great actress. And God forgive me, I thought she was right."

Tears trickled down her cheeks. I dared press a kiss to her forehead. "You were the best of all, Mrs. Wolff. You were, in truth. I'll never forget you. Here is Coleman. He'll look after you now. I wager he always will."

*** *** ***

Life was not tidy, with every problem put away into neat boxes when all was done. I felt as I had when I'd packed up the pieces of my old life in Grimpen Lane—as though I'd emptied everything hodge-podge into a crate and nailed it shut.

The danger was gone, Abigail free to return to

Drury Lane. Pomeroy and Spendlove had searched the Holts' house and found several more of the incendiary devices, which Mr. Holt had kept locked in a strong metal box in a cupboard.

Both the Holts had confessed to hiring Ridgley, and Mr. Holt confessed to killing Mr. Perry. The man and wife were in Newgate now, awaiting their fate. Because Holt was a successful businessman, he had the money to pay for private accommodations for himself and his wife. But they'd hang.

Pomeroy complained that Spendlove would horn in on the conviction reward, though he admitted Spendlove had been helpful in obtaining the confession. I did not like to think how Spendlove had done so.

Spendlove was, of course, forced to drop the idea that I'd killed Perry. He still had his eye on me, though, he said, and on Denis. He promised to pot the both of us with one blow someday. I had no doubt he would, but in the first days after the investigation was over, I scarcely cared.

I never did discover why Mrs. Carfax had so readily told the magistrate she'd seen me entering my rooms the night of Perry's death. Whatever knowledge Spendlove held over her, Mrs. Carfax was not telling. Miss Winston had been unable to discover the secret, and I dropped the matter.

As for Grenville, I did not see him for a few days after the arrests. When he finally invited me to his house to take a midmorning meal with him—a creation of Anton's—he was despondent.

"How did you know?" Grenville asked me. "I'll never forgive you for not sending for me when you made the arrest, but perhaps that was best. They had more incendiary devices, you say, in their *house*? Were they mad?"

"I believe they were," I said, scraping up the sauce of orange liqueur that Anton had poured, flaming, over my crepe stuffed with cheese. "They'd convinced themselves they were Mrs. Wolff's protectors, that they had to look after her at all costs."

"At all costs." Grenville blew out his breath. "Good Lord. But how did you discover what they'd done? I never thought of them, to tell the truth."

"I hadn't thought of them either. When I met them they seemed pleasant but not very clever. But when the device went off in Donata's chamber, all the pieces seemed to rise and form together in my head. I had a flash of how Mr. Kean can transform himself from a small, hunched nobody into a great orator in the space of a moment. He's excellent at it. When I met Mr. Holt, I remembered thinking him a small, hunched nobody—but what would happen if he straightened up and changed his manner entirely? In the next second, it occurred to me that Mrs. Holt had been an actress—she'd know about donning costumes and changing her appearance, and perhaps her husband knew something about acting as well."

"A good point," Grenville said. He leaned forward, no longer downcast, his eyes alight with interest.

"Holt might have been on the stage himself," I said. "Or perhaps he picked up tricks from his actress wife, or from living with an actress as skilled as Hannah. We were looking for a man and a woman, remember. The woman who had hired Ridgley to make the device, and the man who fetched it and took it to the delivery company. Both were described by distinctive things — golden curls and clothing much like Marianne's; the man with large teeth and hands. Mr. Holt's teeth are not large, but I will wager they were false. When I first met the Holts, I remember he sat very quietly, making no gestures. False teeth can be got rid of, but hands are another matter. He took care to hide his from me." I took the last bite of my crepe and wished for another. "Ridgley apparently did not reveal to Denis that he made more than one device for the Holts. I will have to tell him."

Grenville shivered and took another sip of coffee. "Holt kept them about to use on people who stood in his way? Fool. He might have done himself real harm."

"I do not believe either he or his wife cared. I think they'd convinced themselves that anything they did to protect Hannah was just. Even going to Newgate and the gallows. Even destroying themselves."

"Well, God save me from protectors such as they." Grenville sighed and clicked his fine porcelain cup to its saucer. "What about Marianne? She is still in Berkshire?"

"I believe so. She's remaining with Mrs. Collins until Mrs. Collins feels ready to return. Marianne will enjoy the long visit with David."

I spoke lightly, but Grenville gave me a grim look. "I've been a bloody fool, haven't I?"

"A bit." I leaned back in my chair, wiping my mouth on my handkerchief. Another excellent meal. I would begin riding in the park this very day, I vowed. "Though I cannot put the blame entirely on you. Marianne can be maddeningly stubborn."

"If she is determined to leave me, I will let her. I am weary of this. Make certain she comes to no harm, Lacey, and tell her I will continue the keeping of David. Our quarrels are not his fault."

I did not argue. I knew Marianne and Grenville cared for each other, but I was no longer certain how to settle their battles, if I ever had known.

"Perhaps you will take up your travels again? Egypt?"

I felt a pull when I named the place. Grenville had once said he'd take me with him on his next journey there. I longed to travel the world again, and if he'd asked me two years ago, I'd have already been downstairs waiting for him in his carriage. But these days I had much to keep me in England. I had a wife, and I'd found my daughter. I looked forward to spending the rest of the spring with Gabriella, who would make her debut under Donata's care soon. I did not want to rush off to foreign lands at this moment.

Grenville lifted his cup again. "It is too late to plan an expedition this winter. By the time I could set everything in motion, the season would be drawing to its end, the weather growing much too hot. I will begin plans for next winter instead. Shall I include you in them?"

Next winter was comfortably far away, yet near enough for excited anticipation. "Yes," I said. "Do."

"Very well. We will go." Grenville said the words in quiet resignation, a man mourning his present rather than contemplating his future.

"Do not give up," I said as Matthias poured me more of the heady coffee. "Marianne is not an unreasonable woman. She simply wants you to trust her."

Grenville gave a short laugh. "Apparently, I am lacking in this area."

"You are," I said. "You have little trust in your fellow beings, especially the ones you care most about. You are only now beginning to trust me. I know it is a difficult thing for you to swallow, but we are not parasites waiting to stab you the moment you turn your back."

"A mixed metaphor."

"But it makes my point. Think on it."

I returned to enjoying the rest of the meal, including a bowl of bright hothouse berries that must have cost a fortune. They were juicy and sweet, and I relished them. Grenville did not have much of an appetite, so I finished his share as well.

My lecture on trust made me contrite about my own failings in this area. That evening, Donata, in a lacy peignoir, sat curled on a divan in my bedchamber, cigarillo in hand.

Her own chamber had been severely damaged by smoke and the fire before Bartholomew and Barnstable had managed to put it out. Particles of plaster had shot around the room like bullets, pock-marking the elegant cream-colored walls. Mr. Denis had sent a letter of condolence to Donata, commiserating with her and offering to send over the workmen who were repairing his rooms.

Donata had been unhurt, for which I thanked God most fervently. She'd decided to move into my chamber until hers was repaired, which was fine with me. She seemed as usual tonight, unruffled, though I knew her well enough to see she'd been shaken by the incident.

"Actresses," she said now as we discussed the end of the case. "Paying for roles, sharing husbands, nearly killing rivals, and all for the joy of the applause at the end. Too exhausting. I am happy I never felt the need to tread the boards."

"I believe I considered the idea very briefly when I was about thirteen," I said. "Anything to remove myself from my father. But the army was a better stage for me."

"No doubt."

I came to sit near her on the divan, and she put her feet in my lap as she liked to. "And now I must tell you the rest," I said.

Donata fixed her gaze on me as I related how I'd searched for Felicity to question her and found her at the tavern, with Stubbins standing over her, playing his sickening game. I told her I'd beaten Stubbins down, and he'd retaliated with the challenge, which I'd accepted.

Donata drew on her cigarillo as she listened to the tale. When I finished, she let out her last breath of smoke and gracefully dropped the spent cigarillo into a porcelain bowl. "Good. Stubby Stubbins needs to be taken down a peg. Do pot him one, Gabriel."

I remained still. "You are not about to have hysterics and beg me not to attend?"

"Not at all. It would be dishonorable in the extreme to refuse the challenge, and I have faith in your steady hand. Were you a sickly man, more likely to trip over your own feet and shoot yourself in the leg, I would try to dissuade you. But I have every confidence. It is only a shame that ladies are not allowed to attend. I would enjoy the show."

"Dueling is illegal," I pointed out.

Donata dangled her shapely fingers from the arm of the divan. "It is why I have solicitors."

I smiled at her. "You are an astonishing woman."

"So you have told me."

I loved her. My horror upon seeing her reach to open the package returned with force, and I rested my hands on her legs. "I thought I'd lose you. God was good to me yesterday."

Donata's eyes tightened. "You mean He was good to *me*. You pushed me away so you could take the force of the blast. Thank heavens Bartholomew was quick to think of hitting you with a rug. A husband blown to bits is rather useless to me. When you are in my bed, I would prefer you to be in one piece."

I warmed, even as I remembered the pain of the burns, the smothering folds of the carpet, before darkness had consumed me. "Are you saying you are fond of me?"

"Damned fond."

I reached out and traced her cheek with my fingertip. "We are a sentimental couple. I prefer you in once piece as well."

"Let us endeavor to keep each other so." Donata's eyes softened as I caressed her, then she loosened herself from my hold and rose. "I have something for you."

I watched, too tired to come to my feet, as she walked into the dressing room and returned with a walking stick in her hands. The cane was polished mahogany, the head gleamed gold.

"Mr. Pomeroy returned this," Donata said. "It was proved not to be the murder weapon after all. According to Mr. Holt's confession, Mr. Perry brought this one with him and dropped it when he was struck down. And so, I give it to you once more."

I took it, turning the head so I could read the inscription: *Captain G. Lacey, 1817.* "Thank you," I said. "It is a fine gift."

I'd said the same when she'd presented it to me, almost a year ago, and I had not changed my opinion. She'd given me a better gift this year— herself. In Donata, I'd found a lady who was intelligent, brave, adventurous, trusting, and strong.

And not afraid of passion. This last she demonstrated to me in the large bed as we settled down to each other. Donata's blue eyes warmed as I loved her, her touch gentle as down.

The gods had truly smiled upon me.

End

Please turn the page
for a preview
of Captain Lacey's next adventure

Murder
in
Grosvenor
Square

Captain Lacey
Regency Mysteries
Book 9

Chapter One

March 1818

I had an appointment on Lady Day, not half a week away, to face a man in a duel.

My opponent was one Lord Andrew Kenton Stubbins, known to his intimates as Stubby. The reason for the appointment was because I'd come across him beating a young woman he'd hired for his pleasure. I'd indicated to him, by snatching the strap from his hands and giving him a taste of it, what I'd thought of his choice of pleasures.

Stubby had subsequently challenged me, Lucius Grenville had agreed to be one of my seconds, and I'd been fitted with a new suit for the occasion. I thought it ridiculous to waste new clothes on what was certain to be a messy business, but both my wife and Grenville, the most fashionable man in society, assured me it was the done thing.

Today, I was on my way to the Strand to fetch a walking stick I'd sent for repair the Saturday before. During my adventures this January, the stick had been stolen from me before turning up again lying beside a corpse. The stick had been exonerated of any wrongdoing and returned to me by a Bow Street Runner, but I'd discovered eventually that the sword inside it had been bent.

I did not use the sword much, and so did not hurry to repair it. But I complained of it until Donata, in exasperation, told me to please get the blasted thing fixed.

I'd taken the walking stick to its birthplace — a shop in the Strand — explained the problem, and left it with them. This morning, I'd had word that the stick was in good repair, and I'd come to collect it. Being a man of Mayfair now, I could have sent a servant, but I used the excuse to get out for a bit of exercise.

I had the stick now, as fine as ever. I was particularly fond of that walking stick, as it had been a gift from Donata, who only two months before this had done me the honor of becoming the second Mrs. Lacey. After I collected it, I decided to walk up and down a while before returning home, delighted to have use of the stick again.

Spring was gradually creeping over London, kinder winds replacing the harsh ones of winter. March meant green creeping mist-like over trees in the city parks, bulbs pushing their leaves through the ground. It meant rain and fog as well, but also days like this, blue-skied with a promise of sweeter weather to come.

March also meant a whirl of soirees, supper balls, musicales, dinners, at-homes, and other such functions beloved of my new wife. Donata, formerly the Dowager Viscountess Breckenridge, was a hostess to be reckoned with. Now that she had a husband to stand beside her, one she claimed looked fine in his well-kept regimentals, she doubled her efforts to best every other lady in Mayfair. Hence my eagerness to run an errand to the Strand this afternoon, and my excuse to linger and enjoy the first flush of spring.

"Captain?" A voice at my elbow pulled me back from my airy contemplations of the weather. I would be writing poems to skylarks soon.

The young man who'd addressed me had brown hair and small brown eyes set close together. He was well dressed in an expensively cut coat and kid gloves, his hat as fine as any Grenville would own.

"Mr. Travers," I said in true delight, taking his offered hand.

I'd met Gareth Travers while investigating the affair of Colonel Westin, a murder with roots in the Peninsular War. Travers was the close friend of Leland Derwent, whose family invited me to dine with them once a fortnight, where they'd beg me to entertain them with stories of my army life. Now that I was married, they'd extended that invitation to my wife as well.

The Derwents were a family of innocents, looking upon the world with benevolence, never noticing its darkness. Travers had a bit more cynicism in him, but I imagined he enjoyed their unworldly companionship as much as I did.

"Well met, Captain," Travers said. "I am pleased

to have been walking along this same stretch of pavement. I've been meaning to call on you."

"What can I do for you, Mr. Travers?" I liked Travers, who seemed intelligent and sensible, though I did not know much about him.

He hesitated. "There is tavern not far from here. Perhaps . . . ?"

"Of course," I said politely. A chance to stop for a good pint would delay me further from returning home. Donata would host a soiree tonight, and the house was in an uproar preparing for it. My role would be to stand with her at the top of the stairs and shake hands with the crush that shoved their way upward. A friendly ale at a pub was just the thing to fortify me for the task.

We walked along the Strand toward Charing Cross, Travers leading me to whatever tavern he had in mind. As we neared St. Martin's Lane, a strange roar rippled through the spring air. The sound grew and built, flowing down the street to us like a sudden river. A cart horse shied, hooves clattering on the cobbles while the driver tried to calm it. Travers stopped, as worried as the horse.

"A mob?" he asked, his young face drawn in concern.

I sincerely hoped not. Riots sometimes tore through these streets, people protesting — I could not blame them — the cost of bread which seemed to rise out of all proportion to anything sensible. In these times after the war, so many had returned from the army to no work and no wages, cast upon the shores of their native land without recompense. Add to that the cost of grain and men unable to feed their families, and anger built to the breaking point.

Houses and shops were demolished during violence and rioting, soldiers were called in to fire into the crowds and restore peace.

A strained peace, with desperation boiling just below the surface.

If a mob came this way, we'd have to take refuge in a shop or house, begging admittance. I could not outrun a riot on my injured leg, though I had little doubt that Travers could sprint to safety.

"I do not think so," I said, relieved, after listening for a moment. The crowd was excited, but missing the sharpness of fury. "Someone in the pillory, possibly."

Travers relaxed a bit, but only a bit. "Poor bastard."

I agreed. The pillory was for those convicted of crimes of a lesser degree than robbery, murder, and other heinous things, but while the convicted might not be hanged, they could still lose their lives if the mob grew incensed enough. If the person had the crowd's sympathy, he might fare little worse than stiff limbs from the ordeal, but if the crowd despised him, the man or woman could be battered to death.

It became clear as we neared Charing Cross that the fellow in the stocks today did not have the crowd's sympathy. The poor man was already covered in filth from rotted vegetables and dung. His head hung down, and he shuddered when another missile burst upon his back. My pity for him stirred.

I could not get close enough to read the placard that proclaimed his crime. The crowd was chanting, but I could not hear what they said. I turned to a coffee vendor who'd decided this a good place for business today. "What has he done?" I asked him.

The vendor would not answer until I bought coffee from him, so I handed him a coin. He took a cracked mug from his cart, poured thick, steaming coffee into it, and handed it to me.

I took a sip of the coffee and tried not to make a face at its taste. I was going soft, I decided, being served the finest brew at Lady Breckenridge's table every day. Then again, my former landlady had made coffee better than this in her little back-street bakeshop.

"Buggery," the vendor grunted. "So they say."

"Ah." Buggery was a lesser sentence than sodomy, because sodomy, a hanging offense, had to be proved with a witness. Gentlemen who engaged in the practice usually were wise enough to make certain they were completely private. But a charge of buggery could be made against a suspect, and a conviction meant a day in the pillory, at the mercy of the mob.

"Poor bastard, indeed," I said.

"He'll last." The vendor, a large bull of a man, shook his head. "Resilient. He'll be happily poking away at some other bloke in a week or so."

I had no wish to stand and watch the pilloried man be kicked in the backside by youths who found this good fun, so I finished a few more sips of coffee, handed the mug back, and signaled Travers to lead me on to his tavern.

The public house was north on St. Martin's Lane, the interior dark with aged wood, the atmosphere quiet. Travers must be a regular, because men greeted him with nods instead of hostile stares.

"Brutal." Travers looked a bit white about the mouth as we dug into good, thick ale the landlord brought us. "But so many laws in England are."

He sounded like the Derwents—Sir Gideon Derwent was a reformer who threw himself wholeheartedly into making life better for all. His son Leland was following closely in his footsteps.

"Pillory's a bit harsh for the offense, I always thought," I said. "I knew two soldiers during the war who spent the night with each other before every battle. We all knew it but said nothing, because the two in question always fought the more fiercely for each other the next day. I believe the Spartans did much the same."

Travers listened to this revelation in surprise. "You are a reformist then?" A hint of a smile touched his lips. "A radical perhaps?"

"A realist, I would say. I've learned to take things as they come." Or perhaps I had been sanguine because the two gentlemen had never tried to seduce me.

Or I would like to think so. Injustice always enraged me, and I was known to take matters into my own hands. Hence, my forthcoming appointment with Stubby Stubbins.

It was difficult for me not to rush back to Charing Cross, unlock the pillory, and let the pathetic man out, but I knew that such an act could possibly result in my death and his. No, he'd finish his sentence, go home, nurse his wounds, and be more careful in future.

I took another drink of ale and let the bitter taste of hops soothe me. "Why did you wish to call on me?" I asked Travers. "Something for which you need my help?" I was gaining a reputation for assisting those in need.

"Nothing so dire. I simply thought to have a conversation."

This surprised me. I must have had nearly twenty years on Travers and had never considered him interested in conversation with a fortyish ex-army man. When he attended the Derwents' dinners, he rarely spoke to me at all, preferring the company of Leland and Leland's widowed cousin, Mrs. Danbury.

For all his professed interest, Travers didn't seem to know what he wanted to say. He began a ramble about the Derwents—his amusement about how unworldly they were and his admiration for it at the same time, and his worry for Lady Derwent's health. I nodded at intervals, waiting to discover his true purpose in talking to me.

When he started to look at a loss, I broke in, "You've known the family a long time?"

Travers looked relieved I'd taken charge of the discussion. "From years back. Eely—Leland, I mean—and I were at school together, but you knew that. I spent all my holidays with the Derwents, practically lived with them. My own father's a bit threadbare. Clergy, you know, with a small living in the middle of nowhere in Wiltshire. He was happy to have the Derwents look after me."

Travers dressed well to be the son of threadbare clergy. But while his father's living might be miniscule, Travers could have come into trust money or been left a legacy by a friend. Money didn't always travel in straight line—except in my family. Our line of wealth had gone directly to my father and then straight into the ground.

"You are fond of the Derwents," I said.

Travers looked embarrassed. "I am. They have

been very good to me."

"And they've been good to me. They enjoy taking in strays."

"Too true. Eely is an ass about it sometimes. Once at university, Leland tried to help a bloke he found in the street. Took him in, let him stay in our digs, gave the man his clothes, his money, tried to find employment for him. I warned him, but Leland is stubbornly blind sometimes. Of course the chap up and robbed us of almost everything and disappeared into the night. Leland was only sad we hadn't helped him more. He even offered to recompense me for my losses. And then he wanted to go after the man and try again."

Travers laughed, sounding genuinely amused. I imagined, though, that he hadn't been much amused at the time.

"Some people resist being reformed," I said. Well I knew this. I'd tried last year to help a street girl called Felicity, with mixed results. She was the lady in question Stubbins had been beating when I'd caught him.

"Well, Eely won't hear of it. Bless the boy." Travers and Leland were the same age.

"Leland is a kind young man," I said. "Heaven help him."

Travers nodded. "Good thing he has me to look after him. His father is as kind, and sometimes as foolish."

"But Sir Gideon is a man of much power, and he's reached that state by being a philanthropist. Perhaps Leland will end up the same as he."

"Perhaps, but until then, it falls to me to keep the lad out of scrapes."

"He is lucky to have such a friend," I said in all sincerity.

Travers glanced at me a moment, his brows drawing together, as though wondering what I meant by the statement. Then he drained his pint and rose with restless energy.

"Pleased to have met you, Captain." He stuck out his hand as I got to my feet, and I shook it. "I look forward to dining with you at the Derwents. Good day."

As he started for the door, I had a thought. "Mr. Travers, a moment."

Travers waited for me as I grabbed my hat and then walked with him out the door. When we stepped into the fine weather, I spoke to him in a low voice. "How do you feel about settling questions of honor?"

Travers raised his brows but gave me a shrewd look. "Why do you ask, Captain?"

"I need a friend," I said. "One to stand by me, with Grenville. Next week, on Lady Day, early in the morning."

"I see." Travers nodded as he set his hat on his head. "Should I speak to Mr. Grenville about the particulars?"

"Indeed. That would be best." I hesitated. "Perhaps Leland and Mr. Derwent do not need to know of your plans."

Travers shot me a sudden grin, the look in his eyes one of satisfaction, almost triumph, which puzzled me a bit. "I believe I understand you." He shook my hand again, squeezing my fingers warmly. "Well met, Captain." And Travers walked away into the crowd, whistling.

About the Author

Award-winning author Ashley Gardner also writes as *New York Times* bestselling author Jennifer Ashley. Under both names—and a third, Allyson James—Gardner has more than 70 published novels and novellas in mystery, romance, and urban fantasy. Her books have been nominated for and won several *RT BookReviews* Reviewers Choice awards (including Best Historical Mystery for *The Sudbury School Murders*), and Romance Writers of America's RITA. Ashley's books have been translated into a dozen different languages and have earned starred reviews in *Booklist. The Hanover Square Affair* spent weeks as the #1 bestselling historical mystery on Amazon Kindle; the entire series spending months in the top 10.

More about the Captain Lacey series can be found at www.gardnermysteries.com. Or email Ashley Gardner at gardnermysteries@cox.net

The Captain Lacey Regency Mysteries series
The Hanover Square Affair
A Regimental Murder
The Glass House
The Sudbury School Murders
The Necklace Affair (novella)
A Body in Berkeley Square
A Covent Garden Mystery
The Gentleman's Walking Stick
     (short story collection)
A Death in Norfolk
A Disappearance in Drury Lane
And more to come!

6137244R00199

Printed in Great Britain
by Amazon.co.uk, Ltd.,
Marston Gate.